CLOSE
QUARTERS

Copy of a plan from *Residential Closes of England*, by Canon J. D. Judd, D.D. Houses traditionally allocated by the foundation are so marked. Neither the organ shed nor the organist's practice room appear in the original, but they have been inserted for the information of the reader. Detail of the cathedral is not shown.

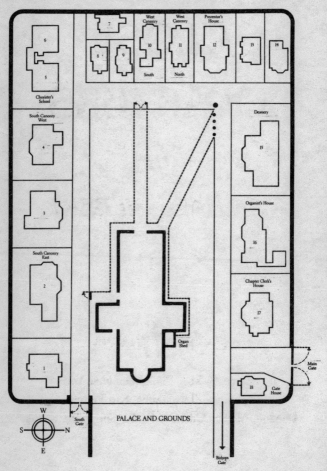

CLOSE
QUARTERS

MICHAEL GILBERT

PERENNIAL LIBRARY

Harper & Row, Publishers, New York
Cambridge, Philadelphia, San Francisco,
London, Mexico City, São Paulo, Singapore, Sydney

The Characters in This Book Are Entirely Imaginary and Have No
Relation to Any Persons Either Living or Dead.

A hardcover edition of this book was originally published in 1947 by
Hodder & Stoughton Limited.

First PERENNIAL LIBRARY Edition published 1988.

LIBRARY OF CONGRESS CATALOG CARD NUMBER: 88-45117

ISBN: 0-06-080936-1

88 89 90 91 92 WB/OPM 10 9 8 7 6 5 4 3 2 1

To
CECIL HEWLETT
Of
KELOWNO, CANADA
IN RECOGNITION OF THE FACT THAT
HE IS THE ONLY PERSON MENTIONED
BY NAME

Contents

Diagrams

Householders of
Melchester Close

THE REV. CANON BLOSS
Late Scholar of Baliol College, Oxford (1st Class
Lit. Hum.), 1895. Canon of Melchester and
Prebendary of Rowstock Parva. Unmarried.

THE REV. CANON BEECH-THOMPSON
Queen's College, Oxford, B.A., 1899, M.A., 1902.
Author of *Stained Glass in the Early English
Period*, *Cromwell—Iconoclast*, etc. Canon of
Melchester. Married. No surviving children.

THE REV. CANON TRUMPINGTON
Late Scholar of Wadham College, Oxford. B.A.
(2nd Class Lit. Hum.), 1900. Principal of Melset
Theological College. Canon of Melchester.
Unmarried.

THE REV. CANON FOX
Educated privately. Edinburgh Theological College, 1902–4. Canon of Melchester. Married. Two
sons; two daughters.

THE REV. H. H. HINKEY
Vicar-Choral and Precentor of Melchester. Rector

of St. Crispins in Melchester. Founder of and contributor to *Cats at Home*. Unmarried.

THE REV. M. J. MALTHUS

Vicar-Choral of Melchester. Chaplain to the Judge in Assize. Hon. Treasurer of "Friends of Melchester Cathedral." Married. Three children.

THE REV. A. G. HALLIDAY

Vicar-Choral of Melchester and assistant of Melchester Choir School.

THE REV. E. V. PRYNNE, M.C., M.A.

Late Scholar of Keble College, Oxford. B.A., 1914. Army Chaplain to the Forces, 1915–18. M.A., 1919. Vicar Choral of Melchester and assistant of Melchester Choir School. Married. One daughter. Wife died, 1930.

C. S. MICKIE, MUS. DOC., F.R.C.O.

Organist and Choirmaster of Melchester. Until 1930 assistant organist Starminster. Married. No children.

L. J. SMALLHORN, B.A., CANTAB.

Headmaster of the Choir School. Associate of the Society for the Preservation of Tombs and Catafalques. Unmarried.

G. H. SCRIMGEOUR

Solicitor. Daniel Reardon and John Mackrell Prizeman. Clerk to the Chapter of Melchester. Late senior partner of the firm of Wracke, Spindrift, and Scrimgeour, Melchester and Starminster. Unmarried.

MRS. E. A. JUDD

Relict of J. D. Judd, D.D., Canon of Melchester, the celebrated author of *Liturgy for the Millions*,

The Book of Common Prayer Done into the Esquimaux Tongue, etc.

D. APPLEDOWN
Head Verger of Melchester. 1887–1900. Deputy Junior Verger. 1900–1 in S. Africa. 1905–14 Junior Verger. 1914 to date: Head Verger. O.B.E. (Civil Division, Coronation award). Unmarried. One brother.

P. H. PARVIN
Second Verger. Appointed 1925. Married. One son.

R. MORGAN
Third Verger. Appointed 1935. Unmarried.

H. K. BRUMFIT
Late Sgt. Royal Horse Artillery. Served India, Egypt, Palestine (1915–18). Appointed constable of the Close, 1920. Married. Seven children.

THE DEAN OF MELCHESTER

I • Decanus Vigilans

THE DEAN, as he lay awake in bed that memorable Sunday night, pondered the astonishing vagaries of the weather. He felt, as a personal presence in the room, the oppression of the coming storm. His windows were wide open, and an occasional breath of hot air stirred the curtains. Heavy clouds had been stealing up since early evening, and by this time the night was pitchy black. The chimes, as Melchester Cathedral clock struck the half-hour between eleven and midnight, seemed muffled and lethargic.

The Dean turned over in bed for the twentieth time and tried to compose his mind. But his mind refused most obstinately to be composed. And he had a feeling that the elements which troubled it were not entirely atmospheric. The approaching storm magnified and made more oppressive troubles which had been lying in wait and which needed only this occasion to rear up and pop up their confounded heads. Feeling certain that he would get no sleep until the storm broke or passed on, the Dean reluctantly brought himself to consider affairs in general.

What *was* wrong with the Close? In the fourteen years that he had been there he could remember no time of such concentrated irritation and unease. First and foremost, of course, this extraordinary persecution of Appledown, the head verger. It had started over a week ago with anonymous letters. These epistles, typewritten and uniformly abusive, had been received by most of the Close community. The Dean himself had not been favoured, but the Precentor had shown him one which he had found amongst his mail on the previous evening. It was a fair specimen of the anonymous writer's style, and had stated in terms which, despite a liberal classical education, had caused the Dean to clear his throat rapidly, that Appledown was not only inefficient but also immoral—indeed, quite remarkably immoral, the Dean could not help thinking, for a man of nearly seventy.

The postmark had been Starminster—a small market town nearly thirty miles from Melchester—but that this was the merest blind had been made manifest by the disgraceful incidents of the previous Wednesday. The wolf was indeed within the fold.

Melchester, like most other English cathedrals, had its own resident choir school. The sixteen cathedral trebles were housed in two fine Queen Anne buildings standing in the south-west corner of the Close. Wednesday had been the Headmaster's birthday. Such a day was traditionally an excuse, the Dean reflected morosely, for a good deal of unnecessary license and excess. An extra half-holiday was inevitable—superfluous food was consumed and superfluous spirits were let off. However, the day's proceedings usually began quietly enough. Morning prayers (weather permitting) were held in the forecourt, and at their termination the school flag (a curious confection of primary colours) was hoisted to the top of the flagstaff by the head boy. This impressive ceremony duly took place in the presence of the Dean, a scattering of Close worthies, and such errand boys as felt disposed to linger on their morning rounds, but was rather marred by the fact that when the flag floated out in the morning breeze it revealed—stitched in white bunting and painfully visible—the words, "BOOZEY OLD APPLEDOWN."

Needless to say this irreverent legend was taken in very good part by the younger members of the audience, and it was with obvious reluctance that they watched the flag being lowered whilst the offending stitches were cut away. It had been apparent to the Dean that the senior verger, worthy man though he might be, was not over popular with the cathedral choristers. But equally apparent to anyone who knew anything of the curious workings of a boy's mind, that none of them were accessory to the joke. Their surprise had been genuine and their appreciation entirely spontaneous.

There had been a further show at Evensong. The copies of the anthem, when opened, had shed a shower of leaflets, all typewritten, and all harping on the same note. "Appledown is past his job" had been the theme of the unknown letter-writer on this occasion. It was curious, the Dean reflected, the psychological effect which a manoeuver of this sort produced. It had crossed his mind more than once in the past six months that Appledown *was* getting old for his work. It was a responsible post, being head verger of a cathedral: and in Parvin, the second verger, they had a younger man well trained to fill the position.

Immediately, however, the anti-Appledown campaign had begun, his feelings veered strongly. The natural reaction to such an underhand assault had been a strong caucus of pro-Appledown opinion. Sympathy and sentiment had united to condemn cowardly tactics, and far from weakening it the whole affair had strengthened the head verger's position considerably. It might even, reflected the Dean grimly, result in Appledown keeping his post some years longer than he would otherwise have done—after he really *was* past it, in fact. This example of the working of Providence the Dean felt to be vaguely comforting, and he settled himself into a fresh position in bed.

There had been other troubles. Why did Malthus always want to be running off at a moment's notice? Malthus was the second of the three vicars choral, and for two weeks out of every six it was his duty to sing morning and evening service in the cathedral. He had other jobs, of course, but what he did for four weeks was his own business. What the Dean objected to was his desertion of his post during the remaining two.

Of course, he had come and asked for permission— but that made it worse, in a way. Almost as if he were pushing the responsibility on to the Dean. Malthus had tackled him in the vestry after Matins that morning. Prynne wouldn't mind taking Evensong for him, and Matins on Monday. His sister was ill, in the country. He must see her. He was sure Prynne wouldn't mind.

The Dean himself was far from sure. In fact he was pretty certain that Prynne would mind. A feature almost as disturbing to the Dean as the constant absence of second Vicar Choral Malthus was the constant presence of senior Vicar Choral Prynne. Whenever he thought of him—which was frequently—the Dean was reminded

4

of the words in which Milton (his favourite poet) describes Belial at the council of the infernal powers:

> . . . *whose tongue*
> *Dropt manna and could make the worse appear*
> *The better reason to perplex and dash*
> *Maturest counsel.*

Decidedly Ernest Vandeleur Prynne, though an able man, as the Dean reluctantly admitted, had proved a sore trial to more than one member of their community.

"Halliday will be back by midday on Tuesday," Malthus had gone on, "and he won't mind taking over the services for the next day or two." Of course Halliday wouldn't mind, or anyway he wouldn't say so if he did mind. A bit rough on him though, having to cut short his holiday and come back to help Malthus out of a hole. Good chap Halliday, cut short holiday, Halliday's holiday, holiday for Halliday, Halliday—holiday. Holiday—Halliday——

The Dean, despite the oppression in the atmosphere, which seemed, if possible, to have increased during the last few minutes, was on the point of dropping off when a vivid flash of lightning lit up the room and caused him to sit bolt upright in bed. It was not, of course—absurd!— that he was afraid of a thunderstorm; but from boyhood's day he had been, as he put it to himself, more susceptible to their influence than most people. He had counted twenty as fast as he dared before the thunder rolled out, and comforting himself (for he was a firm believer in that particular piece of mumbo-jumbo) with the conclusion that the storm was still twenty miles distant, he lay down again and composed himself once more to sleep.

When all else failed he had still one card to play—one home-made panacea to try. Where other people wooed sleep by counting sheep jumping over a stile, the Dean had often found it efficacious to picture the members of his Chapter as they passed through the choir gates on their way to service. First came the inscrutable Canon Bloss. Canon Bloss had a peculiar aptitude—which the Dean had formerly imagined to be confined to Grand Llamas and Victorian ladies' maids—of progressing without appearing to move his feet. Taken all in all, Canon Bloss was not unlike some Tibetan dignitary in appearance—perhaps some rotund and faintly human idol of the middle Buddhist period, with a good deal of dignity and a number of superfluous stomachs and chins.

Behind him ambled Canon Beech-Thompson, demonstrating both by walk and carriage how inevitable it was that he should be known to a select circle as "Jumbo" Beech-Thompson.

It was with greater tolerance that his mind's eye took in Canon Trumpington, third in the procession. He could not conceal it from himself that he liked Canon Trumpington—unprecedented though it might be for a Dean to entertain such sentiments towards another member of the Chapter. "Take him for all in all," murmured the Dean, gagging a little, "as just a man as e'er my conversation coped withal. A sweet-faced man. As proper a man as one shall see in a summer's day." After him Canon Fox appeared as rather an anti-climax. An indefinite person Canon Fox. He appeared and disappeared as unostentatiously as his animal namesake. Of course he hadn't been at Melchester very long, and no one knew much about him. Canon Fox. Shivering shocks. Iron locks. Box and

6

Cox. The Dean was nodding again. Canon Fox (a deadly association of ideas flicked across his mind) hadn't been there long. He had come—now when had he come? A year ago, no more. And why had he come? For a moment his sleepy brain refused to deal with the subject. Why should a new canon come to Melchester? At that moment as icy shudder ran down the Dean's back. It was almost as if a real voice had whispered the answer. "He came because Canon Whyte had DIED."

At that moment a second brilliant flash of lightning filled the room, throwing every detail into sharp relief. A moment later and the thunder again rolled out. Nearer and more menacing. But this time it seemed to be muttering, "Died—died—fell from the roof and died."

The Dean felt something roll down his cheek, and putting his hand to his forehead he found that it was wet.

What, in heaven's name the Dean asked himself fretfully, had brought that business into his mind at such a particularly unsuitable moment? He was convinced now that he would get no sleep at all that night. The death of Canon Whyte had been very upsetting. Nothing mysterious or really sensational about it, mind you. Nothing— with considerable distaste the Dean formulated the exact word in his mind—nothing "police-court" about it. Just simply upsetting for all concerned: for Canon Whyte's family, and his colleagues on the Chapter: and for Canon Whyte too, of course.

It had all happened more than a year ago. Melchester Cathedral, like many others, was a great centre and an attraction for tourists, in the summer months especially. But the ordinary tourist had perforce to confine his attentions to the more easily accessible parts of the building— the nave, transepts, and choir, the beautiful Lady

Chapel, and the stately cloisters, the old chapter house.

But if you could induce one of the vergers to accompany you, you might penetrate the dark little door in the south-west angle and climb up a spiral of well-trodden stone steps. This brought you out on to the clerestory—further steps, and a very low doorway, and then you were outside, in a narrow gallery which had been originally built for the convenience of the workman who put the first roof on Melchester Cathedral, more than five hundred years before. This gallery, invisible from below, ran right round the roof: and it was from this gallery one sunny morning in early September that Canon Whyte had fallen—a hundred and three measured feet—on to the flagstones in front of the newly erected shed which housed the electric motor which supplied the power for the famous Melchester organ.

It was—the Dean thought of it with a grimace—the only time in the sixty-five years of a sheltered life that he had been brought face to face with the unpleasant reality of violent dissolution. His first thought had been that it was uncommonly messy. A scared and breathless verger with a message that Canon Whyte had fallen and hurt himself had brought him on the scene quite unprepared for the realities of the case. When he had rounded the corner of the chapter house and seen what was to be seen on the sunlit stones, it was by a firm exercise of control that he had prevented himself from being actually sick. A moment of shock will sometimes etch a scene indelibly on the mind, and he had only to shut his eyes to see it again. The towering grey walls, dwarfing the little engine shed. The respectful but interested faces of the three vergers—the flat grey stones—the huddled body—blood and the smell of warm tar. He didn't want to think about

8

that. Above them all, two incongruous pigeons preening themselves and cooing.

Accidental death. Naturally. A coroner's verdict had certified so. Canon Whyte very often took parties of adventurous visitors on a ramble round the outside gallery, pointing out the many interesting terminal carvings and gargoyles so characteristic of the period and the building. In fact he had made a special study of them. The coroner had been informed that he was writing a book on the subject. Well, not exactly a book—a brochure. Anyway, he was often up there alone or with visitors. The parapet was high, of course. The coroner had not been up there himself but he had some measurements. Four feet and four inches from the level of the leading. The jury would appreciate that this would come well up to the chest level of an ordinary man. But of course at such a height it was easy to lose one's head. One got giddy. They had heard, no doubt, of people without much head for heights who could not bring themselves within many feet of the top of a precipice or cliff; they entertained a fear that a fit of vertigo brought on by the contemplation of a great depth beneath them might cause them to lose control. No doubt something of the sort had happened here.

In answer to some tactful but obviously leading questions it was established that Canon Whyte had been perfectly happy. That he was an exceptionally sane and balanced man. No, certainly not, he had left no "note" or letter of any kind, or of course the jury would have had it read to them.

The jury had felt strongly that they should assert themselves with a rider, and had toyed with a suggestion that a strong iron fence should be erected to raise the total height of the balustrade to six feet. However, realizing that this was very unlikely to recommend itself to the authorities, they had contented themselves with a verdict of accidental death and a vote of sympathy for the children of the deceased.

It was really surprising, reflected the Dean, how quickly the excitement had died down. Canon Whyte was a widower, and most providentially his two children were in any case due to have left Melchester in the near future, and had in fact done so shortly afterwards. The daughter, Joan, to be married, and the son to enter the diplomatic service.

Downstairs in the Dean's study stood a very handsome medieval Italian triptych. This had come to him under Canon Whyte's will. The money, of course, had all gone to the two children, but most of his colleagues had been remembered with some small legacy in kind. Six fine oil paintings had gone to Hinkey, who was—or who fancied himself to be—a connoisseur of the arts. And to his particular friend, Canon Trumpington, Whyte had left all his books. Not a large library, but some of the volumes were valuable—not the collection of a bibliophile but of a widely cultured man who bought books to read as well as for the pleasure of standing them on shelves. Trumpington had been the natural recipient for these. His friendship with Whyte had started with a common passion for *The Times* crossword puzzle, and ripened when they discovered in each other a mutual admiration for the works of Boswell.

This more pleasant trend to the Dean's thoughts had again made him sleepy. This time he really was on the point of dropping off when it seemed to his drowsy senses that someone had started working on a typewriter. Not a very expert practitioner, thought the Dean drowsily. Tap-

tap—tappity—tap. Picking out the letters with one finger. A staccato pattering. The unseen typist was improving now, and the tapping became faster. A very vivid flash of lightning awoke the Dean to the fact that a succession of huge thunder drops were pattering on to the linoleum through his wide-open window, and further to the realization that the storm was on them at last. He climbed out of bed.

Successive flashes were lighting the world outside with the clarity of full day. The rain was pelting down now and the thunder almost continuous. Looking up, he reflected, not for the first time, on the very real extent to which the people of Melchester Close lay beneath the shadow and protection of the Cross—the great bronze cross on the spire of the cathedral, which even now was attracting to itself the lightnings of heaven and conducting them safely to earth.

As he lowered his eyes a particularly bright flash illuminated the whole Close, and the Dean saw a man standing in the road at the corner of the precinct wall, in front of and a little to the right of his front gate. A momentary impression, then darkness again. Impatiently the Dean waited for the next flash. He was moderately certain that he had recognized the figure. The lightning flared out again, but the roadway was empty. A moment after, however, a light went up in the front room of the cottage on his left. He had been right. Verger Parvin was up late.

Leaving a fraction of window open the Dean turned and made his way back to bed. His feet padded across the linoleum which entirely covered his rather spartan bedroom. He climbed into bed. He suddenly felt very tired. Despite the closing of the window the air was cooler now.

But his mind would not rest. Like a great dynamo that has been turning at frantic speed but from which the motive power has been cut off, the process of his troubled thoughts continued of its own momentum but to a rhythm which slackened and grew slower. "Something is rotten in the state of Denmark," said his mind. And then, "Something is rotten in the Close of Melchester." Verger Appledown, Vicar Choral Malthus, Vicar Choral Prynne, and Verger Parvin. Parvin was out late. "Men must not walk too late." Canon Trumpington, Canon Fox, Canon Beech-Thompson, Canon Bloss, and old Uncle Hinkey and all.

Bloss. Thompson. Fox. Trumpington.

Trumpington. Fox. Thompson. Bloss.

Thud! Thud! Thud! Thud!

The wheels were slowing now.

Outside, the rain streamed down and the thunder cracked and slithered about the darkened sky. The last light in the Close went out, and still the lightning flared and danced round the cathedral cross.

The Dean slept.

And as he slept he had a most disquieting dream. Appledown was running. Running for dear life across the wide cathedral lawn. Behind him glided the sinister figure of Canon Bloss, armed only with a huge typewriter on which he was typing a message. Against his will the Dean forced himself to look over Canon Bloss's shoulder, but all he could see was a jumble of figures, numbers, exclamations, and percentage marks. This annoyed him so much that he put his lips quite close to Canon Bloss's left ear and bellowed, "What does it all mean?" Upon which Bloss turned into Vicar Choral Prynne and answered slowly, "It means anything you can make out of it—take it or leave it."

When the Dean woke next morning it was bright and cool. He remembered that he had had a disturbed night, but the details were blurred. He knew from experience that he would pay for his broken rest by an overwhelming lassitude at three o'clock that afternoon, but at the moment his mind felt particularly clear and vigorous. He viewed his troubles and found that they had shrunk.

This cheerfulness lasted him over his solitary breakfast, and it was a summer morning's face that he turned on the housemaid when she came to clear away the plates, and volunteered the information that "'Ubbard was in the 'all and would like to see 'im." William Lovejoy Hubbard, the Dean's gardener and factotum, was a man of parts—a massive northcountryman and a native of the most phlegmatic county in England. He appeared to be faintly upset.

Without a word he led the Dean out of the front door and across the lawn. A mellow wall of the same grey stone as had made the cathedral separated the Dean's front garden on the east from that of Doctor Mickie, the organist. When he had reached the wall and adjusted his spectacles, the Dean fully understood his gardener's distress. For painted on it, in great red letters nearly two feet high, was the legend:

WHO FORGOT TO LOCK THE CLOISTER DOOR?
APPLEDOWN, OF COURSE.

Master and man digested this surprising sight in silence for some seconds.

13

"It'll take a deal of getting out," said Hubbard morosely.

"Has anyone else seen this?" asked the Dean.

"Not yet," said Hubbard. "They will, though. I don't see 'ow they can 'ardly miss it."

The Dean thought rapidly.

"You must do your best to scrape it off," he said finally. "Cover it up for the moment as well as you can."

In his guilty haste he felt almost as though they were two Eugene Arams disposing of an unwanted body.

"What a scandalous thing!" Absent-mindedly he ran a finger over one of the vivid letters. The wall was still wet from the rain of the night, but the colouring was dry and set.

With a profound sigh the Dean returned to the house and shut himself in his study. He acknowledged the crisis. Gently but very firmly had Fate laid on the last straw.

The forebodings of the night before, which had vanished for a moment at the touch of the morning sun, were back again now with a vengeance. Where was it going to end? asked the Dean. But all the time he had a most disquieting notion of how it *might* end.

Appledown was an old man: and old people are at the same time more susceptible to the barbed shafts of this poisonous sort of persecution and more ready to take the easy way out. Illogically, perhaps, but unpleasantly, the Dean here thought of Canon Whyte's crumpled body lying on the flagstones. He felt that action was demanded, and for the first time he faced the unpleasant thought of the police. They would have to be brought in—perhaps they should have been brought in before.

His hand was actually stretched out for the telephone when he had an inspiration. Bobby Pollock! Bobby was the Dean's nephew, the youngest son of his youngest (and favourite) sister. Bobby had joined the Metropolitan Police Force, and not through the pleasant portals of Hendon College either. The Dean had not seen him for some years, but had heard that he was attached to Scotland Yard and doing well.

A lack of knowledge of police procedure caused the Dean a moment's hesitation. Could one call in Scotland Yard over the heads of the local police? The Chief Constable of Melchester, the Dean remembered vaguely, was an ex-regular, with strong ideas on the importance of his own position and the necessity of closing licensed premises on the stroke of ten. He did not imagine him to be the sort of man who would take kindly to any usurpation of authority.

But stay—why make it an official matter at all? Why should not Bobby take two or three days' holiday and stop with his uncle? A discreet inquiry by a trained man would quickly settle the affair, and if not, at least it would frighten the practical joker, and it could all be extremely unofficial. The Dean reflected that he possessed at least one influential connection at the Home Office. He felt confident that the matter could be arranged.

Leaving the telephone, therefore, he sat down to compose three letters. Firstly, an official invitation to Bobby to visit Melchester for a few days, which could, if necessary, be shown to inquisitive superiors. Secondly, a less official one, setting out for Bobby's edification alone the true facts of the case. Thirdly and lastly, a highly official one to Sir Marmaduke Pelling, O.B.E., one of His Majesty's Under-Secretaries of State for Home Affairs.

"And that," said the Dean, "shelves the matter for twenty-four hours at least."

The thought was premature.

A letter came for the Dean that night. It was in a plain, unaddressed, rather cheap envelope, and an unknown hand pushed it through his letter-box some time after seven in the evening. It was written in a thin, unformed hand on cheap lined paper, and stated simply:

"Mr. Busybody Appledown has lived too long. Someone will get him soon if he doesn't look out."

But unlike the other effusions this one was signed with a bold "J. B."

II • Clearing the Ground

The evidence of vice and virtue are not confined to famous accomplishments: Often some trivial event, a word, a joke, will serve better than great campaigns as a revelation of character.

PLUTARCH

"EVEN A STRAW," concluded the Dean, "will show you which way the wind is blowing. And as there's never smoke without fire——"

"Nor bricks without straw," agreed Sergeant Pollock of the Criminal Investigation Department pleasantly. "Let's have all the facts."

Uncle and nephew faced each other across the table in the Dean's library-cum-study. It was a pleasant room—tolerant, not over-academic. Marcus Aurelius and Jeremy Bentham looked down from adjacent shelves. Benjamin Disraeli, the Dean's large black cat, reclined across the round patch of sunlight which fell on the carpet and watched the two men with a deceptive leer.

He was a knowing animal, incredibly wise in the ways of mankind, and he realized that these two beings—apparently addressing themselves briskly to the work in hand—were really engaged in the age-old pursuit of summing each other up: as he himself had summed up many a possible ally or potential rival in his moonlight

17

rhodomontades and dark witches' sabbaths.

How the lad had grown, thought the Dean. The power of the young to grow was a constant source of surprise to him. It seemed a very short time ago that he had been visiting him at school with a half-sovereign. A few years in London had not only added inches to his stature —they had hardened him and refined him into something which looked to the Dean uncommonly like a man. He seemed competent. Not officious, exactly, yet very efficient. For a moment the Dean experienced the touch of disquiet. Here was no kindly nephew who would ask a few questions for his uncle and then retire discreetly, but a modern police officer. The sort of man who probably delighted in leaving no stone unturned. And underneath stones—large flat stones—even the stones of Melchester—there lived all manner of slimy things. Would it not perhaps be better to send him back—now, immediately? Laugh the matter off. A foolish old uncle, making mountains out of molehills. It could be done. It would be so easy to say that the culprit had confessed; that the Chapter had decided, in the best interest of the cathedral, to hush the matter up. Give the boy a few days of real holiday. The Dean, had he known it, held a good deal of human happiness and unhappiness in his hands at that moment.

Sergeant Pollock secretly approved of his uncle. Indeed, he admired in him several most worldly qualities which that cleric would have been the first to disclaim, but he was determined not to be put down by him. This was to be an ordinary routine job, quite uncomplicated by any considerations of affinity.

It was going to be awkward enough without anything of that sort. Anonymous letters! Broadsheets! Unknown sign-painters and comic flags! The thing was miles removed from an honest job of police work. He was not even sure what particular crime or misdemeanour any of the incidents amounted to. Obscenity? Threats with intent to procure—what? That was the question. There must be some reason behind the silly business. Criminal libel? On the whole, it would be better to pin it to the letters. "Misuse of His Majesty's mails" covered a multitude of sins. However, there were consolations. It should prove a respite. A real and badly needed holiday after that rather beastly affair which had been occupying his attention for the last two months. Melchester would prove a decided contrast to Kentish Town. Of course, even in that affair Hazlerigg had done the real work. Good old Hazlerigg. He was the man to have behind you on a nasty case. As solid as the Tower of London, with a first-rate brain behind that deceptively sanguine façade. The finest chief inspector at the Yard. Well—he could manage a little case like this off his own bat, thank you. As a dabbler in amateur psychology he had already classified the affair as "spontaneous social combustion": the result of a community thrown too much into its own company. It would have been difficult for him to have been more completely wrong.

The Dean consulted his diary.

"We'd better take the letters first," he said. "I'm afraid most of the recipients destroyed them as soon as they got them, but I've collected two for you. And mine makes a third. As a matter of fact it was only when the business became public property that I discovered about some of them. As far as I can make it out the sequence was as follows: Canon Hinkey, our Precentor, got the first—it came on the morning of September the ninth. Two days later Canon Bloss got one."

"Then Parvin got one, on the fourteenth. A very unpleasant little letter accusing Appledown of consorting with Mrs. Parvin. He naturally brought it to me, and actually that was the first one I saw. I advised him to burn it and forget about it. I'm afraid," added the Dean parenthetically, "that a good deal of valuable evidence was destroyed in that sort of way, but I suppose that's always the way at the beginning of an affair like this."

He referred again to his diary.

"Canon Trumpington got one on the fifteenth, and Canon Fox got one the day after. Neither of them said anything to me at the time, and I'm fairly certain that both letters were destroyed. Mrs. Judd was the next. She was very upset about it and brought the letter over immediately. It was then that I made inquiries and found out about the earlier ones. There was a lull after that, but I have a note that Canon Prynne showed me one he had received on the morning of Monday the twentieth. He seemed rather pleased about it than otherwise and proposed publishing it in the Diocesan *Gazette*. However, I dissuaded him from such an unseemly course, and he handed it over to me. That was the last letter."

Pollock checked over the notes he had made.

"Before we go on," he said, "I had an idea that you had only four canons at Melchester."

"That is correct," agreed the Dean.

Pollock looked puzzled, and referred again to his notes.

"You have already mentioned five," he said.

"I might have mentioned eight," said the Dean kindly. "Let me explain. We have four principal canons. But the

Precentor in this foundation is a minor canon—as are also the three vicars choral. They are all referred to as canons indiscriminately."

"I see," said Pollack guardedly; "then which are your four canons-in-chief?"

"Canons residentiary," corrected the Dean gently. "Bloss, Trumpington, Beech-Thompson, and Fox. Hinkey is Precentor and minor canon. Prynne, Malthus, and Halliday are the vicars choral and minor canons also. Their job is to sing the services. They are on duty for a fortnight at a time—or are supposed to be," he added, as the defection of Canon Malthus crossed his mind.

Pollock did not accept the gambit, but simply remarked:

"That doesn't sound as if they were overworked."

"Of course, they have other jobs as well—chaplaincies in the town. Prynne and Halliday both teach at the choir school."

"Choir school," said Pollock, looking up sharply, "I didn't know you kept schoolboys in the Close. You don't think perhaps that they may have been responsible—"

"Certainly not," said the Dean firmly. "The tone of some of the letters! Most improbable. You'll understand when you read them."

"Still, it's a possibility," persisted Pollock, who worked in a district in London where "small boy" was synonymous with all the dirtier and more tiresome types of mischief. "Please go on."

"The headmaster, Dr. Smallhorn, has a house next to the school. The boys sleep in the school building itself. There are only sixteen boarders—all choristers—besides a few day boys. A most respectable type of lad," he added severely, for Pollock's unworthy suspicions still rankled.

"Many of them sons of the clergy of the diocese. Canon Fox's eldest son has just entered the school," he went on, in the tone of one who plays a trump card.

"Masters?" suggested Pollock, with a vague idea of an irresponsible undergraduate element in the Close.

"Only a visiting master—who comes in the morning," said the Dean, "and, as I said, Prynne and Halliday help with the teaching. The musical side is run by our organist, Dr. Mickie—he has the house next to mine, by the way. I'll take you out and point out the lie of the land in a moment. The vergers, Appledown, Parvin, and Morgan, all have cottages."

The Dean paused; and Pollock, who had been scribbling desperately but methodically, looked up.

"By the way, who was that massive warrior who saluted me at the gate when I came in?"

"Sergeant Brumfit," said the Dean. "The Close constable. A most reliable man. I am sure he'll give you any help you want. Anything that he can do, that is," he added more doubtfully. Somehow, excellent though he was with hawkers, canvassers, and circulars, he did not see Sergeant Brumfit tracking an anonymous letter-writer to his lair. "He has a cottage just inside the gate—and that completes the roster. No—wait a moment: I'm sure I've missed somebody. Oh, yes, Scrimgeour. He's the chapter clerk. A real old-fashioned solicitor. He has the little house next to Mickie's: and that really is the lot."

One of Pollock's chief assets was an almost photographic memory.

"Mrs. Judd?" he suggested, without apparent reflection.

"I was coming to her," said the Dean reluctantly. Rather in the manner of one who dis-cupboards a tiresome skeleton. "Her position here is really most irregular. We are not a residential Close, in the sense of Canterbury or Salisbury. We are not large enough. The accommodation is very limited, and the houses are allocated by rule. Mrs. Judd is the relict of old Canon Judd. You may have heard of him. A great scholar. His life's work was the translation of the *Book of Common Prayer* into the Eskimaux tongue. When his publishers complained that it would have a very limited sale in England he did a re-translation into English to accompany it—a distinct improvement on the original in many places, I believe. Well, when he died there happened to be a cottage vacant and we allowed Mrs. Judd to move in—just for a few weeks, whilst she looked round, you know. That was twelve years ago. We tried everything short of force, but she just wouldn't go. She's a very determined old lady—though getting a bit shaky now."

Pollock conducted a rapid mental roll-call.

When he had found all present and correct he asked a question which the Dean had been expecting for some time.

"Is there any reason," he said, "for confining our attention to the inhabitants of the Close?"

The Dean smiled complacently: this was naturally a point to which he had devoted a good deal of thought, and he was not averse to a little disquisition.

"In the first place," he said, "you will concede that it would be natural to look for the author of such an attack amongst Appledown's—I won't say friends—nearer acquaintances. Some of the letters show that the writer was quite familiar with his private affairs: and you may have noticed that many of the attacks are directed against him in his official capacity—imputing failure to do his duty as a verger."

"Not quite the usual anonymous dirt," agreed Pollock.

"But there are far stronger reasons," went on the Dean. "Reasons which, taken together, amount to a certainty. First, the flag which was tampered with. It's kept in a locker with several other flags and pennants in a shed in the school yard. The shed is not locked, so I suppose it's just conceivable that a stranger might have got hold of it, but less likely that he should have known where it was kept."

"When was that particular flag used last?" asked Pollock.

That the Dean could not tell him. He passed on to the anthem incident.

All the music was kept in cupboards in the vestry. Any visitors to the cathedral might have slipped in and inserted the offending notices, but the Dean implied that he thought the contingency most unlikely, and Pollock was inclined to agree with him.

A thought struck him.

"Surely," he said, "no outsider would know in advance what anthem was going to be sung at any particular service."

"I'm afraid that won't do," said the Dean regretfully. "A list of the anthems and services is made up a week in advance and posted in the porch; it also appears in the local paper.

"But," he went on, "there is a third point which is, I think, decisive. After seven o'clock it is impossible to get in or out of the Close unobserved."

He waited complacently for some expression of incredulity, but Pollock contented himself with saying,

"Surely you mean very difficult—not impossible." He had observed the high smooth stone walls and the massive gate. Also he knew something of the medieval régime of a Close.

"Nothing is impossible," agreed the Dean, "but I suggest that entry to this Close after dark is so nearly impossible that you may rule it out of your considerations altogether."

"I was impressed by your walls," agreed Pollock, "but even for twelve-foot walls you only need a twelve-foot ladder—and a little luck."

"It's more complicated than that, I fear," said the Dean. "On the east of the Close lies the Bishop's palace. The Bishop, by the way, is at the moment in Switzerland —for his health." (The Dean's explanation was not entirely unsatirical.) "The palace is shut up. That is the most inaccessible side, since an intruder would not only have to climb two walls—the outer Close wall and the palace garden wall—but at the foot of the outer wall runs the river, which is both swift and deep at that point owing to the constriction of the water between the wall and an embankment on the other side. I think we may rule out the south approach. To the north and west and east the walls give on to well-lighted public roads. This is the residential quarter, and innumerable front parlour and bedroom windows overlook every inch of the perimeter. All three roads are patrolled regularly by the police. To my mind it is quite inconceivable that anyone could come along, plant a ladder against the wall, climb up, and pull the ladder up after him—unobserved. And if he *had* been observed you may be very sure we should have heard about it the very next morning—with embroideries and additions."

"I don't think it's impossible," said Pollock slowly, "but I agree with you that no one could *rely* on doing it and getting away with it—which is good enough from our point of view."

He shifted his ground.

"When are the gates shut?" he asked.

"Evensong," explained the Dean, "finishes at about six-thirty. People leave from all three gates—south gate, bishop's gate, and the main gate—that's the one you came in by. When Brumfit thinks that everyone has had plenty of time to get clear he walks across to the south gate, warning any people who may be loitering about." (The Dean was referring tactfully to half a dozen brace of lovers—hardy amorists who pursued their courtship on the benches which the Dean and Chapter had so thoughtfully set up in the precincts for admirers of early English architecture.) "When he has shut the south gate and shepherded the last straggler out of bishop's gate and shut that too, he comes back up the east path to the main gate, arriving there a few minutes before seven. He has a little office attached to his house, facing the gate, and he's 'on duty' in it until eleven, when he locks up and goes to bed. If you want to get in after that time you have to ring the bell and he will come down and open the gate for you."

"He must have rather a disturbed night," suggested Pollock.

"Why?" queried the Dean innocently. "We are generally in bed by eleven, you know, and we don't visit much outside the Close."

Reflecting that those few simple words told him more of the community into which he had strayed than hours of questioning, Pollock went on to his next point.

"Do you mean to say," he said, "that Brumfit sits solidly at his post from seven-thirty till eleven, keeping such a watch on the gate that no one can possibly slip in unobserved?"

"He has seven active and vigilant assistants," explained the Dean. "I don't say that the good sergeant doesn't take his ease in front of the fire with a pipe, but if he does so you may be sure that one or other of his seven children is on sentry-go, doing Father's work for him. Not that they look on it as work, of course. In fact, I believe it is a great privilege in the Brumfit family to 'take the gate'. Anyone who wants to go out or in after seven simply signs in the book, crossing out their name when they come back. So Brumfit can see at a glance if any of the residents are still out when he locks the gate."

Considering this arrangement critically—and admitting to himself that the vigilance of childish eyes was often the most difficult to escape—Pollock was fain, for the moment, to accept the impregnability theory.

"I take it," he said, "that two of the incidents—the two which concern you—must have taken place after seven o'clock."

"There's no doubt about that," said the Dean. "My letter-box is cleared by the maid at seven o'clock after the evening delivery. She takes out all the letters and puts mine in my study. The letter wasn't there then. I found it myself at about ten past eight. As regards the other business, it's more mysterious still. I was in my garden, talking to Mickie, until after half-past seven: I remember now, it was the evening of the storm, and very hot and sticky. I dined with the windows wide open. And no one could possibly have come into the garden or painted that disgraceful message until quite a late hour, or I should have been certain to have noticed them."

"Did you, in fact, see anybody in or near your garden?" asked Pollock.

"Yes," said the Dean, "I did." And he told him what he had seen in the storm. "It looks as if Parvin might have to explain his movements."

"Wait a minute," said Pollock. "You never actually said that you saw Parvin. First a flash of lightning—a figure standing on the road outside. Then darkness for some minutes. Then the light goes up in Parvin's front room. That's correct, isn't it?"

"It was Parvin, all the same," said the Dean stubbornly. At this juncture a remarkably pretty housemaid announced lunch.

After lunch Pollock inspected the letters but could make little of the first two. They simply confirmed his opinion that people read too many detective stories, being efficient products of the only really foolproof style of anonymous communication in which letters and words are cut from a printed page and pasted on to paper. The third—the Dean's letter—was much more interesting. It was written in a thin characterless scrawl—yet not an illiterate hand, Pollock would have said. Most probably disguised. But what gave him great hopes was that he fancied that he could detect a faint and smudgy print on the glossy surface of the envelope. It might be the Dean's, of course; and then again, it might not. It seemed, on the face of it, incredibly careless of the writer to leave his sign manual on his work, but in Pollock's experience wrongdoers often were just that: incredibly careless over the things that really mattered.

He laid it carefully aside and asked to be shown the celebrated garden wall. Here he had yet another demonstration of the Dean's unrivalled ability as a destroyer of evidence. Hubbard had carried out his orders faithfully, and a raw and roughened area was all that remained to mark the scene of the crime. A hope which he had entertained, of taking a sample of the paint and having it analysed, faded.

The Dean appeared quite impenitent over his unprofessional conduct: indeed, his chief feeling seemed to be one of gratification at the prompt removal of such a public display of bad taste.

"Now that we're out here," said Pollock resignedly, "perhaps you could point out where these people live. I may have to go round and see some of them this afternoon. By the way, do they know who I am and why I'm here, and all that sort of thing?"

"The Chapter know," said the Dean. "I mean of course, the Lesser Chapter, my four residentiary canons."

"Of course," said Pollock, "I suppose you had to consult them about getting me down here."

"Naturally," agreed the Dean smoothly. He did not feel it incumbent on him to explain that he had consulted his Chapter after the event—as he did on most matters of importance. "But everybody," he went on, "must know by now about the Appledown business. And I'm sure that they will be as helpful as they can: we all deplore it deeply."

"Of course," agreed Pollock, wondering not for the first time whether he was a bigger fool than his uncle took him for. "And now that you've given me such a very clear 'Who's Who,' perhaps we might have a 'Who's Where'?"

Pollock extracted from his pocket a printed plan. It had come from the front of a little book called *Residential Closes of England*, and he had already subjected it to considerable study during his journey down. As the Dean talked he filled names into the outlines in his neat script.

"Starting at the main gate," said the Dean, "we have Sergeant Brumfit's cottage, and facing it across that small dividing lane is Scrimgeour's house. He's a bachelor and lives with his sister; they've both been away for more than a month, but I think they're due back next week. Between Scrimgeour's house and mine is Mickie's. He is married but has no family. That big out-building you can see at the back is the practice room which the choir use on Monday, Tuesday, and Friday nights—other practices are in the cathedral. Those two cottages in the north-west corner belong to Mrs. Judd and Parvin."

"Parvin's being the outer one, I suppose," said Pollock.

"A deduction," smiled the Dean, "based on the fact that I could see his front windows from my bedroom."

"Correct," agreed Pollock with a grin. "Has Parvin any family?"

"His wife lives with him—I think there was a boy, but he's grown up and gone. The first of the three big houses on that side is Hinkey's—he's a bachelor. I can't imagine how he manages to use all that rambling great place. He has three cats, and they used to say that each one had his own bedroom, sitting-room, and bathroom. The middle house is Fox's, and the farther one belongs to Trumpington. By the way, they are known officially as the West Canonry North and the West Canonry South. Trumpington's a bachelor. Fox is our family man: he's got four children—two small girls, a small boy—and the older boy, as I told you, at the choir school. The little cottage next to West Canonry South—you can just see it—is Appledown's, and the house beyond that is Halliday's. Halliday is another of our bachelors."

Pollock's Plan: Showing the names of the present occupants.

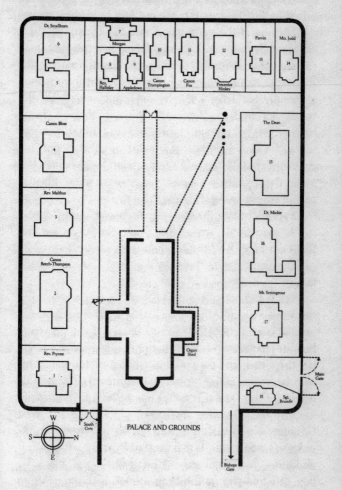

"Is Appledown a family man?" asked Pollock.

"Hardly," said the Dean. "In fact, I should say that Appledown had very little use for women. He lives with his brother, who is older than he is, and I fear rather a disreputable person. He keeps house for Appledown. And, I shoud imagine, liquidates a good deal of his pay. Morgan, the junior verger, has that little cottage you can see over Halliday's garden wall. The rest of the south-west corner is taken up with the choir school and Smallhorn's house. Along the south side you can see that there are two large houses, alternating with two smaller ones. First comes the South Canonry West—that's Bloss. He lives with his unmarried daughter. The first small one belongs to Malthus—he's married and has three children. Next to that is the South Canonry East: Beech-Thompson— wife but no children. Last of all, before you come to the south gate, is Canon Prynne's house. He's a widower and lives with his unmarried daughter."

"Thank you," said Pollock a little breathlessly: he went back over the eighteen houses and their occupants and was pleased to find that he could remember them perfectly. The arrangement of the south side of the Close was particularly gratifying to an orderly mind. Big house, little house, big house, little house. Canon, minor canon, canon, minor canon. Like a huge ecclesiastical sandwich with alternate layers of jam and cream.

As they walked back together to the study Pollock considered his best plan of action. First, he wanted at least an hour alone with his notes, and possibly a pipe of tobacco. Then he thought he would like to begin by doing a little elimination. Here the Dean was again able to help him. Scrimgeour, it appeared, had been away the whole time —both he and his sister were in London, and the house was shut up. Halliday and his sister had gone away on Wednesday, September 8th, and should have had three weeks by the sea, but had had to curtail it because Malthus had insisted on running off on Sunday evening. He imagined that Halliday had just got back—anyway, he was due to take Evensong. Canon and Mrs. Beech-Thompson had got back on Monday evening; they had been away on holiday since September 6th.

"Of course," said Pollock thoughtfully, "we mustn't go too fast. Just because one of these people was away on holiday, that is not enough to exempt them from all suspicion with regard to some of the incidents—in the matter of the letters possibly rather a contrary inference might be drawn."

"You mean," said the Dean slowly, "that whilst Beech-Thompson or Halliday or Scrimgeour was supposed to be on holiday, he might have had an opportunity of eluding his family, or friends, and slipped over to Starminster and posted these letters."

Pollock looked up sharply He had not been mistaken. The Dean was laughing at him.

"I am sorry if I appeared to treat the suggestion with levity," said the Dean. "It was just that I was trying to picture Beech-Thompson leaping on to his bicycle each night and pedalling over to Starminster with his pockets full of anonymous letters. A sustained course of such conduct would—or so I should have imagined—have rendered him a little conspicuous."

"The same would apply to anyone living in the Close," said Pollock after a pause in which he, too, endeavoured to visualize the aged clerical bicyclist skimming along the moonlit road with venom in his heart and a selection of vindictive missives in his pocket. "But I

fancy," he went on more briskly, "that we shall find some
quite simple explanation of the daily posting in Starminster. There are a number of ways in which such a thing
might be arranged."

At this point the Dean looked at his watch and discovered that he was already five minutes late for the League
of Pity Needlework Committee, at which he was to take
the chair.

Having rapidly conferred upon Pollock the freedom of
his household and warned him that dinner that evening
would be at half-past seven ("no need to dress"), the Dean
snatched up some papers which he later discovered to be
a transcript of his sermon for next Sunday, and departed
in a well-organized flurry.

At the door he turned for a moment and looked back.

Pollock was motionless in his chair. He was already
deep in his notes and a cloud of tobacco smoke encircled
his head. It struck the Dean that he had not yet mentioned the unfortunate business of Canon Whyte. But on
second thoughts, why should he? It had nothing to do
with the matter in hand.

III • Cathedral Evensong

And love the high embowed roof,
With antick Pillars massy proof,
And storied windows richly dight,
Casting a dimm religious light.
There let the pealing organ blow,
To the full voic'd Quire below
In service high and Anthems cleer

HEAD HAPPILY WREATHED in tobacco smoke, Pollock
collected his thoughts into logical sequences. He assembled his dramatis personæ and paraded them for a critical
inspection. Four canons (residentiary), a precentor, three
vicars (choral), a headmaster, three vergers, an organist,
and one old-fashioned solicitor. Behind them—a rather
more shadowy rank—he ranged their womenfolk.
Canons' wives and daughters (not forgetting that celebrated relict, Mrs. Judd). To complete the caste he added
at one end Appledown's disreputable brother and the
worthy Sergeant Brumfit, and at the other, withal reluctantly and with a certain sentiment of family disloyalty,
his uncle the Dean.

He was already, it will be noticed, tacitly accepting the
theory that this was an "inside job." He could not have
explained in so many words why he was certain of this: he
had a feeling about the matter which depended little on

facts like high walls and locked gates, and a good deal on mere intuition.

He also felt that it was a one-man (or one-woman?) show. Here the balance of his experience was in favour of the proposition. It had been his melancholy duty during his short term of service in the police to investigate a number of anonymous slanderings and "poison-pen" cases, and he could not call to mind a single example of complicity in such affairs. They were, by their very nature, a product of "a mind diseased." People with obsessions: often, he had found, rather lonely and pathetic people.

He considered the letters themselves. An obvious point was the difference between the last letter—the Dean's—and the others. Why should it be in handwriting, where the others were of the cut-out-and-paste-on variety? And what was the point of the initials? Was it a piece of stupid bravado, or something more subtle? The Dean, assisted by an adult voters' register, had already ascertained that there was no J. B. living in the Close. Brumfit was Sergeant Albert Alfred Kitchener Brumfit, whilst his wife, to complete a patriotic household, bore the name of Elizabeth Florence Nightingale Brumfit. Canon Bloss, the other possible candidate, was Herbert Patrick, and his as yet unmarried daughter was Monica Berwyn.

Pollock felt most strangely that he was, in nursery parlance, "getting warm." That these startling discrepancies in the last letter contained a real key to the business, a key which he had not yet the skill or the knowledge to manipulate. Still, the thumbprint might be helpful.

Granting the truth of his own hunch that the culprit had no accomplices, and the soundness of the Dean's contentions as to the inviolability of the Close after seven o'clock in the evening, it became obvious that the vital incidents were the writing on the Dean's wall and the letter which an unknown hand had thrust into the Dean's letter-box at some time after seven on that Monday evening. It seemed strongly probable that anyone who was out of the Close on Sunday night, or who could produce an alibi (why, he wondered, did it seem slightly incongruous to him to think of clergymen with alibis?) for the period of seven to eight-fifteen on Monday evening, could be eliminated.

"Sound elimination," as his old Chief Inspector used to say, "is the basis of all detection." Good. He would start by eliminating as many people as possible. According to the Dean the entire Beech-Thompson, Halliday, and Scrimgeour *ménages* had been away on holiday, whilst Vicar Choral (and minor canon) Malthus had departed at teatime on Sunday to visit a sick relative. Pollock placed a neatly pencilled cross against each of them in his notebook and registered the determination that his first port of call should be the South Canonry East. He would see Beech-Thompson and Halliday, and ask them a few tactful questions about their holidays.

Under the normal headings of motive and method Pollock could find little to help him. He supposed that it might be to the advantage of either the second or the junior verger to get Appledown removed from office in order to step into his place and superior emoluments. But he could not help reflecting that if Parvin or Morgan had instituted the persecution with such an object they were likely to achieve very little by it.

Anyway, motive was likely to prove a broken reed in a case like this. Obsession mania—complexes of all sorts.

One talked glibly of them—especially if one had read the latest popular approach to psychology. But they were difficult to diagnose in practice: more difficult still to detect. The most saintly countenance might mask a seething fury of inhibitions. The most ordinary-looking breast-pocket might contain a poison pen.

As a rough plan of campaign Pollock felt that the first thing to do was to obtain the fingerprints of every resident in the Close and send them to London with the Dean's anonymous letter for expert scrutiny. This was plain police routine, and yet somehow he shrank from it. What was straightforward in Wapping became a little complicated within the classical purlieus of Melchester. A second step was the elimination of those with sound alibis for Sunday and Monday night: Pollock rose to his feet with a sigh and collected his notes.

Some minutes later he was knocking at the front door of the South Canonry East.

A thin parlourmaid opened the door, accepted Pollock with a practised glance, and showed him into a frigid morning-room. Here he was left kicking his heels for just long enough to imply that, after all, he had called without making an appointment, and then the same maid ushered him into the holy of holies, the canonical library.

Canon Beech-Thompson, once he understood that he was speaking to the Dean's nephew, thawed considerably. He was a robust-looking man of about sixty, with a mop of white hair and a skin of that smooth and satiny pinkness which comes from a complete lack of worry and many hours of healthful sleep.

Pollock opened with a few general inquiries as to the health of the canon and his wife (which, as he was doubtless gratified to learn, was in both cases excellent) and passed on to their recently concluded holiday (extraordinary weather for the time of year!). At the first faint and tentative approach, however, to the real business of his visit, an unmistakable frigidity crept into the atmosphere: and when Pollock admitted that besides being the Dean's nephew he had also the questionable taste to be a member of the Criminal Investigation Department, he was aware almost physically of the drop in temperature. Feeling quite uncomfortably like the hero of a Bateman drawing, he ploughed on with his questions.

Reluctantly, as a man who is losing his last few teeth, the canon admitted a bare minimum of information to be extracted from him. Yes, he and his wife had been at Bournemouth for the last three weeks. Yes, the whole time. They had stayed at the Esplanade Hotel—everyone knew the Esplanade Hotel. On the night of Sunday, September 26th, he had been in bed of course. Where else did Pollock expect him to be? He always retired to bed at ten o'clock precisely. Pollock's nerve failed him at the mere thought of asking whether his wife could corroborate this part of the canon's alibi, and he passed on hastily.

On Monday evening they had attended a concert of classical music in the hotel. He failed to see entirely what concern of the police his movements (or those of his dear wife) might be. Yes, he knew that certain frivolous and disgusting letters had been received in the Close, but since he had had nothing to do with them he was at a loss to see why he was being questioned. Pollock admitted that his visit was a mere matter of routine and took a hurried farewell. He was beginning to perceive that detection in the Close might have its own difficulties.

He made his way towards the modest house of Vicar Choral Halliday.

The door was opened by a wizened, determined-looking woman. To Pollock's cheerful good afternoon she replied dubiously—and a little inconsequentially—that she would see if Mr. Halliday was in.

"Tell him that a Mr. Pollock would like a word with him."

The name clearly meant little to her, for she shook her head angrily and pattered off down the passage.

A few minutes later she reappeared.

"What name, please?" she barked.

Pollock repeated the information.

"He won't insure his life," retorted the old lady with great determination. "It's insured twice already."

"And very rightly," said Pollock approvingly. "You can't be too careful these days."

"Sun Alliance, and Moon Equable Incorporated," said the old lady resignedly. "I dare say they're as bad as each other."

Pollock was just wondering whether he had stumbled unexpectedly into Alice in Wonderland when a hearty clerical figure appeared at the end of the passage.

"All right, Biddy. Excuse me, I'm Halliday. Let me see, do I know you?"

Pollock got an impression of muscular Christianity, and advanced resolutely past the still suspicious Biddy.

"I'm Pollock," he said (thinking how silly your own name sounded when you had to repeat it three times in as many minutes). "The Dean sent me over to talk to you about a small matter which has cropped up. I'm his nephew, you know."

"Oh, come in," said Halliday more genially, opening the study door and revealing an untidy room. "It's quite all right, Biddy you run along and help Miss Halliday with the unpacking. I'm afraid we're rather in a mess, you know," he went on sweeping two tennis rackets and a pair of sand-shoes from the nearest chair. "Just back from our holiday. Won't you sit down." As Biddy backed out of the room, her gaze still fixed suspiciously on Pollock as though she expected him at any moment to blossom with pink proposal forms and premium schedules, he added, "Now what can I do for you?"

Feeling that in this case there would be no harm in trying the approach direct, Pollock said, "I shan't keep you very long, I dare say. As a matter of fact, I'm a police officer from Scotland Yard. I understand that you and your sister have been away from Melchester for some time, so you mayn't know much of what has been going on, but during the last few days somebody has been sending some rather stupid and unpleasant messages to people in the Close—mostly about your head verger, Apple-down."

"I had heard something about it as a matter of fact," said Halliday slowly. "Trumpington, he's one of the canons, you know, wrote to me. Something about a flag and the anthem at Evensong. And now that you mention it I remember that he said he'd had an anonymous letter."

"Letters have been sent," said Pollock carefully, "and it would seem from their nature and contents that they constitute a criminal offence. The evidence would seem to point to the fact that they were written by a resident of the Close."

"Good gracious," said Halliday mildly. "What a very extraordinary thing."

"You'll appreciate," went on Pollock more informally, "that I have to question everyone. I'm starting by trying

to eliminate those people who weren't here. I wondered——"

"You'd like me to prove an alibi," said Halliday cheerfully, coming to the point with such crude abandon as
momentarily to take Pollock aback. "For what time or
times?" he added ingenuously.

"Well," said Pollock cautiously, "it would be a help to
start with, if you would let me know what you were doing
last Sunday evening."

"Preaching," said Halliday, and seeing a slight look of
mystification on Pollock's face he added, "I don't often
take a proper holiday, you know. Too hard up. But I
sometimes do locum for an old friend of mine who has a
tiny little parish in North Devon—seventeen inhabitants
and a three-by-four church: you know the sort of thing.
Just Sunday services, and a very good golf course opposite
the front door. Evensong (with sermon), at six-thirty till
about seven-thirty. Last Sunday, after evening service, my
sister and I went back to dinner with the local big-wigs.
I'm afraid we sat it out a bit late as I knew their eldest son
at Cambridge, and he was spending the week-end with
them—I suppose we were back before one o'clock in the
morning, and then——"

"Have you got a car?" interrupted Pollock.

"Afraid not," said Halliday. "Can't afford it, you
know."

"In that case," said Pollock with a smile, "and seeing
that we are at least two hundred and fifty miles from
North Devon, I don't think I need trouble you for any
detailed account of how you spent the rest of the night."

"Well, that's lucky anyway," said Halliday with an an-
swering grin. "Old Evershed's vintage port being all that it

is I don't remember much myself until breakfast at nine-thirty the next morning."

"What did you do on Monday?" said Pollock.

"Golf with the chap I was telling you about from Cambridge, tea in the clubhouse about five."

"All right," said Pollock. "Subject to verification, I think that disposes of you. You'd better let me have the name of the man you had dinner with."

"Sir Lionel Evershed. The Red House, Tawton, North Devon."

"Thank you, I'll make a note of that."

"This is really rather fun, isn't it?" said Halliday unexpectedly. "I mean I've read so often in books of people being asked to account for all their movements on the night of the thirteenth of April, and I've always rather wanted to be asked to account for my own. In fact, I sometimes wondered if I should be able to remember exactly what I'd done on a particular night after, say, six months."

"It's not very difficult," said Pollock, "as long as there's something to fix it by and you don't have to be exact about times."

"If you want to eliminate someone else who has been away," suggested Halliday, "why not try your arts on Canon Beech-Thompson?"

"I have questioned Canon Beech-Thompson," replied Pollock shortly.

"And got an imperial raspberry?" said Halliday with a most unclerical grin. "I suppose he went all Crockford at once. He's not such a bad chap really. Very good-tempered if you rub him up the right way. You know they all call him 'Jumbo'? I think his trouble is really that he suffers from a bit of an inferiority complex, and that's always inclined to make you brusque to strangers, don't you think?"

Pollock, who was beginning to like Vicar Choral Halliday, agreed with this diagnosis and rose to take his leave, but was pressed to stay to tea; and as it was nearly five and he guessed that tea at the Deanery was now a thing of the past, he agreed readily. Over this meal—served by the still suspicious Biddy—he made the acquaintance of Miss Halliday, a pleasant coltish girl, a little younger than her brother, he guessed, and learned among other miscellaneous items of information that Canon Bloss was "very mysterious" but "rather a dear" (this from Miss Halliday). That Vicar Choral Prynne was universally disliked (and yet Pollock got an illogical impression that Miss Halliday rather admired him). That Malthus was notorious for always being hard up—having a large family to support; indeed, that all the vicars choral were hard up, being scandalously underpaid, whilst the canons apparently received salaries a good deal in excess of their capabilities. That the same inequality extended to the vergers; as far as Halliday knew, Appledown—for some obscure reason connected with the foundation and having its origin in the shadowy recesses of diocesan history—got considerably more than both the other vergers put together.

At this point the sound of a distant bell brought Halliday to his feet, and glancing at the clock Pollock saw that it was twenty past five.

"Don't you go—that is unless you have to," said his host. "I'm afraid I shall have to dash off. The call of duty, you know. Evensong, five-thirty. I have to sing the service; it should really be Malthus, but he had to push off, and so I'm doing it for him."

He said nothing of a holiday curtailed by this good

Samaritanism, and Pollock rather admired him for it.

"Do you mind if I come with you?" he asked. It was an idea which had occurred to him some minutes before, that as an unobtrusive spectator at Evensong he might have a good opportunity of observing some of his prospective victims—or perhaps "clients" was the more appropriate word. He wondered for a moment whether it was quite seemly to make a stalking-horse out of a religious service, but comforted himself with the thought that the end might justify the means (and anyway there was no harm in just having a look at them).

Halliday appeared to welcome the suggestion. "Come and sit up in the choir," he said: and again voicing Pollock's thoughts with disconcerting clarity he added, "Then you'll be able to have a good squint at all of us."

It was beginning to get dark as they left the house and cut across the road into the precincts. The light, almost transparent, mist of an early autumn evening enhanced both the quiet and the beauty of the setting. For the first time Pollock saw Melchester Close as a place of tranquillity and secrecy. Lights were springing up in drawing-room windows. Eighteen households: eighteen separate little entities making up a community.

And how quiet everything was! The clack of the gate behind them as they entered the precincts sounded startlingly loud. They left the path and struck off across the grass for the south door, and their footsteps were deadened in the turf. There was a faint but pleasant smell from a bonfire of leaves in Canon Bloss's garden.

Ahead of them, through a chink in the big west door, showed a soft gleam of light, and in the stillness Pollock could hear the sound of the organist playing the voluntary. In silence he followed his guide round the south-west corner of the cathedral, into the south porch, through a swing door and into the cathedral itself.

His first impression was that the building was completely empty. Rows and rows of chairs but no congregation. Halliday seemed to find nothing surprising in this, for he plunged off up the south aisle without a word and Pollock followed. When he got closer to the choir screen he saw that his first idea had been erroneous; there was a congregation. It numbered seven. Six old ladies and one very old lady.

"Quite a good muster for a weekday," whispered Halliday enthusiastically as he strode across the south transept with Pollock breathlessly at his heels. "That's old Mrs. Judd—marvellous old lady—comes to cathedral every morning and evening. Can't hear a word. But regular as clockwork. Must leave you now—find yourself a seat in the choir."

Pointing a vague finger towards the north he plunged into a room from which was audible a cheerful but subdued babble, and which Pollock took to be the vestry. Bereft of his guide, and feeling as an outsider that he had no right to a seat in the choir at all, he glanced anxiously round him in the gloom. Behind him was the bulk of the organ—now working up into a breathless crescendo. He advanced a few uncertain paces, passed through a gateway and found himself "within the choir." This, as he began to realize, signified no more than the space to the east (or on the altar side) of the screen. It contained a vast number of finely carved stalls and was absolutely empty. Pollock seated himself in comparative obscurity, opened an enormous tome on the ledge in front of him—it turned out to be a volume of Bishop Hooker's sermons—and breathed a sigh of relief. So far, so good. He felt that he had entrenched himself within the inner citadel of Melchester.

He had barely established, as it were, his *pied à terre* when a general movement in the body of the cathedral warned him that the choir and clergy were coming in. In front of the little procession came the sixteen choristers themselves; two by two, eight demure couples: pictures of boyish innocence, the blandness of their shining countenances and immaculately parted hair equalled only by the stiffness of their well-starched frills. Pollock felt his erstwhile suspicions to have been unworthy. How could anyone gazing on this display of composite piety entertain even for a moment the thought that they might have been mixed up in the sordid mischief of the past fortnight? How divorced they were from all notions of brutality or violence. It was only when they got closer that Pollock noted that the boy in front of the file on the left had a rich and quite unmistakable black eye.

Behind the boys came what Pollock took to be the choirmen. He had understood from the Dean that they lived in the town, and he therefore passed them over with a cursory inspection: he noted Halliday just behind them, followed at a slight interval by a thin cleric, a stouter cleric and a very stout cleric. The middle one he knew— it was the rustic and unsociable Canon Beech-Thompson. The very stout one he assumed rightly, from the Dean's description, to be Canon Bloss. The thin one in front baffled him. It might be one of the other residentiary canons—Trumpington or Fox: or it might be the Precentor.

Behind Bloss, and almost entirely obscured by him, came a verger, carrying his wand of office. Behind the verger was the Dean, and behind the Dean a second

verger of such patriarchal and benevolent appearance that
Pollock put him down without a second thought as Appledown. He was interested to note that the vergers, having shown the Dean and canons into their seats, removed
themselves and took up their seats outside the screen,
presumably to keep an eye on the seven old ladies.

Halliday was intoning the service—and, thought Pollock, doing it very well. He had a fine singing voice, deep
and full and confident, and the choir responded to the
lead with precision. It was a pleasing scene, comfortable
and comforting. His thoughts wandered. How still Canon
Bloss was sitting! He did look like a graven image. There
were five seats facing the altar, with their backs to the
screen. The Dean had one of the two seats on the north
side, and Beech-Thompson the other. Canon Bloss occupied a seat and a half out of the three on the south, the
others were unoccupied. Assuming that they belonged to
Trumpington and Fox, the thin man must be Precentor
Hinkey. His Adam's apple had a fascinating wobble when
he attempted a high note. He had a fringe of sandy hair
and rimless glasses. Pollock put him down for a kindly
and inoffensive soul.

Ah, the Dean had spotted him! He had wondered how
long it would be before that happened. He thought he
noted a faint look of disapproval on his face, and grinned
to himself. So he didn't think that this was quite playing
the game, didn't he? Well that was his look out. Actually
he misjudged his uncle. The Dean's irritation had been
caused by the fact that he had seen one of the choristers
fidgeting. In fact it looked very much as if the boy at the
end of the row had passed something to his neighbour.
The Dean frowned and made a mental note that he must
have a word with Dr. Smallhorn.

The choir was now embarked on the one hundred and thirty-sixth psalm: the chant was one which Pollock knew and liked, and he overcame his nervousness to the extent of joining in the swinging refrain:

Oh give thanks unto the Lord for he is gracious
and His mercy endureth for ever.

"The SUN to rule by day," squeaked Cantoris' trebles.

For His mercy endureth for ever,

roared the basses.

The moon and the stars to govern the night

answered Decani demurely.

For His mercy endureth for ever.

Emboldened by the comforting volume of sound Pollock tried out his reedy tenor and divided the Red Sea in two parts. (*For* His mercy endureth for ever): he also made Israel to go through the midst of it, or had started to do so when he discovered that it was a treble solo, upon which he retired behind Hooker, blushing hotly. The choir, however, were either too well mannered to take any notice, or more probably well inured to the vagaries of musical visitors, and Pollock recovered sufficiently from this contretemps in time to take a cautious seat by the waters of Babylon and hang up his harp upon a tree.

After the "Confitebor Tibi," to a strange chant (and outside Pollock's musical compass), Canon Beech-Thompson ambled out to read the first lesson. Beyond the fact that it lay in the Sixteenth Chapter of Ezekiel and the forty-fourth verse (which he knew because he had

read it in the service list) he heard little of this master-
piece of declamatory literature. It was not that Beech-
Thompson was a bad reader, but he spoke in a round
confident boom, and the villainous acoustics of the
building did the rest. However, everybody, as far as Pollock could see, was reading the passage for themselves,
except for the choristers who had relapsed into complete
vacuity and an elderly tenor who appeared to be filling up
his Saturday's football pool.

Magnificat followed. There was an unaccompanied
treble solo on the words "He remembering His mercy
hath holpen his servant Israel," and Pollock, who in his
early days in London had heard most of the famous so-
pranos, was struck by a quality in the tone. He fumbled
about for the right word and decided that it was imper-
sonal. The words meant nothing to the boy. He was producing a note as pure and beautiful as that of a trained
canary, and with as little feeling.

The Dean read the second lesson. His quieter voice
suited the building. Nunc Dimittis. Prayers. No sermon:
the anthem: and only one hymn. Almost before it had
started the service seemed to be over, the organ boomed
forth, and the choir were filing out. Pollock realized with
a start that he had been too interested in the service to
fulfil his real purpose of watching the participants. Technically, he reflected, a most finished performance. Spiri-
tually it had meant nothing to him, but that was probably
his fault. Did police officers have souls, anyway?

He walked slowly down the now deserted nave and out
of the west door. It was dark outside, and the wind was
getting up. It would probably rain before morning.

He turned to the right outside the cathedral, passed

the dim bulk of the cloisters on his left and emerged from the precincts a few yards from the Dean's front gate. It was then about half past six. Pollock felt that he had done enough for one day and dozed comfortably in front of the study fire. The Dean, when he came in a few minutes later, respected the truce and conversed until dinner on Roman history and the chances of Chelsea in the coming league contest; he seemed to be considerably better informed than Pollock on both subjects.

After dinner Pollock decided to sample the night life of Melchester, which resolved itself into a choice between (about) sixty public houses and one cinema. After visiting a few of the former he came to the conclusion that solitary beer drinking was one of the gloomiest forms of dissipation and fell back on the attractions of the screen. The film, which was modestly described as the Perfect Mystery-Comedy-Thriller, so shocked Pollock's professional eye by the improbability of its police routine that he slept soundly through the last six reels.

It must have been at about this time, or possibly a little earlier, that Mrs. Mickie had a fright. She was sitting by the fire darning a sock when she heard the front door open with a crash. The wind was now blowing great guns, and thinking that the servant had carelessly left the door unlatched she hurried into the hall. There she stopped in astonishment. Her husband—whom she had imagined to be quietly working in his study—was standing in the doorway, his hair dishevelled, a mackintosh flung loosely round his shoulders, and his face as white as death. He swayed on his feet, and for a moment she had a horrible suspicion that he had been drinking: then she realized, being a woman of some sense, that he had simply been badly frightened.

"Why, Charles, my dear," she said quietly, "whatever has happened? You look as if you'd seen a ghost."

"I have," said Mickie slowly.

IV • Murder

THE GREAT QUIET of Melchester Close proved unexpectedly disturbing to an ear attuned to the roar of London traffic: and his cat-nap in the cinema had made Pollock feel wakeful. In the case beside his bed he found an assortment of books on religious matters (for the Dean's clerical visitors, he guessed) mixed indiscriminately with a large number of the works of the late Edgar Wallace. After hesitating for a moment between *The Fellowship of the Frog* and *Three Devotional Aspects of Abstinence*, he selected the latter as the one which would most usefully fulfil the prime function of a bedside book and embarked on discourse number one—"Fasting as an Incentive to Thought."

The Dean's spare-room bed was soft, and there was something very soporific in the quarterly chiming of the cathedral clock. On the last stroke of midnight he laid his book aside and turned out the light.

He remembered hearing the first quarter after twelve and noticing that the rain was now coming down steadily. His thoughts dwelt—with the sympathy of experience—

on the policeman on his beat, and he snuggled down farther into bed. It seemed a very long time before the half-hour struck.

The wind was dropping off as the rain thickened, filling the long lead gutters on the cathedral roof, and running off into the overflow pipe above the cathedral engine shed where a jackdaw had started, and abandoned, an ambitious nest. The steadily rising water was filling the blocked pipe, and at the precise moment that Pollock followed the example of the wind (and himself dropped off) the overflow splashed down on to the asphalt. It fell with a muffled drumming sound on to something soft and yielding.

Pollock awoke to a clean and rain-washed morning. He found the Dean already well on with breakfast and hastened to catch up. He had already disposed in gratifying succession a bowl of porridge, an excellent plate of ham, and two boiled eggs—and was, in fact, in the very act of refusing a third when the dining-room door opened to admit—not the trim parlour-maid—but the truculent figure of Hubbard.

The Dean looked both surprised and disapproving. The gardener, however, was plainly the bearer of such momentous tidings as to be beyond fear or favour. In a hoarse whisper—and including Pollock with a sideways movement of the head—he announced:

"Morgan to see yer." And in even hoarser tones he added, "Someone's done Appledown."

For a few seconds he stared at them somberly, and then, as if realizing that the time had come to relinquish the stage, he opened the door wider and revealed Morgan, the junior verger, a sheepish figure, his pink youthful face glowing with exertion and excitement.

Breathlessly he confirmed and amplified Hubbard's cryptic announcement. He had been out early with a brush and a hoe cleaning the runlets round the cloister wall . . . as the Dean might know he did most of the small gardening jobs in the precincts . . . he had worked round as far as the corner—the corner that was between the east wall of the Chapter House and the north wall of the cathedral, when he had seen something lying on the ground by the engine shed door—just a black heap. (Followed a brief resumé of his harrowed feelings on discovering that the black heap was Appledown, very wet and indisputably dead.) Being himself a keen student of detective fiction (Pollock groaned) he had refrained from touching the body—and had retraced his steps, only this time he had kept to the asphalt path, so as not to confuse his own steps with those (Pollock waited patiently to see if he could say it—and with an effort he did) with those of the murderer.

"Come, my man," said the Dean keenly, "how did you know he'd been murdered?"

Pollock was justifiably annoyed at this usurpation of his authority. He had, of course, noticed the assumption of foul play when it had been made earlier on by Hubbard. But he had not had any intention of asking a question—not at that juncture, anyway.

"Never mind that," he said brusquely. "Show me the body, if you please."

In answer to an inquiring look the Dean said, "That's quite all right, Morgan. This is Sergeant Pollock from Scotland Yard."

Morgan lead the way out in awestruck silence. Possibly he was overcome by the speed and perspicacity of modern police methods which enable an officer to get to the scene of a crime before it is even committed.

Pollock found himself a prey to conflicting emotions. His professional instincts told him that the local authorities would have to be informed without delay: there is a form and an etiquette in these things, and he who disregards it is sowing for himself the seeds of a mighty crop of obstructiveness and local jealousy. On the other hand an opportunity of getting at a real corpse before the boots of the constabulary had trampled the ground flat was a tempting one: especially as Pollock, in common with most London men, held to the (perhaps prejudiced) view that the Yard was never called in to a provincial crime until every clue was obliterated, every suspect warned and every trail cold—until, in fact, it was too late for Scotland Yard to do anything but take the blame for another unsolved mystery.

And besides, was it not really his case, anyway? He had been called in to deal with the persecution of Appledown: and now, if one looked at it that way, the persecution had taken an eminently practical turn. But the question was whether the Chief Constable would look at it that way. There was a telephone in the hall, and by the time Pollock reached it professional etiquette was in the ascendancy: with a deep sigh he unhooked the receiver.

A few minutes later, following Morgan, and closely followed by the Dean and Hubbard, he was rounding the north-east corner of the chapter house. Here he paused.

What he saw was immensely gratifying to him as a policeman. It was a beautiful set of footprints. They came in a straight line across the grass from the north boundary wall and joined the path at the point where they were standing. Morgan was positive that they weren't his. His early morning weeding had taken him across the west lawn, but from that point onwards he had been on the asphalt path.

These prints were blurred and muddy (on closer inspection Pollock inclined to the view that they had been made by someone coming away from the cathedral, and not towards it as he had thought at first), and had obviously been produced by someone passing across the turf at some time after the rain had started soaking it on the previous evening. Hubbard and Morgan were dispatched post-haste to the Deanery for flower-pots to cover the precious prints, and Pollock turned his attention to the body.

When he met his death Appledown had been wearing a blue Burberry-type mackintosh and a bowler hat, which had rolled off his head and lay on the path beside him. The cause of death was obvious. What had once been the back of Appledown's head was now nothing but a mess. Pollock felt cautiously with his fingers. The bone yielded in all directions. A powerful blow, he thought. There had been a good deal of bleeding, and the rainwater had added to the mess.

He raised the head gently and examined with interest a rough scrape on the cheek and chin: the eyes were closed, and Pollock, who had seen a good deal of violent dissolution, was surprised by the benignity of the verger's expression. Replacing the head he got both hands under the body and lifted it slightly on one side. It struck him that it was quite dry underneath, and he was about to roll the body still farther on to its side when a loud and authoritative voice announced: "Here, you mustn't do that, young man."

The local police had arrived.

The "homicide squad," as the Dean mentally dubbed them, consisted of a solid-looking sergeant, a solid-look-

ing constable, a thin gentleman with a toothbrush mous-
tache and a motor coat (police doctor, diagnosed Pollock
correctly) and a photographer. Pollock introduced himself
briefly. He felt that he could spare any longer explanations until the inevitable hour arrived when he had to
tackle the Chief Constable.

Sergeant Parks and Constable Potter accepted his cre-
dentials affably, but he fancied they looked relieved when
he suggested that he would leave them to get on with the
job whilst he "just had a poke round." This consisted of a
minute inspection of the surrounding paths and lawn.
Apart from the tracks which Hubbard and Morgan were
now busily covering with a selection of pots, dishes, and
soap-boxes (to the amazement of MacFisheries and the
Home and Colonial, who had been arrested by this unusual spectacle on their morning delivery round), the results were entirely negative.

He went back and found the photographer concluding
his task with three close-ups of the wound. Sergeant Parks
was seated on an upturned section of drain-pipe complacently finishing his notes whilst Constable Potter drove in
skewers to mark the positions after the body had been
removed. This crucial operation was performed soon after
his arrival, and the mortal remains of Appledown were
laid on the Dean's garden truck for removal to the police
ambulance and thence to the station mortuary. This part
of the job the sergeant handed over to Constable Potter:
he himself seemed to be in no hurry to leave the scene of
the crime. Reinforcements in the shape of two more uniformed policemen arrived at this juncture and were
posted—one at the corner of the chapter house and the
other at the south-east corner of the cathedral, to ward off
casual intruders. The sergeant reseated himself on the

drain-pipe and watched Pollock, who was making a second and even more thorough search of the terrain. As he watched he sucked hard at his pencil. It seemed to afford him some comfort.

The engine shed outside which the body had been found was the one which housed the little electric engine which supplied the power for the cathedral organ. It was an ugly plank and studding affair—plain twentieth century and contrasting oddly with the Gothic pile against which it rested—and it occupied the angle formed by the north wall of the cathedral and the east wall of the transept. The whole arrangement formed a narrow cul-de-sac to which the lower bulk of the chapter house made a third side. It was almost entirely floored with what is commonly called asphalt but is really only tarred chips. The exception was a narrow strip along the wall—though it was not quite clear whether this had been designed as a flower-bed or was merely the result of the workmen running short of material before finishing the job.

"Come and have a look at this," said Pollock. The two sergeants stared for some time in silence at his discovery: it was nothing very exciting: sixteen little holes had been made in this patch of hard damp earth. They were close together, almost up against the shed, about an inch deep and a third of an inch wide. They looked fresh.

"Very odd," said Sergeant Parks who clearly made nothing of it. "Very odd indeed." He returned to his seat. "In fact," he concluded, "you might call the whole thing very odd."

"Quite a rum go," agreed Pollock. "Anything particular occur to you?"

"Well, now," said Sergeant Parks—not ill-pleased at such unexpected deference: "The body, very wet on top, very dry underneath, in a manner of speaking. And the ground quite dry too. Which suggests to me," he went on kindly, in case Pollock had missed his point, "as if the poor gentleman was killed afore it came on to rain."

"A sound conclusion, I think," agreed Pollock. "And that, I take it, would give us some time about eight o'clock yesterday evening as the latest possible."

"A little after eight," amended the sergeant. "Say ten past."

"Another thing," went on Pollock. "Didn't it strike you that the body was very wet? Quite uncommonly wet, I mean—especially as it was lying in such a sheltered place."

"It was a very wet night," said the sergeant. "Very wet indeed. I was out in it," he added.

"Rotten luck," said Pollock absently. His gaze was fixed on the drain-pipe with its overhanging spout. "If you were to give me a leg-up do you think I could manage to get on the roof of the shed?"

The sergeant acquiesced with a dubious grunt to this proposed acrobatic feat, and a minute later Pollock was balancing on his broad shoulders: after a perilous wobble and a frantic grasp he drew himself up, and was standing on the flat roof of the engine shed. From here he was able to get a very satisfactory view of the gutter and the top of the pipe. The mystery of Appledown's extreme dampness was a mystery no longer.

"Chock full of sticks," he shouted down. "Nest of some sort, I think. The poor chap must have been lying under a regular shower bath half the night."

"Ah," said Sergeant Parks gaping up at his colleague, "smart work that." Thoughtfully he spat out a twig which Pollock's foot had dislodged into his open mouth.

"It wasn't entirely guesswork," explained Pollock when he had safely regained terra firma. "There's a sort of damp mark on the stone which often means a blocked pipe."

"Ah," said Sergeant Parks. He reseated himself on his favourite seat and continued to ruminate.

Here Pollock left him. He felt that the time had come —in fact, might well be over-past—when he would have to explain himself and his doings to the Chief Constable. Of one thing he was determined: no amount of "choking off"—nothing short of a direct order from headquarters —would make him leave go. The whole affair was most interesting. An assassin who walked across the grass backwards, clothes which were too wet, and a bowler hat which was much too dry. Sixteen little holes in the ground. A case after his own heart. He hoped the Chief Constable would not prove too impossible.

"I must confess," said Colonel Brabington (late Indian Army and the present Chief Constable of Melchester) in one of his less affable tones of voice, "I must confess that at the moment it passes the bounds of my imagination— my very limited imagination—to discover how you came into this case at all."

In moments of irritation he was apt to indulge in an almost Chinese form of self-depreciation.

"Staying with my uncle, the Dean, you know," explained Pollock patiently for the third time: "and he asked me—quite unofficially, of course—to look into the question of these anonymous letters. Quite unofficially, of course."

"Irregularly," amended the Chief Constable unhelpfully.

"Well," said Pollock mildly, "I don't know that you

could call it that exactly: it never was meant to be an official investigation, you know——"

"My knowledge of police procedure is, of course, rusty," snapped the Colonel, "and not to be compared with yours." With a Serbonian glare he challenged Pollock to agree with him. "But I was under the impression that the correct procedure was for the Chief Constable to be consulted before our experts from London were called in."

"Unofficial investigation," mumbled Pollock.

The Chief Constable proceeded to explain at some length his theories (his very ignorant and doubtless ill-founded theories) on the proper observance of police procedure and etiquette. The Dean, though a man whom Colonel Brabington personally admired and respected, had shown questionable taste (Pollock gathered) in having a nephew in the Metropolitan Police Force at all. In his young day constables were constables (correct him if he was wrong) and not public schoolboys playing at being policemen: and even worse taste in bringing the said nephew down behind the backs of the local force.

Things seemed to have reached a deadlock, and Pollock was on the point of playing his final card and asking the Chief Constable whether he proposed to make an official application to have his offending self removed and the matter placed wholly in the hands of the local authorities; he felt convinced that the Colonel did not really want to go as far as that (he might succeed in calling his bluff); and the words were just about to be uttered which would make or mar this very promising case when he observed that the Chief Constable had fallen silent and was glaring at his tie.

"What year were you up?" he snapped.

"Twenty-six to thirty-one," mumbled Pollock.

"House?"

"School House."

"Ha ha," roared the Chief Constable unexpectedly. "Ha ha, that's very good, very good indeed. Here have I been slating you like God knows what and hauling you backwards over the coals, and I never spotted you were an old boy yourself. I was there, you know. Before your time, of course. In School House myself."

At this moment Pollock had an inspiration born of some casual and distantly remembered research into the school archives.

"Of course, sir," he said, with a suitable blend of deference and surprise. "You must be *The* Brabington. The one who broke the half mile record in 'ninety-six."

"Well," replied the Colonel, highly gratified. "I must admit, since you've discovered the fact, that that was me. Couldn't do it now, of course. But sports were sports in those days. None of our damned specializing; we ran every race and jumped every jump on the card. But tell me—is old Marjoribanks still going strong? Wonderful old boy—why, I remember——"

Pollock settled himself down and prepared to swop improbable and disreputable reminiscences—an exercise so dear to the hearts of Old Boys the world over.

The public school system had proved its worth once more.

Three-quarters of an hour later, when Colonel Brabington had concluded his account of the epic steeplechase which he had won in a snowstorm in 'ninety-five, he returned regretfully to the matter in hand. Of course in the circumstances it would be perfectly easy to have everything on a regular footing. He suggested that he (the

Chief Constable) might phone Scotland Yard and invoke their assistance in the matter of the murder of Appledown, whilst Pollock could phone them simultaneously and request a recognition of his position in the affair in view of the increased seriousness of the case (Colonel Brabington would be only too pleased to send this request if Pollock thought that this would be a sound move).

Pollock thought it would be an excellent move. He thanked the Colonel effusively and withdrew to the nearest telephone booth. He had a second, more private call to make.

"Don't say anything to anyone under any circumstances," had been Pollock's parting injunction to the Dean, who had hurried off to morning service at the same time that Pollock had left to play Daniel to the Chief Constable's lion. "If anyone misses Appledown tell them that he's ill in bed, broken his leg—anything."

Vain are the hopes of man.

In his more than metropolitan ignorance he overlooked the peculiar character of a Close. As a sounding-board it is unique. It outshines even the whispering gallery in St. Paul's. There the lightest whisper is audible to everyone. In Melchester Close they hear things before they are whispered. Thoughts are read. Gestures speak words. Looks are interpreted. The interpretation is then twisted by a dozen busy tongues—and that which no one dreamed of whispering in their innermost closets at dawn is shouted from the house-tops by midday.

The thought, therefore, of keeping anything of a sensational nature quiet was—and the Dean must have known it—purely fantastical. Two large policemen standing at the east end of the cathedral! Stretchers! Am-

bulances! Flower-pots! Signs and portents. MacFisheries
and the Home and Colonial had a protracted round that
morning, and by the end of it every housemaid knew,
with varying embellishments, that Appledown was no
more.

The rumours spread and grew.

A well-known detective from London—something to
do with Dean—someone climbing about on the roof—
someone had heard someone else say that the cathedral
plate was missing. "Wilder still and wilder ran the shrill
alarm." Appledown had been caught rifling the offertory
box, and after a thrilling chase had thrown himself from
the roof of the cathedral, practically into the arms of one
of the Big Four from Scotland Yard (or was it Big Five?).
Anyway, this man had come down in response to an
anonymous letter in order to arrest him. The Dean's connection with the business, though well established, was
vague. Most people held, with an approximation to truth,
that the Scotland Yard detective was the handsome young
man who, as everybody knew, was staying with the Dean
—being in fact his illegitimate son: whilst there was a
small but powerful minority who was sure that the dear
Dean had been—or was about to be—arrested as Appledown's accomplice.

The indisputable appearance of both the Dean and the
altar-plate at morning service proved rather a set-back to
both schools of theorists.

V • Figures of Speech

"The one before you is a high official," returned Wong Tsoi with appreciable coldness. "Were he a dog, doubtless he could follow a trail from this paper in his hand to the lair of the aggressor, or were he a demon in some barbarian fable he might perchance regard a little dust beneath an enlarging glass and then stretching out his hand into the void withdraw it with the miscreant attached."

Kai Long by ERNEST BRAMAH

"DECEASED," said the doctor austerely, "died from the after-effects of severe cerebral injury and general shock arising directly from a concussive blow in the cranial area. In other words," he added, relenting a little as he noted Pollock's puzzled expression, "someone hit him on the head and killed him."

"And what was the sole cause of death?"

"What more do you want?" said the doctor, becoming even more unprofessional. "If you're looking for the mysterious puncture of a hypodermic syringe or the traces of that hoary old poison-unknown-to-science, you're wasting your time. This chap wasn't strangled, drowned, stabbed, suffocated, or frightened to death by a headless horror. He was killed by a blow on the torus—and what a blow. I don't want to teach you your job, old man, but I should start by ruling out all women, however suspicious their actions or heavily veiled their faces."

"Thank you," said Pollock, "we haven't any heavily veiled females yet, but I'll bear your words in mind in case I meet one. Seriously, though, would you say from the nature of the blow that we might rule out any possibility of it having been struck by a woman?"

"I should say so," said the doctor. "Quite definitely. It was a very hard, heavy blow—a most deliberate stroke. Apart from anything else, the direction of the splintering in the skull would indicate that the striker was as tall or taller than the deceased."

The two men were standing warming their hands in front of the charge-room fire at Melchester police station. Pollock had had a busy morning. Leaving the Chief Constable he had made two telephone calls to London. The first had been a personal one for Chief Inspector Hazlerigg. For though no mere mortal can influence the decisions of the powers that be at Scotland Yard, the probability is that, if suddenly called upon to dispatch a chief inspector into the distant provinces, they will be more likely to dispatch a chief inspector who is handy at the moment and panting with eagerness to be dispatched, than an equally worthy chief inspector who may perhaps be inspecting dog licences in Upper Tooting or even sleeping the sleep of the just in his maisonette in Lower Balham. Which is only another way of saying that it's the dog on the spot that gets the biscuit.

The second call had been longer and more difficult, and had dealt with the vexed question of how an unofficial investigation into anonymous letter-writing could be turned overnight into an official investigation into a murder. However, Pollock had eventually trusted to the good offices of the Chief Constable, and rung off.

He had then, after a great deal of heart-searching, transferred his belongings to the Bear Hotel. The Dean had taken this official gesture in very good part and approved the thought that underlay it. "After all," said Pollock, "murder's different."

And for some time after he had gone the Dean sat in his study staring at the Italian triptych which had once belonged to Canon Whyte. Yes, he thought, murder *was* different. He was just beginning to realize that.

The doctor was on the point of going when Pollock remembered something he had meant to ask him. "Whereabouts is the torus?" he said. "Or is it just another name for the skull? You know, when you were talking about the blow——"

"Scientific accuracy," replied the doctor, "is my middle name. I said the torus and I meant it. It's another name for the occipital bone, which is what your hat sticks on at the back if it's rather too small for your head."

"I see," said Pollock. "But look here, how could Appledown get a blow like that if he was wearing a bowler hat?"

"That's for you to work out," said the doctor. "I hadn't considered it. I don't think it's impossible, if you presume that the blow which did the trick also knocked the hat off. But it must have been a sideways swing; not so likely, I agree. But since you found his hat lying beside him he may have been carrying it all the time."

"Or perhaps," suggested a thick square man with a brick-red face, who had inserted himself into the room at that moment, but appeared to have picked up the thread of the conversation, "he raised his hat out of sheer politeness when he saw the murderer was ready to begin."

The doctor looked a little surprised at this interruption, and Pollock introduced him to Chief Inspector Hazlerigg.

"So that's that," said Pollock, extinguishing the stub of his third cigarette.

It had been a long story, starting over an excellent mixed grill in the dining-room of the Bear Hotel; Pollock talked and ate: Hazlerigg ate and listened. A noble Stilton cheese came and went. Pollock consulted his notebook occasionally. Coffee was taken in the lounge. Hazlerigg smoked and listened. Pollock talked and smoked.

"Do you think," said Hazlerigg, breaking a long silence, "that the writer of the letters is the murderer of Appledown?"

"Yes," said Pollock, so firmly that he surprised even himself. "I do. I know that there's an almighty difference between a practical joker and a killer, but if the two aren't connected in some way I shall be very surprised."

"Three possibilities," said Hazlerigg. "We'd better have them all before we start getting prejudiced. First, a man with some crazy obsession: he starts in by slating Appledown anonymously: this doesn't seem to be having quite the desired effect, so he lays for him and bashes him. Second, someone wants to kill Appledown for good but extraneous reasons and sees this anonymous campaign as useful cover. Third, the two things are quite unconnected, but I must say that I agree with you, on the whole, that that is unlikely on the grounds of probability alone. However, we mustn't sit here gossiping and wasting the ratepayers' money. Let's go and have a look at Appledown's cottage."

"Artful" Appledown opened the door to them himself.

He was, thought Pollock, a disreputable parody of his brother. The family likeness was striking, but where the head verger's white hair had lain in smooth and venerable respectability, Artful's stood in untidy wisps. His eyes were bloodshot and lips petulantly clenched. In deference to the conventions he had torn a strip from an old black umbrella and bound it round his upper arm, but apart from this striking piece of mourning he appeared to be sustaining the death of his only brother with some fortitude.

"Poor old Dan," he said, as soon as Hazlerigg had introduced himself, and before he had had time to ask any questions. "Poor old Daniel. Little did I think, when I left him at two p.m. yesterday afternoon, that when I returned to hearth and home at twenty-five minutes after ten precisely this morning I should find him cold and dead. Not that I did find him myself—to put the matter in exact words—but I heard the sad news very shortly after my return. It's a dreadful warning to us all."

"Quite so," said Hazlerigg. "Now if you could tell us exactly what you did yesterday, and when you saw your brother last, it would be a great help to us, as you'll appreciate."

"It'll be an important statement, I suppose?"

"Most important," Hazlerigg assured him.

"Then," said the old man with an apologetic leer, "it'll be better to have no mistakes about it," and he pulled a greasy notebook from an inner pocket. "Two o'clock—that's yesterday afternoon—left house, having previously prepared evening meal of cold viands and left some handy in the kitchen. Two-fifteen—depart in charabanc with other members of Brotherhood."

"Brotherhood?"

"Christian Works and Self-help (Melchester Lodge)," explained Appledown rapidly. "Our fortnightly outing, every other Tuesday. Went to Windsor this time, to see the historic sights. Arrived in Windsor three-thirty. Observed sights, such as castle, celebrated Etonian College, deer park, etc. Started back five-thirty. Arrived Melchester eleven forty-five."

"How on earth," said Pollock, "did it take you an hour and a quarter to get to Windsor and over six hours to get back?"

Appledown looked at him pityingly, and Hazlerigg, who had understood that Christian Works and Self-help did not necessarily imply total abstinence, contented himself with saying, "But you didn't come home to sleep."

"I was not wishful," said Artful Appledown virtuously, "of disturbing my old friend Sergeant Brumfit. I, therefore, slept with a friend in the town, as is my custom on such occasions."

"So you've made the trip more than once before?"

"The Brotherhood arranges an outing on the second and fourth Tuesday of every month," agreed Appledown. "I make every effort to support them—very often I am late in returning and thus spend the night in the town."

"And does your brother sit up for you?" asked Hazlerigg.

Artful looked a little confused at this simple question: he scratched his head for a moment or two, and then contented himself with saying, "Daniel was a very good brother to me, very thoughtful. If he was to go out himself when I was away, he'd always leave a note saying when he was coming back. Most thoughtful and kindhearted."

"I suppose he didn't leave a note yesterday?" asked Pollock eagerly.

"Of course he did," said the old man, turning a beady eye in his direction, "as you could see if you had eyes in your head. Pinned up beside the front door. I left it there when I came in—as I said to myself, 'Never touch anything when the police are about, and then you can't go wrong.'"

Disregarding this fresh exponent of detective procedure, Pollock hurried to the front door. Sure enough, pinned to the lintel was a half-sheet of notepaper; on it, in an untidy scrawl, the laconic (and under the circumstances, singularly untruthful) message, "Back soon." The signature was D. Appledown. Pollock unpinned it carefully and took it back to Hazlerigg.

"Of course it's my brother's writing," said Artful scornfully when they questioned him. "No one else writes as badly as that." He hunted out some other specimens of the late head verger's vile calligraphy, and Pollock was inclined to agree with him. Hazlerigg pocketed both note and specimens and piloted the old man back to the main thread of the discussion.

"You left your brother's evening meal ready for him?"

"Ham, lettuce, gherkins, military pickle, prunes and cold shape," interjected Artful rapidly.

"And it was all eaten when you came back this morning?"

"Every crumb," said Artful, "except for three prunes," he added conscientiously. "Poor Daniel always had a good appetite. He never had no tea, you see. He'd be over at cathedral getting ready for evening service. Left the house every day at four o'clock regular as clockwork, and back by a quarter to seven. Then we'd sit and smoke and talk until, perhaps, half-past seven, when we could relish a nice supper."

Hazlerigg consulted Pollock with a glance, but Pollock could think of nothing further.

"His papers and effects will have to be searched," said Hazlerigg, "though the Lord knows whether we shall find anything helpful. If it comes to that, I don't yet know what we're looking for. I think the local force might do that. I want you to look up Sergeant Brumfit. Make a copy of all the entries in the register yesterday evening. Then find out about the keys of the gates and ask him exactly when he locked up last night and at what time he was on duty himself. And whilst you're about it you might sound him as to his opinion about people climbing in and out of the Close—if anyone really knows whether it's possible he will. I want to see your uncle. You'll probably find me there when you've finished."

Brumfit made a good witness, and it took Pollock less than a quarter of an hour to collect the information he wanted—mostly of a negative character. The sergeant was positive that no one could possibly get in without him knowing. As to keys, there were only three in existence. There was the same lock on all three gates: a fine new seven-lever Maxwell-Gurnet, fitted less than a year previously. Two of the keys were held by the local police. The Chief Constable had charge of one; the other was entrusted to the policeman whose night beat took him through the Close. The sergeant had the third. The sergeant had locked the gates as usual on Tuesday. The last one (the main gate) he had locked at perhaps two or three minutes after seven. No stranger had come in or out. After seven (Pollock guessed that the upsets of the week before had tightened up regulations in the Brumfit household) the sergeant himself had been on duty the whole time except for twenty minutes when he had been at supper—that would be ten minutes to eight until ten past.

Pollock found Hazlerigg with the Dean, and passed this information on to him, together with a copy of the "in" and "out" entries in the lodge-book. The Chief Inspector glanced at these with an unusually expressionless face and pushed the paper into his capacious inner pocket.

"Your uncle," he said, stooping to tickle Benjamin Disraeli, who seemed to have taken a great fancy to him, "has kindly offered us the use of the chapter house; it will be very handy for interviewing possible witnesses."

"And you want me to make a statement after Evensong this evening?"

"Nothing very much," said Hazlerigg. "Just that Appledown has met with an unfortunate accident."

"And asking everyone who spoke to him or saw him after Evensong on Tuesday to come to the chapter house?"

"That's right," said Hazlerigg. "It'll sound better coming from you. People are always a bit shy at first about making statements to the police."

He underrated Melchester Close. The first witness was already on her way up the garden path.

Mrs. Judd was a small but immensely penetrative sort of woman, dressed in greens and daffodil yellows, which seemed to suggest springtime and heyday, rather than the autumn of existence: there was, in fact, very little of the sere and yellow leaf about Mrs. Judd, and her speech was as abrupt as her movements.

"Which is the detective from Scotland Yard?" she demanded, almost before she was inside the door.

Hazlerigg and Pollock introduced themselves and indicated that they both claimed that honour.

"I have an important statement to make. I am Mrs. Judd, widow of the late Canon Judd." (This went with rather a defiant look at the Dean.)

"In connection with the death of Appledown?"

"Murder," said Mrs. Judd with some relish. "Face facts, Inspector—murder."

Pollock glanced hastily at his notebook, and Hazlerigg said impassively, "Well, ma'am?"

"I sit," said Mrs. Judd, "in my little front drawing-room in a chair in the window and watch people going backwards and forwards. I see everybody, and if a stranger comes past I ask questions and soon find out who he is. It is very providential that the only pillarbox in the Close should be placed at the corner nearest to my little house." She said this rather as an elderly tigress might comment on the proximity of the only drinking-pool to the mouth of her den.

"Nothing escapes me," she went on. "I observe everything. Especially now that I have my telescope."

"Your what?" said Hazlerigg, shaken out of his composure.

"My nephew, Albert, who is in the Royal Marines—I call him a nephew, but he's really a great-nephew—spent some days with me in the spring, and he kindly fixed it for me. It has rather a limited field of vision, of course, extending from the pillar-box on the near left to the front door of dear Canon Malthus's house on the far left. I could see into two other houses, were it not for the west end of the cathedral."

Hazlerigg had recovered by this time. He agreed with Mrs. Judd that this arrangement indicated a lack of foresight on the part of the builders of the cathedral, and asked her what she had seen on the previous evening.

"It's not so easy after dark, you know. More interesting, but not so easy." She collected her thoughts, pursed her lips demurely, and then said:

"Well, first the dear Dean coming back to his house at a few minutes after half-past six. Then, at least ten minutes later I saw Appledown come from the cathedral, cross the road in front of his house, and go in. Canon Prynne was coming past at the same time, so he must have seen him too. Dear Cannon Bloss left dear Canon Trumpington's house a little before half-past seven and went back to his own house. A few minutes later dear Canon Trumpington came out too, and went into Canon Beech-Thompson's house. Between twenty-five and twenty to eight Parvin went out. Oh, I forgot to tell you: he had only come back at seven o'clock. I have no doubt he went straight from the service to some low public-house. Soon after half-past seven he came out again and went along to Appledown's house."

"You're sure that was where he went?" said Hazlerigg.

"Of course I'm sure. I can use my eyes," snapped Mrs. Judd. "He hung around the house for a few minutes, like the shady character he is, and then went in."

"What time would that be?"

"It was a few minutes before a quarter to eight—for I had my own dinner then—so that is all I can tell you. I heard the boys come past at eight o'clock. They might tell you something; sharp, inquisitive little creatures."

Her mission accomplished, Mrs. Judd got up and made for the door.

"I'm sure that if you attend carefully to what I've told

you," she said, "you'll have no difficulty in catching the murderer."

"I'm sure we're very grateful to you for your kind assistance and observation," murmured Hazlerigg.

Mrs. Judd paused at the door and turned round.

"That was all that I saw," she said, and her voice was so altered that it startled the three men. "But I've still got good hearing. I can use my ears, and I heard things, wicked things, wicked whispers. Late that night. Much later, footsteps creeping, doors creaking. It's been coming for a long time. I'm very sensitive to these things."

As suddenly as she had come she was gone.

"Good gracious," said Hazlerigg mildly.

"I'm afraid," said the Dean weightily, "I'm very much afraid that she is getting just a little bit—you know what I mean—odd lately. It's living alone, no proper company or companionship—has that effect on a lot of people."

"I wonder how much reliance we can place on all this," said Pollock helplessly. "I really thought we were beginning to get something definite."

"Even if untrue," pronounced Hazlerigg judicially, "that statement of hers is likely to prove very useful: if it only starts a hare or two. And once the hares start running"—he raised an imaginary gun to his shoulder—"Bang! Bang! Over they go."

He looked, thought the Dean, like a jolly red-faced farmer out for a day's sport.

"When I first heard of Appledown's decease," said Dr. Smallhorn, joining the tips of his fingers and looking severely at Pollock, "I made it my business to institute a discreet inquiry amongst my boys. I did this for a reason. It is my firm intention that whatever investigations may be set on foot the scholars under my care shall not be subjected to unpleasant cross-examination."

Pollock refrained from pointing out, as he might have done, that in the last resort the majesty of the law might override even the wishes of a headmaster. He himself had a profound mistrust of boys as witnesses and was quite prepared (for the time being) to collect his information at second hand.

"You should understand," pursued the headmaster, "that on Mondays, Tuesdays, and Fridays we have what we call 'late practice' nights. Full choir practice takes place in cathedral, of course, but these evening practices are for the boys alone. Rather late, you will say, but we find it difficult to fit everything in."

Pollock had the impression that the headmaster had forgotten for the moment that he was addressing a police officer and not a prospective parent.

"On these evenings the choir, after finishing Evensong at six-thirty, return to the school for an evening meal of cocoa and bread and butter."

After this orgy it appeared that the choir marched over to Mickie's house for practice, arriving there at about seven o'clock, returning to the school on the stroke of eight to retire to their virtuous slumbers. As the headmaster rolled forth his leisurely periods Pollock made an occasional note and allowed his eye to rove. The photographs of classical statuary on the wall and a modern filing cabinet in the corner. A methodically arranged desk; on top of it photographs of boys, three calendars, and a model in compressed paper of the Duomo at Florence.

"In the past," Dr. Smallhorn was saying, "I have had to take a Firm Stand on the subject of the punctuality of their return. Ten hours' sleep is essential to the growing boy. I have usually found that choirmasters have little sense of time. The artistic temperament, one supposes. Mickie, however, is very good in *that* respect. Very good indeed. You will appreciate, therefore, that I can say with absolute accuracy that Appledown was still alive at one minute to eight yesterday evening. The boys passed him on their way back from practice."

Pollock came back to mental attention with a jerk.

"Passed him? Let me see. He was going towards the main gate then?"

"He was not, as I understand it, going anywhere: when I used the word 'passed' I intended to imply that the boys were moving whilst Appledown was static. In point of fact he was standing on his own doorstep apparently engaged in pinning a slip of paper to his doorpost. As to what the paper contained I cannot, of course, speak——"

"Thank you," said Pollock, "we know about the paper." He added casually, "I wonder if you could let me know roughly what you were doing yesterday evening?"

"With the greatest of pleasure," said Dr. Smallhorn. "I did not attend Evensong. Morgan, our junior verger, also does odd jobs about the school and garden, and I was talking to him for the greater part of that time and watching him dismantling and cleaning the dining-room stove. As I recollect, we discussed calceolarias. Then the boys came back (that would be about half-past six), and I superintended their tea-time. At five minutes to seven they left for Dr. Mickie's, and I sat here in my study, correcting Latin exercises until they returned."

"No one disturbed you during that time," suggested Pollock.

"Fortunately, no," replied Dr. Smallhorn courteously. But Pollock, as he took his leave, was wondering whether or not it would prove so fortunate: of course, it was a ground-floor window—it might have been open. He went in search of Morgan.

"Talk!" said Morgan. "He'd talk the hind leg off a donkey. Him and his calceolarias. Still, I've known worse in that line of business, and the boys like him. Yes, he's quite right: I raked out the stove after the boys left for evening service. That would be about twenty past five, and so soon as it had cooled down I got to work on the back damper joint. One of the screws had come adrift and the damper was jammed open, and that made the stove draw too hot and used up a lot of coal, which wasn't to the liking of the doctor, and seeing as he has to account for every penny he spends to the Chapter you can hardly blame him, can you? I worked at that joint for the best part of an hour, and whilst I was working he was talking in a haughty cultural way—not that I can remember very precisely what he said, but now that you mention it I do recollect the calceolarias. Then the boys came back and I went home. I have my tea and supper together—high tea you might call it. And when I'd finished that I set to mending my wireless—never happier than when I'm patching or fiddling with something. My front window—you'll see when we go indoors—looks right into the doctor's study across the road, and all the time that I was working at my old wireless I could see him doing the same—working, I mean, at his desk. I often watch him in the evenings correcting the boys' books, and I can tell whether they've done well at their work or not—that surprises you! When a boy does well the doctor never lifts his pencil off the book but writes slow and smooth. But if he spots a mistake up comes his pencil and—jab! Down on the paper, like as if he was digging a hole in it. So just by watching his pencil I can almost mark the work myself."

"Do you mean," asked Pollock, "that you can't actually see Dr. Smallhorn from your front window?"

"I told you," said Morgan aggrieved. "I can see his hand and his pencil. What more do you want?"

To this Pollock could find no suitable answer.

VI • Pollock Asks Questions

Sᴇʀɢᴇᴀɴᴛ Pᴏʟʟᴏᴄᴋ was walking back towards the deanery when he observed two girls: one was fat and the other was thin, and they were sitting side by side on the precinct wall. As he came up he heard one say urgently to the other, "Don't be such a sneak." To which the other answered in a piercing undertone, "It's not sneaking, it's murder. Murder's different."

Both then stopped talking and glared at Pollock, who tried at the same time, and unsuccessfully, to make it appear that he had not heard what they were saying, that he had no idea what they were talking about, and that even if he had heard he would have been far too well mannered to have taken any notice of it.

He was spared further embarrassment in this complicated deception by the stout one, who said, "I'm Miss Bloss. This is Miss Prynne. I take it you're the C.I.D. We were wondering what those soap-boxes and flower-pots were for?"

"Not me. I wasn't. Speak for yourself," muttered Miss Prynne, who appeared to be in the worst of tempers.

"We supposed that they must be covering up some footprints," continued Miss Bloss placidly.

"Well," said Pollock guardedly.

"We only wondered," said Miss Bloss, with a glance at Miss Prynne which met with no response, "why you should trouble to cover up Dr. Mickie's footprints?"

"Sneak," said Miss Prynne audibly.

"And what makes you think they are Dr. Mickie's?"

"Well, of course they are. Didn't you know that?" said Miss Bloss with such round-eyed surprise that Pollock nearly laughed. "Look at them! They come straight from his house to the organ shed—and anyway, he's always fiddling about with that blessed old engine. Besides, he's the only man I know who runs with his feet straight in front of one another—like a horse on a tight-rope," she added graphically. "We've watched him sprinting across that grass hundreds of times when he's been late for service, haven't we, dear?"

Miss Prynne said nothing, but annihilated a hurrying ant viciously with the heel of her broad and sensible shoe.

Pollock, studying the line of the prints, noted this idiosyncrasy for the first time. It was quite true: they were not like an ordinary set of prints which alternate, first to the right and then to the left: they lay in a straight line. He admitted to himself that this point had escaped him, and being a generous and fair-minded young man he decided to thank his informant.

"Sharp eyes you've got, Miss Bloss," he said genially. "If you notice anything else of that sort be sure to tell me, won't you?" He passed on his way.

"You've made a conquest," said Miss Prynne acidly.

Sergeant Pollock, as has been explained, had been on

his way back to the deanery, but now he altered his course. It occurred to him that he would like a word with the organist and choirmaster of Melchester Cathedral.

He found Mr. and Mrs. Mickie, as it were, "drawn up to receive him" in the dining-room. Pollock was, in fact, peculiarly sensitive to "atmosphere" in the people he interviewed, and he would have needed to have been very dull indeed not to have noticed the sense of restraint and anticipation which greeted him as he came into the room.

He introduced himself briefly and said in his most noncommittal voice, "I have a few questions to ask you, Dr. Mickie, as a matter of routine. I dare say you can guess in what connection."

"Yes," said Dr. Mickie.

"Well, if you wouldn't mind . . . Let me see. You were at Evensong, of course, and saw Appledown there——"

"When I left the cathedral after locking up the organ," said Dr. Mickie, "Appledown was still in the vestry—I pass the door on the way out. That would be quite normal, since he always stayed behind for some time after everyone else had gone—counting the collection, tidying up, and turning out the lights, and so on. When I left the cathedral I came straight back to my house——"

"When you say straight," interrupted Pollock, "I suppose that your quickest way would be along the path to the north-west gate—or do you find the north-east gate quicker?"

"There's very little in it. Of course the quickest of all is to come straight across the grass, but I don't take that way often because it leads to an awkward scramble over the wall." He started to laugh, failed, and cleared his throat.

"Of course," said Pollock. "Well now, which way did you come this time?"

"The north-west gate. I remember I had a letter to post. I must have been home by twenty-five to seven. We have a very early meal on Mondays, Tuesdays, and Fridays, because of choir practice. The boys arrived over here on the stroke of seven and left a minute or two before eight."

"And were you here during the whole of that time?" said Pollock, turning to Mrs. Mickie, who looked a little surprised, and said, "I think I slipped down to the town for a few minutes . . . yes, that must have been yesterday —I had a book to change at Smiths. But I wasn't away for very long. Our maid has the evening off on Tuesday, and I usually make the coffee myself. We have a cup together when the boys have gone. Then Charles goes to his study to finish——"

"I think Dr. Mickie had better tell me about that himself."

"Why," said Mickie, "there's really nothing very much to tell. We had coffee in the drawing-room, and then, at about a quarter-past eight I removed myself to my study —no, not actually composing, it's a little book on plainsong that I'm writing. I rejoined my wife in the drawing-room at about ten o'clock, and shortly after that we went to bed."

Mrs. Mickie concurred in this statement with a nod, and there was a short interval of silence whilst Pollock debated tactics.

He felt that what he had heard was not all true. Most of it was true—the arrival and departure of the choir were fixed times and capable of being checked. But there was a constraint in Mickie's manner which told him that he had not heard the whole truth. He tried a direct approach.

"What shoes were you wearing yesterday?" he asked.

The tension was unmistakable now.

"I have two pairs of black shoes and one pair of brown shoes. I wear the black pairs alternately during the week."

"So that the pair you wore yesterday——?"

"They would have been cleaned this morning and put in the cupboard in the hall."

"I should like to see them, please."

In silence Mickie led the way out, and after some fumbling under the stairs produced a pair of well-worn black shoes. They were spotlessly clean.

"A well-trained maid," observed Pollock.

"As a matter of fact," said Mrs. Mickie sharply, "I cleaned them myself. I try to save Eva as much trouble as possible. We've only the one maid, you know, and she has enough work to do about the house."

Very reasonable, again thought Pollock. But he also knew a tag about ladies protesting too much. He decided to advance his siege-works a yard or so nearer to the fortress.

"Someone," he said, "ran across the cathedral lawn last night in the direction of your house."

"Well," said Mickie steadily.

"It has been pointed out to me," said Pollock, "that these prints have one peculiarity. The runner who made them has a habit—a rather unusual habit—of throwing his feet down one in front of the other in a straight line. I may add in fairness also that though the prints are not distinct enough to be accurately measured they might easily have been made by a shoe of this type and size." He weighed the black shoe carefully in his hand and looking at it rather than at Mickie said, "You are quite sure that you haven't forgotten anything that happened last night? You wouldn't care to add to your statement at all?"

There was a moment of silence, and then Mickie said, "No, I can add nothing to what I have told you."

Pollock replaced the shoe and took a thoughtful departure.

When he got back to the deanery his uncle was out.

The house was quiet, but from the kitchen quarters at the back came a rumble of conversation, in which male voices predominated. Pollock moved quietly down the passage, guided by the sound, and found himself outside the kitchen door. Opening it he peeped in.

"After all we'd been through," Hubbard was saying, "I can't hardly say as I was surprised. When it comes to messages being writ up by night on a man's own garden wall—well, you can imagine what I felt; a man has his feelings, and messages on the garden wall are wounding to same. Huge, staring letters, a foot high—Letters of Blood."

On this dramatic note he paused, and the two young men at the kitchen table (clad in dirty motor-cycling coats and with faces like intelligent Cairn terriers) nodded pleasantly and scribbled hard. At this moment the housemaid, who had been an enthralled listener to Hubbard's recital, caught sight of Pollock, and the meeting broke up in disorder.

"Now boys," said Pollock, "that's hardly playing the game, is it, questioning a man's servants behind his back?"

"I was granting an interview to the press," said Hubbard loftily. "There's nothing to be ashamed of in that, I suppose?"

Pollock turned to the intruders.

"You ought to have come to us, you know—we'll always give you a statement." At the sound of the word *statement* the eyes of both reporters gleamed, and two pencils were poised. "Now you come round to the Bear Hotel this evening and you shall have all the facts. It'll do you no good pestering these people, so run along like good chaps. They don't know anything, anyway—you shall have everything this evening."

He shepherded them out of the back door, talking hard, and took the precaution of seeing them clear off the premises before he returned to the study, where he found that the Dean had returned.

"Hubbard," he said, when Pollock told him, "has been presuming for years on the fact that he is the only man in Melchester who really understands chrysanthemums. Some day he will go too far."

Since Hazlerigg had not yet returned, Pollock set forth once more on his round of interrogation. The next on his list was Vicar Choral Halliday. His house appeared to be slightly tidier than it had been the previous day, and since Biddy had by this time made up her mind that he was not an insurance salesman, hawker, or circular, he was admitted at once. Halliday was with his sister in the drawing-room, and with a good deal of heart-searching and mutual prompting they produced a schedule of their movements on the previous evening. Halliday had come straight back from cathedral, and had then, as was his custom, spent a few minutes at his private devotions, after which he had helped his sister to unpack and they had sat down to dinner at seven o'clock. Seven sharp—perhaps a little before, as the Foxes were coming to play bridge later in the evening and they wanted to get tidied up before they arrived. After dinner Miss Halliday was upstairs "tidying up," whilst Halliday set out the card-table. The only exact time he could fix was when he had been talking to Biddy in the hall, and they had both heard eight o'clock strike. Shortly after—at about ten past eight, say —the Foxes had arrived, and they had stayed until about half-past ten.

Pollock, who had already detected that the critical moment in the affair was eight o'clock, asked for further details, and Biddy was called in. She was able to add some valuable evidence. She had been in the kitchen washing up, and had thought she had heard a bell ring. Fearing it might be the Foxes arrived before they were due, she had tied on her best apron and hurried out into the hall. However, she must have been mistaken, because when she opened the front door there was no one there. It was then that Mr. Halliday had come out into the hall and they had heard eight o'clock striking.

Pollock asked, "Could you see Appledown's front door?"

"No," said Halliday, "our own door opens out to the left, and neither of us went outside."

"But you could see down the south side of the cathedral. Can you remember if anybody crossed the lawn or went down the path whilst you were standing by the open front door?"

Neither Biddy nor Halliday had seen anyone. Pollock thought rapidly.

If Smallhorn's timing was correct, then Appledown had been at his front door at a minute before eight—yet at eight o'clock Halliday and Biddy had commanded a clear view of the south side of the cathedral and had not seen him. Therefore, he must have turned left outside his front gate. Why, then, had Mrs. Judd not seen him? Of course! She was having dinner—just at the one time when she might have been useful.

But if Appledown was heading in that direction he might have been going to see Parvin. According to Mrs. Judd's evidence Parvin had been at Appledown's house some time between seven-thirty and eight, and possibly he was returning the visit. Anyway, Parvin was clearly the next person to see.

The second verger Pollock recognized as the smaller of the two he had noticed in cathedral on the previous evening. He was a small, dark, rather unprepossessing man with a face like an intelligent rat, and it did not need his speech to tell Pollock that he was a native of the principality. He greeted the detective effusively and showed him into a shabby and overcrowded sitting-room. When he had seated his guest safely on a tubby red plush sofa he shut the door (thereby partially excluding the ruling aroma of stale cabbage) and placed himself at the disposal of the law.

Pollock withdrew his gaze with difficulty from the leer of a dropsical kitten whose portrait adorned the southern wall of the Parvin living-room, and put his cautious opening query.

"What did I do last night, you are wanting to know," said Parvin. "Well, and that's not such a very great time back to remember."

"Marking time," thought Pollock uncharitably.

"I finished my duties in the cathedral at half-past six and then I went along to meet a friend in the town." He looked a little embarrassed. "I won't deceive you, Sergeant Pollock—it was a public hostelry that I went to; I like a small half pint in the evening to clear the cobwebs out of my brain, as they say."

Pollock accepted this hitherto unknown property of beer and asked for the name of the public hostelry.

"The Victoria and Albert is the name—a very respectable house, though kept by a dissenter, and not above five minutes from the gate of the Close, which makes it handy to slip out and in. But I'll not seek to conceal from you, Sergeant," and Parvin wrinkled up his face into a sharp-toothed grin, "that some of the people in this Close are as narrow in their ideas that they would gladly grudge a man even a simple drop of beer of an evening."

"Could you," said Pollock patiently, "give me some idea of your movements yesterday evening?"

A slight extra tenseness added itself to Parvin's naturally sharp face, and a curious timbre was noticeable in his voice. It was not exactly, thought Pollock, that he was preparing to tell lies, but he was going to be very, very careful indeed of what he said. If his thoughts had been put into words they would have been, "How much shall I tell you, young man: and more important, *how much do you know?*"

"I was back from the Victoria and Albert by the hour of seven for my evening meal. A fine tender end of lamb stewed with onions and pearl barley—my wife is a fine hand with a stew. I finished and lit my pipe, just as I might be doing now, and sitting in this very same chair —which I had from my grandmother who died by lack of breath, rest her soul, forty-two years ago to the day!"

He added this last telling detail triumphantly as though it finally corroborated all that had gone before.

Having done so he stared glumly at the carpet, but Pollock would give him no help.

"And then," he suggested.

"And then," said Parvin, looking as if he was ready to burst into tears at any moment, "I walked along to see Mr. Appledown."

"The time, as I take it," said Pollock consulting a previous note, "would be about five-and-twenty minutes to eight?"

This little bit of pantomime was not lost on Parvin, and it seemed to cheer him considerably.

"It is little use," he said with exaggerated fervour, "attempting to keep anything from you gentlemen of the London police force, I can see. Yes, I went along to see Mr. Appledown about a little matter of duty—nothing that would interest you."

He paused invitingly, but Pollock said nothing.

"Well, it would have been about fifteen minutes that we were talking of this and that——"

"Where were you—I mean, in what room?"

"In the kitchen it was. Mr. Appledown pecking and picking at the poor victuals provided by his scamp of a brother—out on the booze himself, I've no doubt," he added virtuously.

"When did you leave?"

Parvin's manner became even more guarded.

"That is a very different question," he opined.

"Very," agreed Pollock dryly. "Perhaps, if you can't fix the exact minute when you left the house, you can tell me where you went to, and when you got there?"

Parvin brightened considerably at this suggestion. "It's a funny thing you should mention that," he said, "for I went straight back to the Victoria and Albert, and I happened to notice the time when I was ordering my first glass of beer. It was a few minutes after eight."

"And how long does it take you to reach the Victoria and Albert?"

"A little more than five minutes from the gate of the Close," said Parvin promptly—almost too promptly from the viewpoint of total abstinence. "Eight or ten minutes from Appledown's door, according as you hurried or not."

"Then," said Pollock, "we may take it you were off the premises by about ten to eight."

"Right," breathed Parvin, with fervent admiration for the keennees of Pollock's mathematics, "that's quite right. I must have been away by ten to eight."

"Did you pass anyone?"

Again Parvin hesitated.

"Plenty of folk about in the streets," he volunteered.

"In the Close," said Pollock impatiently.

"No one."

"You're sure?"

"Not that I can remember," said Parvin unhappily.

"Come, man," said Pollock sharply, "it was only yesterday."

"Well, so it was now," said Parvin, as if this put it in quite a different light. "Well, I'm sure, now I think of it, that I didn't see a soul about in the Close. They were all at their dinner, no doubt."

"No doubt," agreed Pollock grimly. "Only you didn't seem very sure about it when I asked you just now."

"I was casting my mind back," said Parvin, who seemed to have recovered his assurance, "and it's plain to my memory now that I met no one. I remember remarking to myself how deserted the roads were."

"I see. Well, that's quite plain then. Would you mind calling your wife?"

Parvin went to the door and bellowed "Meg" whilst Pollock resumed his study of the distended kitten. It had an enormous pink cable of ribbon round its neck, from which was suspended a bell massive enough to have immobilized a mastiff. The title ran round the top in Gothic capitals, and Pollock (who had first made it out as "The Family Fiend") had just disentangled the additional "r" in the last word from the tendrils of a rose-bush, when he was brought back to reality by the slamming of the door.

Mrs. Parvin was a bold, black-eyed, handsome slut, and Pollock could well imagine that she found Close life wearisome. His mind reverted to the anonymous letters: there had been one, he remembered, which accused Appledown of the most strictly dishonourable intentions in this quarter. He had not paid much attention to it at the time—but he had not then seen Mrs. Parvin. The outlines of a *crime passionnel* took sketchy shape in his brain.

The girl waited for him to begin—half sullen, half contemptuous. Pollock knew that type of witness well, and tackled her in his blandest manner. Her information, when extracted, was corroborative of her husband's, but amounted to little more. She had been at home getting the supper ready until seven o'clock. They had eaten together, and then she had cleared the dishes. Whilst she was in the kitchen she had heard the door go. That was a little after half-past seven. She had finished washing up and putting away by eight o'clock. Then she sat in the living-room reading and listening to the wireless until her husband had come back at about a quarter-past ten.

"When else would you expect him?" she added shrewishly, "with closing time at ten o'clock."

"And that's all you can tell me about yesterday evening," said Pollock conventionally, as he rose to go.

He got an unexpected answer.

"Why don't you go and ask someone who *was* out last night?" Mrs. Parvin was on her feet now, her voice shrill with malice and her dark eyes snapping. "Ask old busybody Hinkey why he came creeping home after nine o'clock last night. He thought no one saw him, but I did. And his trousers all covered with mud. Ask him where he'd been, and what he'd been doing."

"Thank you," said Pollock, "I will. Is that all you've got to say?"

He felt that Mrs. Parvin had a good deal more to say on the subject of the Precentor—probably of a sharply detrimental nature. But her husband had silenced her now with a glare.

"Nice people," he thought. "I wonder if Hinkey has been pi-jawing her about morals?"

Said Precentor Hinkey, seated placidly amidst his black cats, "I don't really know that I can help you very much, Sergeant. Of course I will tell you all that I know." He was mild, sandy-haired, and bespectacled, and as he talked he massaged his smooth pink cheek as if hypnotizing his side-whisker to a yet more luxuriant growth. He was so uncommonly like one of his own pets that Pollock expected him to start purring at any moment.

"I got back to my house at half-past six," he went on. "I believe I was just a few steps behind you, Sergeant, on your way back to the deanery. When I got in I put on an old coat and hat, took a stick, and went out for a long walk."

"Good gracious," said Pollock, "but it was almost dark! Do you often do that?"

"I have never done it before in my life," admitted the Precentor. "But I had some very serious thoughts to turn over in my head, and it seemed the best plan."

"Did you meet anyone you recognized?"

"Well, do you know now, I was so deep in my thoughts that I never noticed a soul. In fact, I could hardly tell you where I went, but it was some miles out into the country. Then it started to rain, so I turned round and came home again. That's really all."

Pollock stared down thoughtfully at the mild-eyed man in front of him. The story seemed so incredibly thin and improbable that it might even be true.

"Don't you remember anything more?" he said persuasively. "For instance, what time did you get back?"

"I'm afraid," said the Precentor apologetically, "that I can't tell you even that. I have a clock in the hall, but it stopped at half-past four on the afternoon of our late king's funeral—quite a coincidence." He laughed sedately, and the largest of the three cats jumped softly on to his knee.

Pollock went back to the deanery.

VII • Dr. Mickie Comes Clean

"BEES," said Canon Bloss, "appreciate a warm autumn. Warm and calm. This unsettled weather has been very trying for them."

He was walking with Hazlerigg down the broad grass path which ran the length of his well-kept garden. Hazlerigg thought it one of the most beautifully proportioned gardens he had ever seen; not too broad for its length, and ending under the shadow of the grey stone ramparts of the Close.

Hazlerigg showed no sign of irritation at the discursive style of his host. He found it restful. He had already packed into the preceding two hours what most men would have considered a good day's work.

On leaving Pollock he had visited Canon Fox and had discovered that elusive and nondescript man in the nursery, instructing Prima, Secunda, and Tertius Fox in their Catechism. He had seemed unsurprised at Hazlerigg's visit, and, in consultation with his wife (a sleek, tawny-haired, sharp-toothed lady destined inevitably to be known as the Vixen), had produced a satisfactory schedule of his movements.

Canon Trumpington, interviewed next, had proved kind and concise. Canon Beech-Thompson, on the other hand, had been concise but unpleasant. Canon Bloss could hardly have been said to have evinced any independent tendencies. He had answered Hazlerigg's questions with a great clarity and complete lack of emphasis and had then propelled him into the garden and started to talk about bees.

"A mild spell in September and October," he explained, seizing Hazlerigg by the arm and steering him amongst the little green and white hives, "produces just those conditions favourable to good wintering. The bees can collect a little nectar and pollen to ripen their winter stores."

Gently he raised the roof of one of the hives, and lifting a wad of blankets, invited his reluctant guest to observe the cell formation. Hazlerigg knew nothing about bees, except that one end of them stung, and was relieved when Bloss replaced the coverings as carefully as he had removed them.

"We must on no account disturb them," he explained. (Here Hazlerigg entirely agreed with him.)

"Disturbance of any sort causes a rise in the temperature of the hive: then the bees eat too much food and that may give them dysentery."

He brooded benevolently over his little flock, and Hazlerigg felt compelled to ask, "Do they live through the winter on what they collect in the summer?"

"Good gracious, no!" said Bloss, appalled at such ignorance, and with more animation than he had yet shown. "They have to be fed. Not individually—I don't mean that—but thirty to forty pounds of syrup to each hive."

"Ah, I see," said Hazlerigg. "Thirty to forty pounds of syrup. Not individually, of course."

When he took his leave he was still toying with the picture of Canon Bloss knocking at the hive door at breakfast-time and feeding each hungry little mouth with syrup from a long silver spoon.

Dropping in at No. 3 next door, Hazlerigg discovered that Vicar Choral Malthus had returned from his visit in the country. In fact, as he learnt to his surprise, Malthus had got back unexpectedly the night before.

"I understood from the Dean," said Hazlerigg a little severely, as if it was inconsiderate of Malthus to intrude himself as a further complication in an affair so tangled already, "that you were away visiting a sister who was sick and were likely to be away for some days."

"That's quite right," agreed Malthus unhappily.

"Then may I inquire why you changed your plans? Did she, perhaps, take a sudden turn for the better?"

"Yes: that's right, she did," said Malthus, with such patent insincerity that Hazlerigg almost gasped. "She suddenly got very much better, so I left her. I'm in course, you know," he added as an afterthought.

"In course?"

"In course—I mean it's my fortnight to take the services. Halliday very kindly does them for me when I'm away, but I don't like to trespass too much on his good nature." He plucked off his round gold spectacles and polished them with nervous energy on the edge of the tablecloth.

"Could you let me have the name and address of your sister?"

"Oh, certainly," gasped Malthus, looking as if he were

going to expire on the spot. "I've written it down for you." He fished in his pocket and produced a piece of paper on which was scribbled in pencil: "Mrs. Frampton, Lea House, Park Drive, Bournemouth." "My married sister," he explained. "She has always had a weak chest but finds Bournemouth very bracing." Having delivered himself of this tribute he relapsed into complete silence. Hazlerigg thought he had never witnessed so extraordinary a performance. The man was plainly beside himself with agitation, and though the matter was coherent enough, yet the manner in which he had made his statement would have shaken the most credulous listener. On principle, however, Hazlerigg disbelieved people who looked him straight in the eye, and very often found that a hesitating and nervous reply contained more truth than a calm and concise statement. On these slender grounds he was prepared to admit that Malthus might be telling the truth— or some of the truth.

In that case why was he looking like a badly frightened rabbit?

Very gently—almost as one coaxing a timid child— Hazlerigg extracted the information that Malthus had come back the night before on the six o'clock train from Bournemouth which reached Overton Junction at five minutes to eight, there making a connection with the fast train to Melchester from town (the seven o'clock which reached Melchester at eight fifty-five). He had not had dinner on the train. He thought—and Hazlerigg agreed with him—that train meals were one of the poorest bargains which modern life had to offer—besides, a very dear friend of his had once contracted ptomaine poisoning from eating tinned tongue on a railway journey. He supposed that he had reached home by shortly after nine.

He had walked down from the station. His wife had had a hot meal ready for him; perhaps the inspector would care to speak to Mrs. Malthus.

Mrs. Malthus arrived so pat on this suggestion that it might have been suspected, in a less refined atmosphere, that she had been listening outside the door. She looked altogether more self-possessed and confident than her husband, and Hazlerigg imagined that she was the driving force on the Malthus axis.

"Please don't apologize!" she exclaimed before Hazlerigg had either time or inclination to do so. "I quite understand that you have to ask these tiresome questions. Oh, dear me, no! I wasn't at Evensong. What with one thing and another to worry about, and all the children at home and the shopping to do—well, it doesn't leave you with much time for religion."

"Oh, Martha, Martha!" said Hazlerigg—but he said it to himself.

"I went straight down to the town after tea. I like to do my shopping then—the shops are not so crowded, and one meets a nicer type of person."

"Did you?"

Mrs. Malthus looked surprised, and stopped talking for the first time since she had burst in on them.

"I mean, did you meet anyone you knew? Anyone from the Close, that is."

"I don't think so. Most of them would be at service, wouldn't they? Stop, though, let me see. I did meet Mr. Prynne coming out of Boots. I remember I exchanged a few words with him. After that I was some time in Roberts—beautiful ham they sell and the most delicious cheeses—and, let me see, what did I do next?"

"Never mind exactly where you went—what time did you get back?"

After some consideration she opined that it must have been nearly eight o'clock.

"Rather a long shopping expedition," suggested Hazlerigg.

Mrs. Malthus was at a loss for an answer to this, but at last she said, "Of course I wasn't shopping the whole time. I went into the reading-room in Smith's and sat down with a paper. A shocking waste of time, but you know what we women are." She smiled tentatively.

"I don't really know—you may be a fool or you may be a liar," said Hazlerigg, "but I can pretty soon find out whether that last bit is true or not." But this, again, of course, he said to himself.

Aloud, he added, "And after you got in, Mrs. Malthus?"

"Well, I suppose I sat down and rested for about ten minutes. Then I had the girls to put to bed and the supper to see to. I knew that my husband would need a good meal when he got back."

"You had heard from him during the day?"

"No," said Mrs. Malthus, after a barely perceptible pause.

"And yet you expected him back by that particular train and knew that he would not already have dined."

"I had always understood that he would get back on Tuesday evening, if possible—and I know how much he dislikes train meals."

The answer smooth and natural, but Hazlerigg was not deceived. His eyes had been on Vicar Choral Malthus, and the look of urgent discomfort on the weaker partner's face had not escaped him. However, he saw that at the moment further questioning would be fruitless. "That's their story and they're sticking to it." He murmured the old saying to himself as he took his leave. It was after five o'clock, but he had another call to make before he could think of tea.

"Yes, sir," said the maid at No. 1 the Close (rather surprisingly), "Mr. Prynne's in and he's expecting you."

When Hazlerigg entered the study a tall ascetic-looking gentleman rose to greet him. Guileless eyes regarded him from behind rimless pince-nez glasses. A lean but unexpectedly sinewy hand shot out from a length of snowy clerical cuff, grasped his own hand, shook it, and steered him into a tall wheel-back chair—all with a certain absent-minded grace.

The Reverend Ernest Vandeleur Prynne, having settled his guest, took a short hitch in his own immaculate trousers and seated himself in the chair opposite.

"I have been expecting you," he said austerely.

"So your maid informed me," retorted Hazlerigg. "Would it be indiscreet of me to inquire why?"

Prynne elected to take this question at its face value.

"No," he said, "you can ask me that. My reasons for expecting you were, I think, quite logical. Either you were questioning everyone in the Close—in which case of course I should be included—or else you were confining your attention to those who could give you useful information on the subject of Appledown's movements yesterday evening."

"Short of questioning you in pursuit of method number one," said Hazlerigg, falling in easily with the didactic manner, "how was I expected to ascertain that you qualified with inclusion in category two?"

"You knew," said Prynne, "because Mrs. Judd told you so."

"And did she also tell you that she had told me so?" inquired Hazlerigg, nettled.

"She informed Miss Bloss, who told my daughter, who passed the information on to me."

This remarkable instance of The Close Intelligence System left Hazlerigg a little breathless.

Prynne went on.

"It's no good trying to keep any secrets in this place. And exclusive information is an expression we haven't heard of. Information here belongs to everybody. To that extent alone we really do live the communal life. But I mustn't divert you from your purpose. I suppose you want to know what I was doing yesterday evening?"

"If you please."

"That's simple. I went to the cinema."

"You were on your way there, I presume, when you passed Appledown going into his house. That would be at about a quarter to seven."

"If Mrs. Judd says so," observed Prynne courteously, "I am quite prepared to take her word for it. Personally I never notice the time."

"Could you think back carefully and tell me exactly what you did and what you saw?"

"Why, yes," said Prynne slowly. He seemed a little surprised. "You think it might be important? I thought that it wasn't, until——" He paused.

"Until what, were you going to say?"

Prynne looked at him blandly.

"I shan't answer that," he said. "My thoughts are no one's business but my own."

The smile that accompanied them robbed the words of

their sting. "You were asking me what I saw. Let me think. I was walking along the road—it was dusk, not quite dark. As I rounded the corner of the wall I heard the gate go—the west wicket gate of the precincts, that is to say: it has a most peculiar and characteristic squeak. I looked up and saw Appledown crossing the road—he must have just left the cathedral. By the time I got up he had gone indoors, but I saw the light go on in his front room and immediately afterwards his shadow jerking about on the blind."

For the first time in the interview Hazlerigg shifted sharply in his chair. Prynne waited for him to speak; but if he had been going to say something he evidently thought better of it, and after a pause Prynne continued in his dry pedantic tones.

"That is really all I have to tell you of that particular incident. I reached the cinema in time for the beginning of the supporting picture."

"What time did you come out?"

"As I told you before I never notice the time, so it's no good asking me. I came out after the big picture was over and went straight home. I then read a discourse of Marcus Aurelius—as a mental laxative—and went to bed."

"Casting your mind back a bit, can you tell me what you did before going to the cinema?"

"Before going to the cinema I had a meal, a sort of high tea, at six o'clock. And before that I was down in the town—first to the tobacconist's and then to Boots. I don't know if you're one of those investigators who find an absorbing interest in small and irrelevant details: if so, I may tell you that whilst I was there I encountered Mrs. Malthus, and purchased a two and fourpenny bottle of

Dr. Balsom's Balm for the Bilious."

Hazlerigg's mind was wandering. He was trying to re-capture a shade—an intonation—in Prynne's voice which had puzzled him a minute before. Almost idly he asked, "Did you like Appledown?"

Surprisingly there was quite a long silence. Prynne was looking at him for the first time with a hint of admiration in his cold blue eyes.

"I got an impression that you disliked him the very first time you mentioned his name," went on Hazlerigg. "It's a thing we're trained to listen for. Not very difficult to detect."

"Singular perspicacity! Well, I admit the charge."

"Any particular reason?"

"Nothing to put into black and white," said Prynne slowly. "And, mind you, Appledown was a very popular man. Perhaps some people thought that he was getting a little past his job, but he was such a complete 'faithful old retainer' that no one would have dreamed of mentioning it for fear of hurting his feelings. But to my mind he was much too complete, too benevolent and too benign. In fact, altogether too good to be true. And the choristers didn't like him, you know."

"Did they say so?"

"Not to me—or in as many words. But you can take it from me that such was the feeling. I don't think they had much against him except that he sometimes used to make them run tiresome little errands for him—the sort of petty pilfering of their liberty which often annoys boys more than downright tyranny."

"By the way, you and Halliday teach at the choir school, I understand—is that a private arrangement between you and Dr. Smallhorn?"

"It is a bit unusual," agreed Prynne. "All the minor canons are supposed to lend a hand with the boys' education—God help them! But it usually seems to devolve on Halliday and myself, as 'Kinkey' simply refused to have anything to do with it and Malthus is always too busy— or says he is. Malthus is one of those supremely efficient people who can organize anything except their own daily existence."

"Another of your dislikes?"

"Well, anyway," said Prynne with a smile, "I didn't trouble to conceal it that time."

As Hazlerigg rose to leave, Prynne added apropos of nothing in particular: "When I was going into the cinema last night I stopped for a few minutes to talk to the commissionaire at the door."

"Did you now," said Hazlerigg; "that was very thoughtful of you."

Hazlerigg had one or two matters of routine to look to, and Evensong was over by the time he reached the cathedral. He made a half circuit of the cloisters, pushed through an iron gate into the celebrated slype with its tessellated pavement and broad swing-frame windows, and found himself in the chapter house (one of the lesser glories of Melchester Cathedral). Pollock was already in possession, seated at a table with the results of his afternoon's work spread out in front of him.

"The Dean," he announced in answer to a question from Hazlerigg, "was splendid. We had a very large congregation to-night; as Halliday remarked to me, 'It's wonderful how calamity brings out the religion in people'—or maybe it was just the herd instinct. I don't think anyone else could have said the things he did without seeming sacrilegious."

"I hope he didn't say too much."

"No, no. He was the model of discretion. He began with a sort of appreciation of Appledown—a devoted worker—'good and faithful servant,' and so on. Then he led up to his death—'foully struck down in the course of his duty,' with a rather impressive bit out of Genesis about 'blood-guilt,' which made people sit up and eye each other. When he had got them all worked up he rubbed it into them that it was their solemn duty to tell the authorities anything which might have any bearing on the matter—with the implied threat of hell fire if they hung back (to say nothing of several years of penal servitude as accessories after the fact)."

"I see. And has anyone responded?"

"The response," admitted Pollock regretfully, "has so far been disappointing. As yet no one has come forward to admit that they did it—or even that they know who did it."

He had barely uttered the words when footsteps—audible on the cloister flags—came pattering towards them in a brisk determined rush.

"The harbinger of the fates," muttered Pollock involuntarily.

The steps paused, the door was thrust open, and Mrs. Judd appeared, out of breath but as resolute as ever.

As usual she came to the point without preamble.

"I have two things to tell you, Inspector. I forgot them both last time I saw you. My memory isn't what it used to be. Though I wouldn't have you think that it was failing. I had a cold bath every morning until my husband died."

"You have an addition to make to your previous statement?"

"Yes. First I should have told you that whilst I was having my supper I heard people talking in Parvin's house. Mrs. Parvin—and a man." An indescribable look came into Mrs. Judd's aged eye, malevolent yet impotent. "That dirty slut, the moment her husband's back was turned. The other thing I had to tell you was about Dr. Mickie. I was looking out of my window at a few minutes past nine and I saw him. He was wearing an old mackintosh over his shoulders; I saw him go down the path to the engine shed; I couldn't see him for more than a moment because the path goes out of my sight."

"You're absolutely certain that it was Dr. Mickie?"

"Yes," said Mrs. Judd. "I saw his face by the light of the lamp at the corner." This quiet, matter-of-fact statement was strangely convincing. "And I didn't see him come back again," she added. "I think someone should ask him what he was up to."

She made one of her unobtrusive exits and they heard her feet tap-tapping down the corridor.

"If she's telling the truth," said Pollock, "the case is over. I suppose we must see Mickie." He felt little elation at the prospect.

"So you see," said Hazlerigg firmly, "you must tell me what you know. We've been very fair with you, I think. We might have held up Mrs. Judd's statement and used it against you at"—delicacy shied at the words "police court," so he finished up lamely—"at a later stage."

The two men faced Dr. and Mrs. Mickie across the remains of their evening meal. What a miserable business it was, thought Pollock, hating it. Hazlerigg was immovably polite.

"Mrs. Judd saw you going down the path towards the cathedral. She admits that she lost sight of you after that. Then we have a set of footprints—there can't be much dispute that they are your footprints—running across the lawn, from the engine shed to your house."

He paused invitingly, but still Dr. Mickie did not speak. His face was a ghostly colour, but he had himself well under control.

"Have you nothing to say, Mrs. Mickie?" Hazlerigg turned to the woman.

"Yes, I have, but I don't promise that you'll like it." There was a surprising amount of spirit in her tone.

"You've no right to ask these questions. My husband has said that he knows nothing and that he never left the house last night—and now I suppose you'll make it your business to bully him until he says something different. Those footsteps might have been made by anybody—you said so yourself—and as for Mrs. Judd, she's mad. She's been mad for years, as anyone in the Close would have told you, if you'd taken the trouble to ask them."

The affair seemed to have reached a deadlock, when Mickie surprised them all by breaking into a wan smile.

"It's no good, dear," he said, "but thank you all the same. I think the truth's the thing. After all, I've nothing very much to be ashamed of, except that I ran away from a ghost."

"We all do that," said Hazlerigg.

"Well, I did go to my study at eight-fifteen, as I told you, and started working. I suppose I worked for about three-quarters of an hour, but my conscience was worrying me. I had felt for some time that there was something

110

wrong with the electric transmission in the organ—a sort of powerlessness on some of the stops: it had been particularly noticeable at service that evening, and I knew—or thought I knew—where I could lay my hand on the trouble. Still, it *was* nine o'clock at night and raining into the bargain, and it could easily have waited over till next morning. But as it happened there was a matter of private honour at stake. You know how it is when you funk a thing once, you can't rest easy until you've done it—if it's only to prove to yourself that you aren't a coward. I'm sorry if that sounds a bit cryptic, but I'll explain in a moment.

"Well, the long and short of it was that I put on a mackintosh and let myself out of the front door. It was raining very hard. I went along the road and into the precincts by the pillar-box entrance. It was light enough for me to see my way along the path to the corner of the chapter house, and the cathedral was pretty black. I felt my way along it with my fingers on the wall, cursing myself for not bringing a torch. A few yards short of the door I stopped for a moment to get my keys out of my pocket; by that time my eyes must have got more used to the dark, because quite suddenly I found myself looking at a body. It lay crumpled up on the ground in front of me, so near that I could have stretched out my foot and kicked it."

As he paused for a moment they could see him re-enacting the shock and nausea of the moment.

"I think my heart turned right over. I don't know how long I stood there without breathing. It seemed like hours, but was probably a fraction of a second. Then a large raindrop fell on the back of my neck, and I turned and ran. I must have climbed the wall, but I can't remember anything more until my wife met me in the front hall."

As he paused, Pollock could not resist the temptation to ask the question which was uppermost in his mind. "The body you saw," he said, "was it bare-headed, or had it a hat?"

Both Mickie and Hazlerigg looked surprised. The organist answered, but without any confidence, "Bareheaded, I think. It was very dark, I could scarcely see more than a blurred shape on the ground."

"Yet you knew it was a body."

"There's something very unmistakable about a body," said Mickie dryly.

"So that's the truth at last," said Hazlerigg. "I think you might have given it to us sooner and saved us a lot of trouble. There's one thing, though, that puzzles me. Admitting that it was an unpleasant shock to stumble across Appledown's body under such conditions—lonely place —awkward time of night—anyone might have been excused for taking to their heels: but once you were safe and sound back in your house, do you mean to tell me that you took no steps to inform anyone of what you had seen? That's rather odd, isn't it? Why, for all you knew the man you'd seen might not even have been dead. He might have been badly injured—in need of help."

"It's difficult to explain," said Mickie slowly, "but I was quite sure in my own mind that what I had seen was an hallucination—not of this world. I had some reason for thinking so. A month ago I went over to the organ shed on a similar errand and at about the same time at night. It was raining then, I remember, and as God's my witness I saw then—what I saw last night."

VIII • Night Thoughts at the Bear

"What did you make of that?" asked Hazlerigg.

"I don't think he was lying," said Pollock, "if he was, then he did it remarkably well. I've no doubt he saw Appledown's body last night and ran away just as he described. He kept quiet this morning for fear of implicating himself—until he saw that we knew too much."

"And the body he saw a month ago?"

"Hallucination. A figment of the imagination. What Dr. Smallhorn would call 'the artistic temperament.'"

"I don't believe in ghosts," said Hazlerigg. "We shall find a more rational explanation for that disappearing corpse. Good evening, Sergeant."

"Good evening, sir." Sergeant Brumfit emerged from his cubby-hole by the main gate. "Shall we be expecting you back again this evening?"

"I hope not," said Hazlerigg. "Sincerely I hope not."

"Good night, sir."

"Good night."

The two men passed under the thick stone arch, and the gate clanged shut behind them. It was eight o'clock, and the pavements were nearly empty. Melchester was eating its evening meal, and the second house was not yet out from the cinema.

In the lounge of the Bear Hotel, that comfortable Georgian hostelry, they found two young men awaiting them: two young men looking more than ever like intelligent Cairn terriers.

Pollock felt a slight misgiving at the sight of them. In kindness to the Dean, and in order to expedite their departure from his premises, he had offered them a statement—an exclusive statement; this offer he now felt some difficulty in implementing. Hazlerigg, however, when he learned that they were reporters, appeared almost excessively gratified. He ushered them into the coffee-room, and whilst dinner was being served he talked. It seemed to Pollock rather a curious, lopsided talk— though his listeners found it satisfying enough. There was a good deal of insistence on the campaign of anonymous letter-writing, and full descriptions of the incidents of the anthems, the flag, and the garden wall. The poison pen. The heartless practical joker. Police inquiries into the origin of the letters (I suppose we *have* inquired? thought Pollock). The culminating idea—the theme song, as it were, of this remarkable performance—was that "the authorities were confident" that if only they could trace "the perpetrator of these scurrilous missives" they would have no difficulty in solving the mystery of Appledown's death.

"No," said Hazlerigg, when their visitors had departed, "I wasn't pulling the journalistic leg. Not entirely; though I don't think it's quite as simple as I made out."

"Rather an odd aspect of the case you put to them."

"Didn't it convince you, Sergeant?"

"I think it convinced *them*," said Pollock diplomatically.

"Then it may serve its turn—start some more hares. Keep the old ones running. I understand that the *Melchester Times* has a wide circulation—here and in Starminster. Pass the salt."

In a private sitting-room upstairs, an hour later, the serious business of the evening began. Papers were spread out, pipes were lit, and the committee of two went into session.

"First these canons," said Hazlerigg. "I spent most of my afternoon with them—seeking the bubble reputation, as you might say: and this is what I got. Canon Beech-Thompson was at Evensong—you probably saw him. He wasn't in residence, but feels it to be his duty to go as often as possible as an *example* to the younger clergy. He meant Prynne, whom he can't stand at any price. He got back at six-thirty and sat with Mrs. B.-T. until seven-thirty. He was preparing a sermon. She was painting in water-colour. *Aequabiliter et diligenter.* Next came nice Canon Trumpington. He was not at Evensong. He spent four-thirty to six-thirty at the Foxes, having tea and helping to bathe the baby. Left the Foxes at six-thirty, picked up Bloss, and took him home for a chat. When Bloss left him at seven-fifteen, he was dressing for dinner. He was going to dinner with the Beech-Thompsons, whither he duly proceeded (at seven-thirty approximately). Left for his own house a little before ten. Bloss, you remember, had departed from 'chez Trumpington' at seven-fifteen. He went straight home to his own evening meal, which was served by his ancient female retainer at half-past seven. After dinner—say eight o'clock—he fell into a profound meditation on the Inner Causes of Action (a

meditation which he obligingly retraced for me in detail).
As far as he can recollect it would seem that he returned
to the surface about half-past nine, made a few careful
notes on 'Hibernation in the Hive,' and retired to rest.
Canon Fox, as I have told you, had Trumpington to tea.
After he left at half-past six, Mrs. Fox put the rest of the
brats to bed, and Canon Fox read a detective story for
half an hour. Dinner in the Fox household is seven
o'clock. Coffee was taken in the drawing-room at about
ten to eight, and at five past eight the two Foxes trotted
off to visit Halliday, where they drank further coffee and
played contract bridge. Is that all clear?"

"Beautiful," said Pollock in the enraptured tones of an
artist appreciating a piece of rare virtuosity. "Simply beautiful. They practically cancel each other out. Barring a
complete canonical conspiracy, the only person not
vouched for the whole time by at least one independent
witness is Canon Bloss—from eight o'clock onwards. Of
course, if Canon and Mrs. B.-T. were in league——"

"Don't forget that they were two of the very few people
who couldn't have had anything to do with the writing on
the wall. I think that's important."

"Then Canon Fox may have slipped out whilst Mrs.
Fox was bathing the children. He had half an hour."

"Not he," said Hazlerigg. "The sensible man sat in the
dining-room, and the maid was in and out every other
minute, laying the table."

"Anticipating trouble?"

"It's funny that you should say that," murmured Hazlerigg. He told Pollock of his conversation with Prynne
and of the latter's peculiar insistence on the rather obvious alibi afforded to him by the cinema commissionaire.

"We shall have to check it, of course."

"It does seem a bit too good to be true," agreed Pollock. "If you can't be good be careful—that sort of idea. Well, now, I'd better give you an outline of my afternoon's work."

He dealt in some detail with Dr. Smallhorn, Junior Verger Morgan, Vicar Choral Halliday, Second Verger (acting head verger) Parvin, Mrs. Parvin, and Precentor Hinkey: and the long hand of the clock flew round and quarter after quarter chimed out—faint but distinct—from Melchester spire.

"Very good," said Hazlerigg at last. "Very good indeed. I think we can feel our way forward a little now. Stop me if you disagree. Evensong on Tuesday finished almost on the stroke of six-thirty. Most people were clear of the cathedral within the next five or ten minutes. Mickie was one of the last away at twenty to seven. Appledown finishes clearing up, turns out the lights, locks the doors, and walks over to his own house. Time, a quarter to seven. Witnesses, Prynne and Mrs. Judd. He goes into his front room—his custom being, according to that brother of his, to smoke a quiet pipe after the day's labours. Very nice and natural. Did anyone come to see him then? We don't know. Next definite information shows that Appledown has moved into the kitchen and is 'pecking and picking' at his supper—witness, Parvin. Parvin, by his own account, left Appledown's cottage at about ten to eight——"

"That's been checked," said Pollock, "after a fashion. The local force have been busy, and amongst other reports"—he picked up a paper from the table—"we have Mr. Silas Begg of the Victoria and Albert. He remembers Parvin coming into the public bar at eight o'clock. It appears that Parvin made some jocular allusion to the hand being exactly on the hour."

"Oh, Lord, another of them," groaned Hazlerigg.

"Furthermore, he swears that his clock is the last word in accuracy. Rather unusual for a pub clock, don't you think?"

"If you want to know what I think, I should say that that whole issue collaborated in murdering the poor old man, having first taken care to provide themselves with carefully interlocking alibis—like a silly novel I once read. Never mind, let us persevere with Appledown's movements. At a minute to eight he has finished with his dinner and leaves by the front door, first pinning up a note for his brother. Witness—the whole choir. By process of reasoning (I think your deductions from Halliday's evidence were sound on that point) we know that he turned to the left outside his front gate, and then he walks out of our ken. Not for long, though. He was dead before ten past eight."

He paused.

"I don't think we need indulge in any fancy speculation about the next bit, when the explanation is so plain. Someone or other had induced Appledown to meet him behind the organ shed. He kept the appointment and was killed."

"That's how it happened," agreed Pollock. "I've never felt much doubt about it. And I think I can give you a little bit of corroboration. The murderer did the job with an ordinary walking-stick, possibly one with a rather heavy knobbly head. Whilst he was waiting for Appledown he stood behind the opened shed door, and he must have been a little bit nervous, because every now and again, as he waited, he drove the ferrule of the stick into the hard earth behind him. He himself was standing on the asphalt and left no footmarks, but I found the marks of his stick this morning."

"Well done," said Hazlerigg, "you must be right. And when Appledown shut the door he would present the right side and back of his head. A sitting shot, eh?"

"Rather a cool customer, your murderer."

"Cold-blooded and efficient. I've thought that all along. Well, now, allowing time for Appledown to walk round the cloisters, we can put the murder at not before eight-five, and certainly not after eight-ten, when the rain started. There's no means of telling exactly how long the murderer had been waiting for his victim—say ten minutes at least. Allow him five minutes afterwards to get back home. That gives us an overall period of approximately twenty minutes between five to eight and a quarter past eight. We might do worse than start by checking over the people without definite alibis for that period. I'll tell you what, let's chalk them in on that plan of yours. It's always easier to see a thing if you write it down."

"I've done that roughly," said Pollock. "Here you are. Bloss was in meditation, Hinkey somewhere in the country, Prynne in the cinema (I don't entirely trust that commissionaire), Malthus in the train—so he says—and Morgan at home, and alone. Mickie has only his wife to vouch for him from a few minutes to eight and onwards. According to the doctor the women are out of it. The only two resident men-servants in the Close are Artful Appledown, who was with his brotherhood in Windsor —I've had a check up on that—and Hubbard, the Dean's gardener, who was being the life and soul of the saloon bar at the Cock."

"At first sight not a very likely collection," assented

Hazlerigg, but Pollock could tell by his voice that something had pleased him. "I'll take them separately. Malthus is rather a special case. I'm expecting a phone message about him, so we'll leave him for the moment. First, Canon Bloss. He has an ancient retainer, as I told you—a lady of some four-score years, a little tottery on her pins but still extremely sound and sensible in her observations. She says that 'the master' retired to his study at about eight o'clock. Pressed further, she said not quite eight o'clock. It's a bit of a squeeze but he might have done it. Hinkey has no sort of alibi, but we do know he was out of the Close——"

He was interrupted by the ringing of the telephone.

"Yes," said Hazlerigg into the mouthpiece. "Yes." And "you don't say!" . . . "No, not at all." After a long period, during which the instrument buzzed and crackled inanely, he added, "Thank you very much. We'll expect that in writing some time to-morrow. Good night."

"Malthus!" he said simply. "Listen to this. As soon as I had finished with Prynne I telephoned the Bournemouth police, gave them the address of Malthus's ailing sister, and told them to get on with it. Their report, which they phoned back to the station here, is in front of you. Nothing doing. Miss Malthus seems to have been surprised but firm—unconvincing but unassailable. Then I had another bright idea from something I saw in the evening paper. So I again telephoned Bournemouth and told them to get on to the railway authorities. That was the result which came in just now."

He rubbed his hands one over the other in a genial, circular motion, but his eyes were hard.

"There was an accident on the Bournemouth-Overton branch line yesterday evening. Nothing serious: the up

Hazlerigg's Plan: Showing his estimate of the whereabouts of all male members of the Close community at 8 P.M on the evening of Tuesday, September 28th.

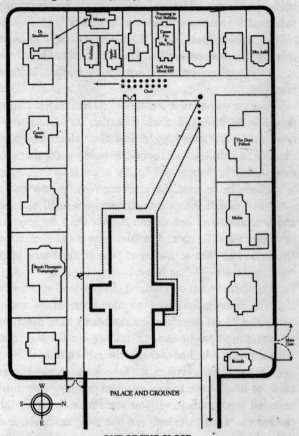

PALACE AND GROUNDS

W
S — N
E

OUT OF THE CLOSE

Name	Where they were	Who says so
Prynne	Cinema	Var. cinema attendants
Malthus	In the train	?
Hinkey	Somewhere in country	?
A. Appledown	Windsor	Drinking companions
Hubbard	The Cock Inn	Ditto
Parvin	The Victoria and Albert	Proprietor (?)

line was blocked by a fall of earth. Train services were held up, though. The six o'clock from Bournemouth didn't reach Overton until after nine o'clock."

"So," said Pollock, "and yet Malthus managed to catch an eight fifty-five connection. How very agile of him."

"Some explanation would seem to be needed," agreed Hazlerigg.

"How do you work it out then?" asked Pollock. "Suppose that Malthus did catch an earlier train—an afternoon train—the four-fifty, for instance, which gets in at six. He wouldn't know about the hold-up on the line then, unless he happened like you to see it in the paper. What does he do next? Let me see. Why, of course, he walks in through the gate unobserved—it's still open—and he lurks about behind the cloister wall. Appledown has been asked to meet him there on some pretext or other. He kills him according to plan at some time after eight, and then——" he paused.

"And then," went on Hazlerigg helpfully.

"Why, then he finds what we have got to find—a way *out* of the Close! After that he returns by back streets to the station, where he has left his bag—collects it, and walks down as if he had come by the eight fifty-five."

"Not bad," said Hazlerigg. "Check up on the earlier train; he might have been seen. And that bag—he must have left it somewhere, as you say. Probably not in the cloakroom, though. It's only got one thing against it, and that is Malthus himself. He didn't strike me as possessing that sort of nerve. And you have still failed to produce a motive."

"I think the motive, when discovered, will be somehow mixed up with the first attacks on Appledown—and come to think of it, Malthus was in as good a position as anyone with regard to that part of the business. In fact, better than most. As vicar choral he would have the anthems under his hand, and I believe he is supposed to be attached to the school as a master. Always assuming, of course, that the anti-Appledown campaign is connected with his murder."

For the first time that evening Hazlerigg's equanimity appeared to have deserted him. He was clearly troubled. "There is a connection," he said doggedly. "I know there's a connection, if only we were clever enough to see it. But we must be terribly careful. We mustn't half see it: or see it from the wrong angle, or it may blind us to what we really do want to see."

Pollock was so unused to this defeatism on the part of the inspector that he must have showed a startled face, the immediate effect of which was to make Hazlerigg laugh.

"We're not done yet," he said, "though the immediate future is obscure. We have a conference with the Chief Constable to-morrow at ten, in order that we may report progress—if any. I propose to set out the bare bones of the case against Malthus: all his movements must be checked. We can hand all that over to them; they'll do it better than we can. But there are one or two things I meant to look at before then. Are you very tired?"

"Not a bit," lied Pollock loyally and suppressing an aching desire for bed. "Never felt more awake in my life."

"First, then, about Appledown's private affairs. It seems that he was either a very methodical or else a very secretive man. You may remember seeing a desk full of papers in the old chap's sitting-room: it looked as if we had a heavy job in front of us there. Well, I handed it over to the local men and I got a report from them this evening. Apparently there's nothing there at all! Nothing at all private, that's to say. Piles of bulb and seed catalogues and newspaper cuttings about everything and nothing, and old service lists from the year dot, and a bundle of receipted bills—all local tradesmen and for small amounts. But as for letters or notebooks or diaries or writings of any sort—they drew a complete blank."

"Didn't his brother show us some specimens of his handwriting?"

"He did," answered Hazlerigg; "they were lists of household duties which he had made out at some time for his brother—rather a nice domestic touch, don't you think? I sent them up to headquarters with the note we found pinned up beside the door. I'm rather anxious to have an expert opinion on the writing. Well, as I was saying, the men who searched the desk had found nothing—in fact they had finished and were giving it up as a bad job when one of them saw a pink edge of paper sticking out at the corner of one of the small escritoire drawers. Something had slipped down behind the back of the woodwork, and they had the devil of a job to fish it out, but I think it repaid their efforts. Here it is."

He pushed over to Pollock a very much crumpled scrap of pink paper. It bore the royal arms and the heading Post Office Savings Bank, followed by a serial number; and it ran: "The Postmaster-General has been notified of the sum of £300 by cheque for the credit of the above described account in the books of this department," followed by Appledown's name and address.

"Acting on the hint contained in the words 'by cheque' they did what we ought to have done already, they went round to see the manager of Appledown's bank. He must have been less obstructive than the genus usually are, for they soon had the information they wanted. Appledown was a wealthy man. He had a current account of over a hundred pounds, and nine hundred pounds on deposit. Further than that, the manager volunteered the information that Appledown had in the past bought a good deal of rather speculative stock through him, though what had become of the certificates he was unable to say."

"And the man who gets it all is that rascal of a brother, I suppose. There's motive enough and to spare."

"But it won't hold water," replied Hazlerigg with a grin. "Wait a minute, I haven't finished with the bank manager yet. He further produced what is indubitably the last will and testament of Daniel Appledown: by it he gives, devises, and bequeaths his entire estate (real and personal) to the friends of Melchester Cathedral for the restoration and upkeep of the fabric."

"But his brother mayn't have known——"

"The witnesses," went on Hazlerigg smoothly, "were the bank manager himself and Artful Appledown."

"Game, set, and match to Appledown," conceded Pollock. "But what a fantastic situation! It amounts to this: if there was one person in the whole wide world who would want to keep Appledown alive and healthy that person was his brother. Yet he didn't appear very worried this afternoon."

"Artful's deep. As deep as the Atlantic Ocean and about as difficult to cross. But he didn't commit this murder."

"Surely," said Pollock, branching off on a new train of thought, "if Appledown was really a man of wealth and means he must have had private papers—unless he kept them all at his bank. Do you think he carried a pass-book with him?"

"I know he didn't." Hazlerigg unlocked his dispatch case and took out of it a gold half-hunter watch, a cheap fountain pen, a wallet containing five one-pound notes and a ticket to the free library, a handful of small change tied loosely in a rather dirty handkerchief, and last of all a bunch of steel keys of all shapes and sizes—some new, some with their wards and barrels worn thin and shiny. Each one had a little bone label, and Pollock read "West Door," "Library" and "Cloisters," cheek by jowl with "Front Door," "Coal Cellar," and even "Larder."

"A careful man, the late head verger," remarked Hazlerigg. "Careful of his own and his master's property. Fast bind, fast find."

"Yet he went off without any precautions to a rather curious and lonely assignation."

Pollock thought at first that the inspector had not heard him: he made no sign of having done so. At last he said, "That's a very good point; I confess that it had not occurred to me."

Pollock wondered what new train of thought had started on his casual remark. He also wondered how long he could keep awake.

Hazlerigg may have divined the thought, for he looked at his watch with a little tchk! of surprise: it was past one o'clock. "Enough for one day," he said.

Pollock felt suddenly dispirited and very tired.

"I can't believe it," he said impulsively. "They all looked so damnably normal. Don't you think it's just possible that we're mistaken, and some outsider did it after all? A tramp asleep in the shed, and annoyed at being disturbed by Appledown, or perhaps a small piece of stone dropping off the top of the spire. I read somewhere in a book that even a lump of sugar would kill you if it fell far enough. Or perhaps Appledown had a thundering apoplexy and fell and hit his head."

"You've been reading detective stories," said Hazlerigg good-humouredly: he seemed quite untired by his day's work. "Find me a piece of stone, yes, even the size of a sugar lump; or some signs of your disembodied tramp who slays head vergers and flies over stone walls—or even a little tiny symptom of apoplexy. I for one should be only too glad to see it. No." His face grew suddenly serious, and Pollock recognized such a quality of determination in the heavy jowl and the shrewd grey eyes as startled him back to wakefulness.

"There's a mind behind this business, make no mistake about that. A very fine brain, cool, calculating, and deadly careful. Every step, every single step, has been thought out beforehand. I have felt that once—twice— three times already to-day. It's all in there, if you care to look for it."

He stubbed a thick forefinger at the pile of papers which littered the table between them.

"Do you know," he went on, "I've got an unchancy feeling about this affair—what the Scots call a 'grue.' There are more than fifty people sleeping over there in that Close—fifty ordinary people, as you say; kindly people, clever and stupid in different ways. But one man isn't sleeping. He isn't sleeping because his brain is turning over and over, considering, probing, questioning. Not the wild thoughts of a half-baked intelligence—the sort of criminal (you know him as well as I do) who gives himself away to the police by his own silly lack of nerve. But the calm and clever thoughts of a man confident in his own ability. Fifty ordinary brains and one with this extraordinary kink in it. Not madness, but sanity—a sort of terrible sanity. When we discover the truth we shall find it as something simple and obvious. Its simplicity will be its strength. No elaboration—no frills—nothing to catch hold of."

"Nothing to catch hold of," repeated Pollock dully, desperately sleepy but hypnotized by the sincerity in Hazlerigg's voice.

"What shall we do about it? We shall come at him again and again, searching for the weaknesses in his plan. And our unknown will be at our elbow helping us— chatting with us—we may sit in his drawing-room, admire his garden, laugh at his jokes. But in the end, if we are clever enough, probe deep enough, look in the right places—it's a slender chance, but we may scare him. And what will he do then?"

"What will he do then," repeated Pollock dreamily.

"He'll make at last—God willing—that one deadly mistake which has brought the greatest murderers to the scaffold. He'll try to improve on perfection. He'll elaborate. He'll begin to wonder whether something hasn't been left undone. Some clue may be staring us in the face. Quick! Out of sight with it! Someone may let drop a remark. Really quite an innocent remark. Our murderer hears it and begins to wonder. Is that man safe? Has he seen something he shouldn't see—heard something he wasn't meant to hear? That man must be extinguished, too. But quickly, on the spur of the moment. No time for elaborate preparation or a careful alibi. And we shall be close on his heels. We shall have him then," he added simply. "For murder, though it have no tongue, will speak with most miraculous organ."

This last remark Inspector Hazlerigg made softly to himself. His audience was asleep.

IX • A Few Short Casts

"To that extent," said Hazlerigg, "we have proved that the murder was probably committed by a resident of the Close. According to your doctor's opinion we can narrow the field further and say a *male* resident of the Close. We can begin from there."

It was a five-power conference. The Chief Constable was in the chair, and besides Hazlerigg and Pollock there were present both Inspector Palfrey of the Melset Constabulary—fat, cheerful, and spasmodically helpful —and the lugubrious Sergeant Parks. The time was a few minutes after nine: the Chief Constable, displaying that unselfish attention to public duty which is typical of an English gentleman, had arisen a full hour before his accustomed time in order to be there.

His manner proclaimed as much.

"I've already told you," went on Hazlerigg, "how we imagine the job to have been done. The time, also, can be settled with fair accuracy. Appledown was alive until about five minutes past eight, but was dead before the rain began at ten minutes past eight. Yet, as you see, at first sight it would appear impossible for any one of our suspects to have murdered him at that particular moment, unless two or more of them did it together, and then they might have combined to rig up an alibi: but that, at the moment, I'm not prepared to believe."

"Then what you say is this." The Chief Constable was displaying a heftyish wit. "Someone in the Close did the job, and yet none of them could have done it, hey? I'm a man of ordinary intelligence, you know, Inspector, but it doesn't seem to me——"

"Quite so," Hazlerigg was unabashed. "But it's too early yet to talk about what's possible and what's impossible. If I may employ a metaphor myself, sir, before we start building we have to do a good deal of demolition. Clearing the site, you might call it. And our big obstacle at the moment is that confounded wall round the Close. It keeps a lot of 'em in, it's true: that's a help in a way; but it shuts other people out, and that's convenient too—convenient for them, I mean."

"Stone walls do not a prison make nor iron bars a cage," suggested Inspector Palfrey happily.

"Yes, well, I want you, if you will, sir, to do this for me. Find out by inquiry amongst your men—after all, I suppose they ought to know, if anyone does—if it's considered possible to climb into the Close. Is it feasible to do it without being seen? Is it possible? Has anyone ever done it, and if not why not? That sort of thing."

"I can tell you the answer to that myself," said Inspector Palfrey. "I walked a beat in Melchester for fifteen years, outside the Close and in, and you can take it from me that climbing over those walls is an impossibility. I believe boys used to do it once upon a time by climbing up the trees and dropping down inside the walls—I never caught them at it. But now they've cut down most of the trees and taken all the branches off the others, it'd be a job to climb the tree itself, let alone the wall. I should say myself that it was the third biggest impossibility in the Close—the other two being to get a rise out of Canon Bloss, or a subscription out of Canon Prynne." He laughed heartily at his own pet apothegm.

"Hum—well, we must leave it at that, I suppose. Now, secondly, I want the commissionaire on duty at the cinema put through it—gently, you know. He will probably tell you that Canon Prynne spoke to him on Tuesday night when he was on his way in. Find out what time that happened—the exact time, if you can. The man may be able to remember. Commissionaires often get asked the time, and when films start and so on. Then I want to know whether he saw Prynne coming out afterwards—at about five past nine, that should be. I want to know whether it would be possible for anyone to leave the cinema and re-enter it during the performance without the commissionaire seeing him. Could someone do that for me as soon as possible?"

Sergeant Parks implied his willingness to undertake the task, and momentarily ceased eating his pencil in order to make a note in his book.

"Thirdly, is anything known about an inn called the Victoria and Albert, and its licensed proprietor—a certain Mr. Begg?"

This innocent query produced a remarkable effect. Sergeant Parks glanced sharply at Inspector Palfrey, and both men started to speak at once. As is common on such occasions each reduced the other to silence, and this afforded a fine opening for the Chief Constable. On a sudden he had lost every trace of good humour.

"That man!" he cried explosively. "I might have supposed we should find *him* in it somewhere: he's the biggest scoundrel in Melchester, that's what *he* is. He's more trouble and nuisance than the whole of the Licensed Victualler's Association rolled together. It's my considered opinion that he's a radical."

Hazlerigg asked what the man had done.

"We've had three complaints against him for keeping open after hours," said Sergeant Parks sorrowfully, "but we've never convicted him. It's a great pity."

"It's intolerable," amended the Chief Constable. It was not entirely plain whether it was intolerable of Mr. Begg to have stayed open after hours, or not to have allowed himself to be convicted for so doing.

"How did he get off," ventured Hazlerigg, "some jiggery-pokery with the clock?"

"Black perjury, you mean." The Chief Constable turned on Sergeant Parks. "It was your case, wasn't it?"

Sergeant Parks agreed unhappily that it had been his case. The memory of it appeared to pain him.

Hazlerigg interposed tactfully. "I don't think we need go into details about it. I take it we may assume that this man Begg is an unreliable witness, and a man who would certainly go out of his way to hinder the police."

"That's right," said Sergeant Parks, "unreliable and nasty."

"Assume it by all means," agreed the Chief Constable. "How is it going to help us?"

"At the moment not at all. It might prove useful if we found any reason to shift our suspicions on to Parvin." Briefly he related to them evidence relevant to the second verger and his movements. "At the moment I think we must concentrate on Malthus. There's almost a prima facie case against him."

"I agree," said the Chief Constable. "On the facts that you've given us, I agree. Now, if you could suggest any possible *motive* for the crime—I should say, take a risk and pull him in. Arrest 'em first and prove it afterwards, eh, Palfrey?"

This frank inversion of police procedure appeared to upset the jovial inspector, who looked deprecatingly at Hazlerigg and ventured his first coherent comment.

"I had a report, sir," he murmured, "about Mrs. Malthus. You know you asked us to check up on her movements. Well, we've found one or two people who saw her about the town yesterday evening, but after six o'clock she seems to have disappeared. Vanished into thin air, as you might say. And she never went into Smith's reading-room, like she said. The young lady there knows her well by sight, and she was most positive of that."

"Curious," remarked Hazlerigg, "curious and suggestive. But it doesn't necessarily prove anything against Malthus himself. I incline to think that we need more evidence before we act; though, mind you, he's got a lot of explaining to do. If we're right in our suspicions we should be able to find someone who saw him arrive by the earlier train—or saw him on his way down to the station. He can't have flown. That's the line to concentrate on. And he'll have to be watched. Discreetly, of course. I leave it to you."

An hour later, as Pollock and Hazlerigg finally left the Chief Constable's office, they passed the door of the station-sergeant's inner sanctum. The only sign of life was Sergeant Parks (back elevation) wrestling like some modern Laocoön with an extension telephone. They attended, with what patience they could muster, to the usual one-sided conversation.

"Ah. That's right. Freedom of the press, eh? Oh, 'e did, did 'e? Just spell it. C-R-U-N . . . what? Oh, M for monkey . . . all right. I heard. Oh, yes, that was the house where . . . so it was." Long pause. "Oh, 'e did?"—inflexion of surprise. "Ah, did 'e, though?"—ditto cynicism.

A succession of neutral h'mps brought the sergeant to something which he evidently considered of first importance, for he produced his ever-ready pencil and inscribed on the back of an old envelope: "He—did—not mind—a—practical joke—but—he—drew—the—line—at—murder."

A final hysterical cackle and Sergeant Parks rang off.

"Message from Starminster," he said; "they've had a man in the station this morning; tells a funny story by the sound of it. Apparently he read an article in the paper—the local paper that'd be—about this business here. It sent him round to the police station in double-quick time, saying he'd been the victim of a practical joke—name of Crumbles."

"What sort of a joke?" asked Pollock.

"Well, it was like this. Some time ago, more than a month, he had a big envelope come by post. He'd destroyed it, of course—they always do. The envelope, I mean. Inside it was another packet of letters and envelopes and postcards, all stamped and written and dated. Pinned on to it was a letter—he had the sense to keep that—it simply said, 'I'm having a joke on some of my pals in the Close. Will you send off these letters on the dates indicated? Enclosed find a pound for your trouble. When the last one has arrived here I'll send you another pound. Nothing criminal about it, just a joke.' 'Well,' he says to himself, no doubt, 'A pound's a pound.' I dare say he read some of the letters—silly from what I can hear, but no harm in 'em. Seeing that article in the paper, though, it puts the wind up him properly."

Hazlerigg smiled the smile of a man who has improved on Providence by casting his bread upon the waters and finding it good and early the next morning.

"We'll get a proper statement from him this evening," continued Sergeant Parks. "There's another thing you might like to hear. About that cinema. I saw the man myself. If you want a thing done properly—you know the old saying. Well, I can't help thinking that this 'ere canon of yours must be a talkative sort of bloke. He spoke to the commissionaire when he was going in, as well as when he was coming out, and twice during the performance. Once he wanted to shift his seat, and once to complain that someone had stolen his umbrella, which was found subsequent, two rows back. He also passed the time of day with the girl who tears your ticket in half and the girl who shows you into your seat. He also bought a box of chocolates, which he left behind, and an ice-cream. I don't know what became of that. And I dare say," concluded the sergeant sorrowfully, "that every now and then he found time to take a peep at the film."

"Holy Christmas," breathed Hazlerigg. "Can that be true?" It was an expression he rarely used, and was the very token and sign manual of his profoundest interest.

X • Prynne Is Almost Certain

WHEN CANON PRYNNE AWOKE on Thursday morning he realized that something very jolly was happening. It took him a moment or two to sort his sleep-scattered thoughts, and then he remembered. As he remembered he glowed and a pure and disinterested enthusiasm.

Appledown had been murdered—so he had! And he, Canon Prynne, knew who the murderer was. And no one else knew. The two policemen from London, to give them their due, had probably guessed—had, anyway, a shrewd suspicion. But suspicions were far from proofs.

For that matter he had no concrete proof. And though he could point the finger and say how and when and where, the why of it eluded him. And to-day being Thursday he was going to have a shot at getting proof and the why at the same time.

He dressed in a mood of thoughtful elation, and went down to his customary breakfast of orange juice and dry toast.

Morning service over, he returned to his house and settled down in his study. It was the best and largest room in the house, and from Prynne's point of view it had one great advantage. It possessed a bow window which commanded the stretch of the road from corner to corner of the precincts.

Having positioned his chair carefully in the window recess he settled himself in it, facing west: on his knees he laid a weighty commentary on the book of Job.

At twelve-thirty he shut the book with a sigh, rose to his feet, left the study, passed through the front hall, and reached down his town-going hat. A moment later he was strolling along the Close walk in the bright sunshine with which September had graced its closing day.

He was so occupied with his philosophic reflections that he did not notice the peculiar behaviour of a stolid-looking man in corduroys who seemed to have been spending a busy morning doing nothing in particular to the lamp outside Mrs. Judd's gate. Not, in point of fact, that there was anything very remarkable about the stolid-looking individual, except possibly the size of his boots. But no sooner had Prynne passed him than he deserted his work on the lamp-post and entered a near-by telephone booth, where he put through a call. (And why not, anyway?)

Pollock was at the police station when the call came, and he took it himself. He listened carefully, and said at last:

"Quite right—but of course we can't make 'em all stop in the Close. Pass the word to Page and tell him to phone me in ten minutes. I'll hang on here."

Ten minutes later the station telephone rang again. Pollock listened with growing excitement and satisfaction. This time he said, "The devil he did! Well, don't lose sight of him. I'll be with you myself in five minutes."

To Hazlerigg, who came in at this moment, he explained rapidly, "It looks as if one of them's breaking cover. I can't quite make out who it is, from the description, but he's up at the station—no, he's not simply meeting someone; Page just heard him book for London. What about it? He says there's an up train due in about ten minutes."

"Then I think," said Hazlerigg, "I really think that you might take a trip to London yourself. It's a beautiful day. There's a police car outside the door. . . ."

"Of course," said Pollock many hours later, when he was making his report to Hazlerigg, "that infernal car would elect to break down just in the middle of the High Street. Even then I should have had loads of time to walk, but the fool of a driver—may he tramp his beat to the black end of eternity—assured me it wouldn't take a minute to put right. It was nearer five minutes. In the end I got the train by the skin of my teeth.

"However, I was out of the train before it had come to a standstill, and dodged quickly into cover behind the paper stall in the middle of the platform. It was at this juncture that it struck me that I didn't know who I was chasing. Gimblett had said 'one of they clergymen from the Close,' and Page had been hardly more explicit: and stare as I might I couldn't see anyone I knew. I had been standing at the extreme end of that paper stall, keeping well down, but now the last passengers were climbing out and the porters were slamming the doors, so I made a move forward. It was one of those two-sided stalls with an opening on each side, and as I moved up level with it I could see right through it, and there on the other side, unconcernedly buying an *Investor's Chronicle*, was

Canon Prynne. He must have been within six feet of me the whole time.

"There was only one thing to be done. I retired to my previous position, hoping that I hadn't been seen. And I don't think Prynne did see me, but a new danger appeared in the shape of a very superior station official who had for some minutes been regarding my conduct with the gravest suspicion. He may have seen me leap from the train. Anyway, I was obviously a suspicious character and 'lurking with intent.'

"By the grace of heaven, before he could get at me, Prynne had bought his paper and was half-way down the platform, his nose deep in his *Investor's Chronicle*. I had time, therefore, to produce my warrant card and explain to the station-master in a blistering whisper exactly what I thought of interfering minor officialdom (rather unfair, really, but it took him aback to such an extent that he never even asked me for my ticket—which was lucky, because I hadn't got one).

"Prynne by this time was through the barrier and drifting up the station. I say drifting, because I've never seen anyone progress with his nose buried so deep in a newspaper—but I daren't give him too much rope, as he was obviously making for the Underground, and I knew by experience the choice which the Waterloo Underground offers, even to an innocent quarry.

"However, he ignored the City line entirely, and kept straight on, and it presently became apparent that it wasn't the Edgware, Highgate, and Morden line that he wanted. That left the Bakerloo, and a balance of probability that he was making for the West End.

"So far, as I have said, no hunter could have desired a more considerate quarry. He never took his eyes off his paper and he never looked back. When he reached the Underground platform he stood well against the wall, and continued to read. There was a fair crowd, and I was well out of his sight, some twenty yards farther down the platform, in the opening of the corridor. All too, too easy.

"Well, I may have been lulled into a false sense of security, because the next bit caught me on the wrong foot. A train came in, and Prynne moved up with the others as if to get in. Then he changed his mind—too crowded for him, I thought, as he moved back to his old position. I stayed where I was, of course. The guard had shouted 'all clear,' and the train doors were beginning to close when Prynne changed his mind for a second time, and showing a most remarkable turn of speed he nipped across the now empty platform and inserted himself between the rapidly closing doors.

"I don't know, to this moment, how I managed to get aboard myself. In fact I don't think I should have done, had not some part of Prynne been caught as the doors closed, whereupon the presiding Deity opened them again sufficiently to clear the obstruction, and this just gave me time to insert my own vile body.

"But I was horribly perturbed, nonetheless, for it stuck out a yard that there was nothing accidental about Prynne's last manœuvre, and it's disturbing to find you have been underrating an opponent.

"But the business presented another curious feature. To start with, I was as sure as I could be that Prynne had never once looked at me. You know how sensitive you get to these things when you are 'tailing' somebody, and there isn't one man in a thousand can prevent himself from giving that involuntary backward glance when he realizes he is being followed.

"By the time we had run through Charing Cross and were approaching Trafalgar Square I had come to the conclusion that either Prynne was a bold and desperate criminal or else I was the world's fool—and neither idea pleased me too much. But then when I saw him pottering off up the platform, still seeming uncommonly interested in market prices, well—the first notion seemed fantastic.

"When we got to the lift Prynne was the last man in—which meant, of course, that I couldn't go in after him: so as the lift shot up I sprinted for the emergency stairs. They were as endless and as filthy as emergency stairs always are, and by the time I arrived breathless at the top I expected that Prynne would be out of sight. However, he was only just leaving the station. He seemed to be in no hurry. He had put away his paper now and was making for the Strand.

"At the first corner we came to I slowed down and took a squint into a conveniently placed shop window; it was lucky I did. Prynne had stopped dead and was backing. Not walking back, but walking backwards, if you follow me. I could only see his reflection, and it looked so odd that I stood rooted to the spot. Another moment and he had disappeared into a doorway—something that looked like one of those back kitchen or basement entrances you see behind big hotels.

"I was wondering whether to go forward (which meant certain discovery if Prynne was merely standing in the doorway) or stay where I was and wait on events, when a hand tapped my shoulder and I leapt round to find—yes, laugh if you like—a common or garden police constable regarding me with owlish suspicion: it was an 'A' Division man, and fortunately I knew him by sight.

"'Now then,' he said, 'I've bin watching you.'

"'Well, Potts,' I retorted, or words to the effect. 'You can something or other well stop watching me this something minute and get on with your qualified job and leave me to do mine.' It's funny how extra savage you sound when circumstances force you to whisper.

"I think he must have recognized me at this juncture, for he grinned toothlessly and started to move off, and suddenly it struck me that here was a heaven-sent ally.

"I quietly explained the situation to him, and told him that he must walk up the next street and glance in the doorway as he did so. 'You probably see a clergyman standing there,' I ended.

"'Ah,' said he, 'I've bin keepin' a hye on 'im too. I thought it looked a bit suspicious, being a clergyman, like: which on 'em are you after?'

"At this I think I stood stock still for a minute, staring like a ninny. At last I said feebly, 'What do you mean, Potts? Are there more than one?'

"'There's two,' said Potts, 'a fack which first roused me suspicions. First a little fat one wearing no hat, with a bald patch to the top of his head like a soup plate, and horn-rimmed specs, and then a long thin one follering him, and then you follering the long thin one, only of course I wasn't to know it was you.'

"Well then, of course, everything slipped back into perspective, and if I hadn't been so taken up with my own misadventures I should surely have seen it all before. Whilst I was following Prynne, Prynne for some reason of his own was following Malthus (I had no difficulty in recognizing him from Potts' graphic description). Seen in this light, Prynne's behaviour became purely rational. His lingering behind on Waterloo platform and burying his nose in the paper and being last into the train and last into the lift were merely his own devices for keeping out of sight of Malthus.

"'Baldy's gone in to have a snack in the grill room of the Imperial,' went on Potts. 'That's the entrance round the corner on the left. Number two's waiting for him to come out, I suppose.'

"That being so it struck me I could do with a snack myself.

"'How long will number one be?' I asked.

"'I'll find out,' said Potts, and disappeared.

"He was back within a minute.

"'Grilled kidneys and braised carrots,' he breathed in my ear. 'Ten minutes to serve and ten to eat, barring he don't 'ave something else besides.'

"I didn't, of course, question the accuracy of his calculation, knowing what I did of 'A' Division and their friends in the West End catering trade.

"I doubled back to a little eating-house I had spotted, leaving Potts on guard, and consumed a quick bacon and eggs. I even spared a thought for Prynne lurking foodless in his doorway, and wondered for the first time what he was after, and what it all had to do with the Melchester affair and the decease of Daniel Appledown. A quarter of an hour later I was back on the corner.

"'Nothing doing,' Potts reported. 'Number two come out once and took an eyeful into the grill room door: he didn't go in, though. I thought he looked a bit hungry himself. They tell me Baldy's going on to mushrooms on toast,' he added. 'That gives you seven minutes more.'

"'All right,' I said, 'now double round and get me a taxi. Have it waiting in front of the Imperial in five minutes' time. You can stand on the pavement at the corner where I can see you, and give me the signal when number one comes out. You'd better blow your nose.'

"Potts barged off, and a minute later I saw him reappear at the corner of the Strand. He stood there woodenly on his heels for a few minutes, moved off to caution a street vendor, directed an old lady to somewhere or other, and at last, when I was beginning to think that something had gone wrong, slowly drew out an enormous khaki handkerchief and blew his nose.

"I was off like a flash and found my taxi ticking over in the next side street. Malthus was plainly visible. He had crossed the road and was waiting for a bus to take him up the Strand. Prynne was still out of sight. I decided to bide my time.

"Malthus ignored the first offer—a number 1—and chose a Cannon Street bus. Still no Prynne. The bus moved off. At that moment there was an angry honk behind us—we were right in the middle of our side street —and a taxi squeezed past. Canon Prynne was in it talking earnestly down the speaking-tube to the driver.

"'Follow that taxi,' I said. 'And you needn't go too fast, because I happen to know that it's following a bus: so you can keep well back.'

"The driver seemed amused at the thought—murmuring 'Just like a ruddy paper-chase' he swung his machine across the bows of a blaspheming Rolls-Royce, and joined the procession.

"Past Chancery Lane on the left and Sergeant's Inn on the right—to say nothing of the best pub in London— and by that time we were about two-thirds of the way down Fleet Street, and Ludgate Circus was in sight. Prynne's taxi pulled up with a jerk. Plainly Malthus had got off his bus. Then Prynne's taxi executed one of those lightning cross-traffic pirouettes that only taxi-drivers seem to understand, and plunged down a turning in the direction of the Embankment. Mine performed the same manœuvre in front of the same bus (I think the bus driver was already speechless with rage) and followed demurely.

"The affair seemed likely to reach a point at any moment. I said to my driver. 'If that taxi ahead of you stops, go on round the next corner and stop too.' Then I sat well back.

"I was none too soon. We turned to the right again and found ourselves in a very narrow street behind one of those mammoth newspaper blocks. The first thing I saw was Prynne himself standing on the kerb paying off his taxi. Malthus was already out of sight.

"My driver said something most uncomplimentary to Prynne's driver, Prynne's driver replied in kind. We mounted the pavement and scraped past. The moment we were round the corner I was out of the cab, slipped ten bob to the driver and ran back. One cautious peep was enough. The street was empty. Evidently the quarry had gone to earth.

"Prynne's man was still there glaring at his scraped mudguard. Stimulated by a further flashing of my warrant card he indicated a door some yards up on the right.

"'That's where they went,' he said, 'both of them.' I saw that the building he was pointing to was part of the big Megatherium newspapers block. 'The big tall one following the little bald one. That's what he told me to do. I can't tell you why. I hope there was nothing wrong in it.'

"'Nothing at all,' I said cheerfully, 'we're doing very nicely.'

"'I dare say they mistook the door,' he went on sadly. 'It must have been a religious paper they were looking for, mustn't it? *Protestant Truth*, or *The Banner*—they're

146

both in this street, you know, but farther up. That one there's nothing but a lot of lady's papers. Fashions and such-like.'

"I left him speculating, and made for the doorway he had indicated. It led to nothing more exciting than a flight of stairs, and since no alternative offered I went up them. In front and all round me there was a sort of murmur and bustle of activity, concentrated but subdued by distance or very thick walls.

"On the first landing I stopped and looked round me. The only door visible was a heavy iron studded affair labelled 'Emergency Exit Only.' It was locked or bolted on the other side—anyway I couldn't shift it, so I went on upstairs.

"This arrangement was repeated on the second and third landing; I had quite decided that I was on the wrong trail—this was clearly nothing but an emergency staircase and leading probably to the roof of the building—and I was on the point of turning back when I noticed something. The stairs so far had been plain stone, grey and undistinguished, but from the landing where I stood and upwards they were carpeted. A small enough point, but it made the place look more inhabited and hopeful somehow. I was utterly beyond speculation by this time, but on tiptoe and with a curious sense of expectation I climbed quietly upward.

"The turn of the stairs showed me a fourth landing— also carpeted—a plain wooden door, and Canon Prynne. He was on one knee, with his back to me, and sad though it is to relate of a canon of the Established Church, his eye was firmly affixed to the keyhole.

"I watched him, fascinated, for a few minutes. Then he straightened up, adjusted his collar, and opened the door. I had just time to hear him say 'So that's your secret,' and then I stepped in behind him.

"I don't quite know what I'd been expecting; an Ali Baba's cave, with Malthus in the midst of it undergoing a Jekyll and Hyde transformation into a master criminal: anyway, it was quite an ordinary office with a desk and some file cabinets, and a shelf or two of reference books, and a huge pile of letters in one of those wire basket contraptions, and a couple of telephones, and in the middle of it all—Malthus sitting in a swivel chair with his waistcoat off. He looked, I thought, both surprised and aggrieved. He certainly didn't look in the least alarmed. When he saw me I thought his eyes were going to fall out of his head: then Prynne turned round and he saw me too: and quite suddenly an extraordinary thing happened. We all burst out laughing. . . .

"'In short,' Malthus was saying five minutes later (we were all seated round his desk by this time in the greatest possible amity), 'I am Aunt Sylvia of the *Woman's Sentinel*. It began years ago when I was a young curate at St. Saviour's Wormwood Scrubbs, and got married; a thing young curates are not encouraged to do. I was extremely hard up, and an old college friend of mine—I can give you his name if you want it—got me this job. He had done it himself for many years, and had to give it up as he was going abroad. I was a little doubtful about taking it on at first, but really, do you know, I found it ideally suited to my needs. They pay me quite an absurd amount of money, and I can do most of the work at odd moments. My dear wife is a great help to me. She has a perfect genius for ferreting out odds and ends of knowledge which I can use in answers to my correspondents. You only have to be a bit careful about copyright and libel and so forth: then, of course, sometimes I don't know the answer and I can't find it out, so I write a nice letter to the person, thanking them for asking such a *clever* and intelligent question, and explain quite frankly that at the moment I can't quite find the best answer. Nine times out of ten they're so pleased at catching you out that they're quite satisfied. As a matter of fact I've only had one persistently dissatisfied customer—in that way—since I took the job; and that's an old lady in Epping, who's been writing to me regularly for the last three years.'

"'What does she want?' asked Prynne keenly: as a matter of fact he'd been listening most attentively to Malthus's little discourse.

"'Well,' said Malthus, 'it's quite an absurd thing, really. She wants to know who was the fattest woman in history. We can't think what possible use the information will be to her, even if we can get it, which seems——'

"'I can tell you that,' Prynne interrupted him. 'It was a Mrs. Robinson, a Mrs. Delilah Robinson of Kansas City; she lived at the end of the last century. Her peak performance was when she turned the scale at fifty-two stone exactly, wearing only a bathing-dress, at the first Chicago Federal Exposition. The sensation was, I am told, unparalleled.'

"Malthus looked just like a shipwrecked mariner sighting land after six weeks in an open boat. 'Really,' he gasped, 'why, that's splendid!' My own private impression, which I didn't confide to Malthus, was that Prynne had made the whole thing up from beginning to end.

"When I could secure their attention I recalled Malthus to the business in hand.

"'Now, look here,' I said rather sternly, 'we are investigating a very serious affair. What I want from you is an account of your movements last Tuesday night.'

"'Why, certainly,' he said. 'Now that you've surprised my little secret there's no point in keeping anything back. It's like this. Whilst I was still in London I found it easy to do my work in the parish as well as this little extra job. But when I came to live in Melchester Close—well, it was a wee bit different. You do see that, don't you?'

"I thought of Canon Beech-Thompson, and also of Mrs. B.-T., and I assured him that I saw it perfectly.

"'Well, it was a bit awkward. I knew that if it leaked out I should have to put up with a good deal of ridicule. I might have had to drop it altogether, and I needed the money badly, with a growing family. Funnily enough,'— and here he gave an apologetic blink at Prynne—'I chiefly dreaded your finding out. I imagined the jokes you might make——'

"'You misjudged me,' said Prynne. 'I respect your work on the *Women's Sentinel*—what I have seen of it— infinitely more than your work in the Church. This is your real vocation, if there's any meaning left in the word. Your advice last Monday to a young wife on how to keep chickens in a fourth-story flat fell little short of genius. And now that I have discovered your guilty secret I promise you my silence—for a price.'

"Malthus gave a squeak like a shot rabbit, but Prynne continued unmoved: 'In future there will be two Aunt Sylvias; I have a wide fund of general knowledge which is entirely at your disposal, whilst you will supply the human touch. Aunt Sylvia as Malthus was good. As Malthus-Prynne she will be the non-pareil.'

"'Really!' cried Malthus, looking both alarmed and

pleased at once, if you can imagine such a thing. 'I don't think my editor——'

"'Your editor need never know,' said Prynne firmly. 'We will consider it settled.'

"If he sticks to his word my own opinion is that the next few numbers of the *Woman's Sentinel* should be worth reading.

"With difficulty I again recalled Malthus to business. I'd better summarize what he said, or we shall be all night. He hummed and hawed a good deal, and Prynne kept interrupting him, as fresh ideas occurred to him for brightening his feature page.

"In short, what he told me was this:

"His first main difficulty was that he had to get up to London at least once a week, usually on Thursday, to see the editor about matters concerning the policy of his 'page,' and to deal with any letters which had come to him at the office.

"We were quite wrong about Tuesday—Malthus never went to Bournemouth at all. He was called up on the Monday for a long 'policy' conference—his page has been such a success lately that you may be glad to hear they are doubling his feature space—and since he was kept late he stayed on until Tuesday. He came back by the seven o'clock from Waterloo. As usual, to short circuit any questions he arranged with his sister the customary fiction that he was visiting her in Bournemouth. That suited him very well, as the six o'clock from Bournemouth made a connection with his train, so there would be no discrepancy if anyone happened to meet him at the station when he arrived. So, unless he took to himself the wings of the morning and flew, it's a stone-cold certainty that he wasn't in Melchester until nine o'clock. He walked straight home and went to bed. I might say now that I went afterwards with him to Waterloo, and since he clings to the pleasant old-fashioned habit of lavish tipping, I easily found the porter who had put him on to that particular train last Tuesday. Incidentally, he also cleared up his wife's movements. When she disappeared yesterday she was paying one of her discreet visits to the free library, to unravel a knotty point raised by a reader in Brighton anent the mating of Leghorns."

When he had finished his story, Pollock added rather despondently, "Another dead end, sir. I suppose we shall have to sit around now and wait for something to happen."

"Not a bit of it," said Inspector Hazlerigg grimly. "It's happened."

XI • A Tea-Party—And After

WHEN POLLOCK DEPARTED for London in pursuit of Prynne, Hazlerigg went and had lunch. Since the lunch was a good one, and was being paid for moreover by his country, he added the small luxury of an Indian cheroot. Fortified thereby he reviewed the case.

An infallible instinct told him when he had reached the storm centre of a disturbance. For the moment a pleasant inaction was indicated—until such time as he heard from Pollock or until the local police saw fit to cry on one of the lines they were hunting so patiently. Ahead of him he saw the breakers, and far, far ahead the passage for which he was steering, half hidden in the mist and spray.

This nautical imagery was so pleasing and the leather arm-chair in which he was sitting was so comfortable that he was on the point of sinking into that lotus-flower coma which is the stepsister to sleep, when he realized that someone had come softly into the room and was standing behind his chair.

Just for a moment Hazlerigg forgot he was in the cathedral city of Melchester. He had been trained in a part of London where wise policemen face strangers at all times.

In a fierce concerted movement he heaved his bulk out of the chair and spun round.

Facing him was a solemn and startled boy. It was Hazlerigg who recovered his poise first.

"Well, my lad, and what can I do for you?"

"Please, sir," said the boy, shifting awkwardly from one foot on to the other after the manner of his kind, "are you Inspector Hazlerigg, and if you are could you come up to the school some time this afternoon if it isn't inconvenient and have a word with the headmaster?"

"I am and I could," said Hazlerigg, gallantly abandoning all thought of a siesta. "I take it that you are one of the choirboys—I'm sorry, choristers. Would it be indiscreet of us to inquire your name?"

The boy suddenly giggled and looked more friendly. "I'm Brophy," he said. "John Brophy. I'm head of the school. I'm leaving this term and going to Marlborough."

"Melchester's loss is Marlborough's gain," said Hazlerigg courteously. "Lead on."

The motion of his legs seemed to have the effect of unlocking John Brophy's tongue. Indeed, his worst enemy could not have accused him of being a difficult person to talk to. Amongst other items of information Hazlerigg gathered that Halliday was "rather a good sort," that Prynne was "all right" but could be "frightfully sarcastic," and that the late Appledown had been "not bad." Even as an epitaph Hazlerigg could detect no conviction in this last statement.

His guide stopped at the last corner before they reached the school. His embarrassment had returned.

Fumbling in a distended coat pocket he produced an autograph book and thrust it into the inspector's hands. It was the first time that Hazlerigg had realized that he possessed even a notoriety value. With a dawning sense of values he signed under Don Bradman but above Somerset Maugham.

Brophy led his visitor into the big schoolroom and left him there whilst he went in search of Dr. Smallhorn. Most of the boys had gone down to the playing-fields, and the place was unnaturally quiet and empty. Sunlight through dusty windows, inkstained desks, a varnished map of the Holy Land, and the mingled smell of mutton and carbolic soap.

Hazlerigg's mind flicked back thirty years to his own early schooldays. He could remember little of his preparatory school except that it had seemed to him a place where the masters were much happier than the boys. No doubt that was all changed now.

At that moment Dr. Smallhorn made a precipitous entry, with Brophy fussing round him like a dog reuniting two dilatory walkers.

"Ah, Inspector. I'm truly relieved that you managed to get here. That'll do, Brophy. You can run along now and change. If you hurry you should be in time for the kick-off. Now, Inspector—could you come this way? Mind the step. We'll go out into the garden, I think: there's less danger of our being overheard. Don't be alarmed, but I've got something rather serious to tell you."

Hazlerigg promised that he would endeavour not to be alarmed. By this time they had reached the back door which gave directly on to the boys' changing-rooms. The headmaster pointed to the door itself: comment was really unnecessary.

"Crude work," said Hazlerigg. "When did it happen?" He fingered the broken hasp of the lock and ran a professional eye over the raw dents and sears in the wood. "Someone's been using a jemmy or something of the sort. Not very clever at it either."

"I found it like this when I came down this morning," said Dr. Smallhorn. "I locked the door myself at eleven o'clock last night. No, no one heard a sound, but then we none of us sleep—— Hi, get off that grass, you little ruffian. How many times have I told you to keep to the path when you're wearing football boots? That's Canon Fox's boy. A very promising Greek scholar. As I was saying, we none of us sleep on this side of the house."

"Yes," said Hazlerigg dubiously. "But it must have made a noise like a pistol shot; young heads sleep sound, eh? Has anything been taken?"

"As far as I know, nothing."

"What's in this next room through here? Just boys' desks. The top form, I see. And you're sure that no one has missed anything?"

"The boys, do you mean?" said Dr. Smallhorn. The thought seemed to surprise him. "I'm afraid it hadn't occurred to me that anyone would want to steal their things. They have very little private property, you know."

He opened a desk at random and revealed a complicated clutter of picture books, meccano, and natural history specimens.

"Not an ordinary burglar," agreed Hazlerigg absently. He was lost in abstracted contemplation of the open desk in front of him. Peering over his shoulder, Dr. Smallhorn could see nothing more remarkable than a dispirited bag of toffee.

"Have you discovered something?"

"No, no. I was just thinking. Tell me, Dr. Smallhorn, how many suits do your boys bring back with them?"

Dr. Smallhorn's first impression was that his visitor had gone mad—then came a happier thought. After all, even inspectors married and had children—a prospective parent!

"I must introduce you to our lady matron," he said affably. "Such a charming woman. A great organizer. Come along. Mind the step."

They found Mrs. Meadows upstairs, folding and brushing clothes. A placid, middle-aged woman of ample proportions. She evidently held to the theory that many hands made light work, for over her shoulder Hazlerigg could see Halliday staggering under a pile of second-best suits. He had the look on his face of one who has entered the toils.

"This is Inspector Hazlerigg, Mrs. Meadows. He wants to know about clothes for the school. Perhaps you have a list handy. By the way, how old is your boy?"

"Six," said Hazlerigg at random.

"Rather young. But still, no harm in that. Six to seven is a very formative age. And, really, Mrs. Meadows is a second mother to all our younger boys."

Mrs. Meadows smiled grimly and produced by sleight of hand a typewritten list starting "Thirty-six handkerchiefs (all clearly marked with boy's name and number)." It was a comprehensive document, embracing spiritual as well as bodily clothing ("Bibles, two, authorized and revised versions"). Hazlerigg examined it with interest.

"Splendid," he said. "I must show this to my—er, to

my dear wife. Two suits for weekdays, I see, and a dark suit for Sundays. That's three, isn't it? I wish I had as many myself. Please don't let me interrupt you, Mrs. Meadows—I can see how busy you are."

So compelling was her personality that he felt that in a very few minutes he would have joined Halliday and be bustling round with piles of underclothing.

"Come this way, Inspector," said Dr. Smallhorn. "Mind the step. I will now show you our sanitary arrangements. . . ."

Half an hour later, as he shook hands with the headmaster and emerged into the forecourt he encountered Halliday, making a furtive exit. He grinned sympathetically.

"Mind you," said Halliday, in answer to the unspoken criticism, "she's quite all right, really. A bit bossy, that's the worst that can be said. But she works so hard herself that it just hurts her to see somebody doing nothing. I was a bit surprised to hear you were married. I'm sorry— that sounds rude—what I meant is that I somehow thought of you as a bachelor."

"You weren't nearly so surprised as I was," said Hazlerigg.

"I expect," said Halliday, apropos of nothing, "that you'll be coming to the Dean's tea-party this afternoon. It's sure to be crowded, but if you don't mind a crowd you ought to enjoy yourself. Everyone'll be there, of course."

"I haven't been invited," began Hazlerigg doubtfully.

"Good gracious me, you don't have to be invited. It's a regular Thursday afternoon 'do.' The Chapter takes it in turns, and everyone in the Close rolls up and eats sandwiches and lacerates each other's characters, and all in the most Christian way imaginable. You'll regret it all your life if you miss it."

Sometimes, afterwards, when it was all over and done with, Hazlerigg remembered this remark. He was inclined to agree with it.

"Glad you were able to come, Hazlerigg," said the Dean. "What have you done with my young nephew?"

"I had to send him up to town," said Hazlerigg, amiably certain that everyone in the room was listening to him. "Business, you know. An unexpected call. He should be back some time this evening."

"Splendid," said the Dean vaguely. He still found it a little difficult to decide whether he should think of Pollock as a jolly undergraduate nephew or the hand of the law. "Do you know Dr. Hinkey, our Precentor?"

"I've heard of him," said Hazlerigg truthfully.

"So difficult, you know," purred the Precentor, "to make up one's mind how to treat this very distressing and shocking business."

(But he doesn't look in the least distressed or shocked, thought Hazlerigg.)

"I think the happiest thing," went on the Precentor, "is to forget about it altogether. I have always found that if you really make up your mind to disregard a thing it ceases to exist. Have you ever noticed what an extraordinary faculty cats have in that direction?"

"Talking of cats," said Halliday, surging up with a tea-cup expertly balanced on one huge palm, "I just heard rather a good story about Prynne."

"Really," said Hinkey. "I don't think we ought to listen to unkind stories about our neighbours." He made, however, no perceptible attempt to depart.

"You remember that Zenana pageant of Scripture that the Beech-Thompsons got up last summer? Of course, as you know, Mrs. B.-T. was running it and pinched all the best parts—Ruth and Bathsheba and so on—most unsuitable. Well, apparently Prynne met her one morning in the Close, and after chatting of this and that he said that he thought it would add just the crowning touch to the pageant if she came on as the Inspiration of the Song of Songs. Mrs. B.-T., overcome with pleasure and gratification, asks just what is it in the Song of Songs that puts dear Canon Prynne in mind of her. Prynne says he can't remember the exact reference, but he thinks it's somewhere about chapter seven, verse four. Mrs. B.-T. hurries home and looks it up and goes off the deep end. She wouldn't speak to Prynne for a month."

There was a desperate silence whilst keen theological brains attempted to locate the snag, and then Hinkey broke into a low musical laugh.

"Splendid," he said, "the older version, of course. 'Thine eyes like the fishpools in Heshbon—thy nose as the tower of Lebanon which looketh toward Damascus.' No wonder B.-T. doesn't like Prynne. Do you remember that time on the choir outing when they could only find two bathing-machines——"

Unfortunately, what promised to be a further entertaining narrative of clerical life was interrupted by the arrival of Canon and Mrs. Beech-Thompson—the latter wearing a hat which the irreverent Miss Bloss immediately dubbed "The Wedding of Hope and Charity." She and Miss Prynne were entrenched in a secluded corner demolishing a plate of savoury sandwiches and the characters of their elders and betters.

"Where's your father?" asked Miss Bloss suddenly.

"No idea. And Malthus seems to have skipped too." Other people had noticed the absence of Malthus and Prynne, but it was left as usual to Mrs. Judd to voice what everyone was thinking. She had arrived a few minutes previously, supporting her tottering steps on ivory walking-sticks.

The Dean, seeing the light of battle in her eyes, had endeavoured to steer her into a safe and secluded armchair in the corner, but she had disdained the suggestion, spurned all comestibles, accepted a cup of China tea, given it immediately to Miss Halliday to hold, and fastened herself to Inspector Hazlerigg.

"Such a funny thing," she shouted in his ear. "I've had a man looking at my lamp all day."

"Indeed," said Hazlerigg uneasily. "I wonder if he found what he was looking for."

"Do you know what I think?" screamed Mrs. Judd, abandoning one stick and clutching at Hazlerigg's lapel lest he should escape her at the eleventh hour. "I think he was spying on me."

"Why should he do that?" asked Hazlerigg feebly.

"I don't like to think," said Mrs. Judd, "but it was a very alarming experience. But I didn't lose my head. I'm not easily frightened, you know, Inspector. I'm sure I did the right thing. As soon as I saw he was spying on me I sent for the police. They soon chased him away."

"That was a sensible thing to do, ma'am," agreed Hazlerigg. "When in doubt send for a policeman."

Mrs. Judd didn't answer him. Her bright, birdlike eyes were darting round the assembled company. A frown puckered her forehead.

"Where's Mr. Prynne?" she exclaimed. "And dear Mr.

Malthus—he's not here either. Have you arrested them, Inspector?"

At this very pertinent question all individual trickles of conversation ceased as though they had been turned off at the main.

"Not yet," said Hazlerigg lightly.

"Come, Mrs. Judd," said the Dean hastily, "you mustn't talk of arresting. You're making us all quite nervous. Besides, the inspector is off duty for the moment. Here's one of your favourite chocolate cakes. Let me cut you a nice large slice." He cut an enormous wedge, and with Mrs. Judd effectually gagged conversation again became general.

Dr. Smallhorn cornered Dr. Mickie and lost no time in expounding his latest grievance to him. "Boys, in my experience," he was explaining, "are very sensitive—I'm sure you'll agree with me there, Dr. Mickie. These disturbances of the last fortnight have had a very deleterious effect on discipline."

"Oh, I don't know," said Dr. Mickie, who on principle always disagreed with his scholastic colleague. "I've found them very well behaved lately. What do you say, Halliday?"

"What do I say to what?" asked Halliday.

"I was saying," said Dr. Smallhorn, "that I've been finding the boys unusually troublesome lately. Only the other day I detected one of them passing a scurrilous note to his neighbour in class."

"Well, look what a bad example their elders and betters have been setting them," said Halliday. "You ought to be thankful they haven't started murdering each other."

"Really," said Dr. Smallhorn stiffly, "I think that's hardly a proper subject for a joke. . . ."

"I racked my brains for the best part of an hour," Canon Trumpington was explaining to Canon and Mrs. Fox, "but still it eluded me. A quadruped of South America discovered in half a swamp with its tail turned up."

"Oh, dear," said Mrs. Fox, "I'm afraid I'm dreadfully stupid about crossword puzzles. Herbert is very clever at them. He once won a pack of playing cards from the *Daily Telegraph*, didn't you, dear?"

"What was the clue, did you say, Trumpington?—A South American quadruped discovered in half a swamp with its tail turned up. Let me see now. No—I give it up."

"Quagga," said Canon Trumpington, with mild triumph. "Half of quagmire (that's a word for swamp, Mrs. Fox) 'quag'—with the addition of the last two letters reversed—the tail turned up, you see?"

"Well, just fancy that," said Mrs. Fox. "Let me press you to another slice of this cake. . . ."

"I was pleasantly surprised to discover this afternoon," said Dr. Smallhorn to the Dean, "that Inspector Hazlerigg is thinking of sending his little boy to our school in the near future. He is young, of course—only six and a half. But better too soon than too late. And young Essington Fox was scarcely seven when he came, and look how splendidly he's getting on. I was telling his father, the day before yesterday, he conjugated 'rego,' active and passive, without a single mistake."

"That's more than I could do," said the Dean with conviction. . . .

"I hear Canon Pritchard has passed away," said Canon Beech-Thompson to Canon Trumpington. "It was indeed sad news. Such a healthy person. In the midst of life we are in death."

"He will be a loss to the diocese," said Trumpington. "How did it happen?"

"It was very sudden, I understand. A stroke of some sort during service . . . ah, Bloss, we were discussing the sad news about Canon Pritchard."

"We mustn't grieve," said Canon Bloss firmly. "It was a very beautiful way to die.

"Far from making us sad," he added sternly, "such an example should inspire all of us. He was a martyr. A martyr to his sense of duty."

He bestowed a severe glance on the company and glided majestically away.

"What a splendid expert witness he would make," murmured Hazlerigg to the Dean.

"Bloss is really a very likeable person," said the Dean, "if you are prepared to discount his alarming manner. Once or twice I've even suspected him of possessing a sense of humour. He lost his only son in the war. I don't think anyone knew how much that boy meant to him. From that moment he froze. I wasn't here at the time, but I knew Bloss as a young man at Oxford and I can assure you that the change must have been astounding. Oh, good-bye, Mrs. Judd, I'm so glad you were able to get here. I hope you've enjoyed yourself."

"Do you think," he added, when Mrs. Judd had gone, "that there was anything in that story of hers about a man watching her?"

"I'm afraid it was one of my policemen," explained Hazlerigg ruefully. "He might have had more sense than to spend the whole time loafing round Mrs. Judd's front gate. Of course, he wasn't watching her. Just keeping an eye on things generally."

"But you're not expecting any more trouble, Inspector?" Hazlerigg reassured him on this point, and since most of the guests had gone, took his leave.

Halliday lingered to the last. He had had an idea, born of something he had heard during the course of the afternoon. Of course, it didn't do to appear too inquisitive, but like the rest of the Close—perhaps even more so than most—he was bitten with the desire to find things out for himself. So he waited until the last guest had taken his leave and then approached the Dean—albeit a trifle shamefacedly.

"I say," he said. "Please don't think I'm being the complete busybody—I really have got a good reason for asking. Have you still got that anonymous letter—the last one, I mean: the one that came on the Monday evening?"

"How in the world," said the Dean, genuinely surprised, "did you hear about that? I have told no one except the police."

"I'm afraid everyone knows, though," said Halliday. "Hubbard saw it, and he told Hinkey's gardener, and Hinkey's gardener told Morgan, and Mrs. Parvin heard Morgan telling Parvin——"

"Say no more. We could hardly have gained wider publicity by publishing it in *The Times*."

"It is rather awful," agreed Halliday, "how these things get about. But, harking back, I wondered if you had kept the original."

The Dean looked a little confused. He appeared to be debating something with himself.

"As a matter of fact," he said at last, "though I had to hand the original to the police—I believe they wanted to test it for fingerprints and so on—I was so struck by its curious appearance that I made a copy of it—it's a tracing." Seeing that Halliday looked a trifle surprised at this admission the Dean added, "In my younger days I was rather a student of handwriting—I was under Dr. Cross the great calligraphist at Oxford, and I read a good many books on the subject. I used to practise on my friends—reading character from handwriting—just a parlour trick, really. But when I saw that note there was something in it that struck me as peculiar—you see what I mean? It was even more marked in the original. It is definitely an educated hand—and yet definitely unformed. It might very well have been written by a person possessing a good neat fist which he was anxious to disguise."

"Or else"—there was a note of suppressed excitement in Halliday's voice—"it might have been written by a——"

He broke off suddenly.

"Is there someone at the door?"

The Dean, mastering an uncomfortable sensation in the pit of his stomach, walked firmly across the room and threw the door open. The passage outside was quite empty.

"Sorry," said Halliday. "It must have been my imagination."

"It wasn't imagination," said the Dean. "I thought I heard something myself. I expect it was Benjamin Disraeli scratching to be let in. What about a game of chess. We're too late for Evensong, anyway."

With which sedate amusement they passed the next hour and a half.

When Halliday let himself out of the Dean's front door it was already quite dark. A soft but persistent wind was rustling the leaves of the old plane-trees as he threw a leg across the low wall and started on the short cut back to his house over the precinct lawns. Despite the darkness he had taken that particular route so many times that his instinct had recorded every step of it and reproduced it without conscious effort on his part. Here he swerved automatically to the left to skirt the memorial cedar of Lebanon (planted in honour of the late king's jubilee and stunted at birth by Canon Beech-Thompson inadvertently sitting on it in the dark). Twenty more paces now and his footsteps would ring out on the asphalt path from the north-west corner. Here it comes. Four steps to cross it. One—two—three—four.

At that moment a most unpleasant thing happened. A second after his fourth footstep had rapped out on the path, in the silence which followed he heard a fifth step. It certainly wasn't his. Someone had crossed the path behind him.

He didn't hesitate for a moment: he started to run. He couldn't tell whether the pounding noise he heard was the sound of pursuit or simply the beating of the blood in his ears. A second later he had crossed the path at the corner of the west wall. And here for a moment he slowed down to listen. If anyone was after him he would hear them crossing the asphalt. The silence was complete. Halliday slowed to a walk. His imagination must be playing tricks, he thought angrily. And yet—he *had* heard something. It was with a feeling of relief that he reached and opened the gate.

His extra sense must have been working overtime that evening, for as his hand touched the gate it caused him, for no good reason at all, to step quickly to the right. The result was that the savage blow which was aimed at his head only grazed his left shoulder. Even in the pain and shock of the moment what chiefly astonished him was the ferocity of the attack. For a moment his assailant loomed in front of him, a dimly seen shape of menace. He threw up his left arm—in the same instant he shouted. The shout saved his life.

As the second blow landed on his forearm a light flared up. Canon Trumpington had heard the shout and, slinging open his front door, came charging gallantly down the front path. He found Halliday leaning painfully over the wall nursing a throbbing arm. In a few seconds he had his story and was helping him towards his house. As they went he kept a careful watch over his free shoulder and grasped his stout walking-stick with tremendous determination. The assailant, however, had disappeared as silently as he had come.

A phone call to the Bear brought Hazlerigg onto the scene, but he quickly came to the sensible decision that no good purpose would be effected by trampling over the ground in the dark. He therefore returned to the police station and arranged for two constables to be on duty in the Close until the morning. He was taking no chances.

XII • Breaking an Alibi and Catching a Tartar

F<small>RIDAY</small> MORNING and Melchester awoke to another fine day—the third in succession. But now the sunlight had a hard quality and edge to it.

Hazlerigg got up before seven and made his way to the Close. He found a bored constable, who reported that everything was exceedingly (not to say excessively) quiet. Dismissing him, he set about a methodical search which, after half an hour, had revealed absolutely nothing.

Halliday's assailant—pursuing his old technique, thought Hazlerigg—had apparently not trodden on the grass at all. The turf was soft enough, even after two fine days, to show distinct traces where Halliday had stepped off the verge and then staggered back on to it again. There was a little dried blood on the top bar of the gate. That was all.

He simply stood on the road and sloshed at him with a stick as he came through the gate, thought Hazlerigg. Safe, simple, and confoundedly unhelpful.

He cast about for a further quarter of an hour but without much hope of result. In fact, he was really killing time until he could decently knock up Halliday and get his story. Knowing the after-effects of shock he expected to find him confined to his bed. He was therefore surprised and a little disgruntled when Halliday rode up on his bicycle with his cassock over his arm.

"I'm a bit stiff," he confessed, "but I had an early service in the town. It's wonderful how it takes your mind off your own troubles if you have something that's got to be done."

"If everyone acted on those lines," said Hazlerigg, "life would be so much easier. Now tell me——"

Halliday told him.

"I see," said Hazlerigg. "You didn't by any chance recognize him?"

"He was tall—I think. And fairly massive, or does everyone look larger at night?"

"They do, rather. Male sex?"

"Definitely—and bareheaded. Wearing some sort of coat turned up at the neck."

Hazlerigg said, "Tell me, Mr. Halliday, why do you think you were attacked?"

Halliday grinned.

"This is going to be awkward. If you really want to know, I think that it all happened because of something I said. Something rather silly. And if that's true—mind you, *if* that's true, I've got a very fair idea of who it was that attacked me last night. But that's not to say that the person who attacked me was the one that killed poor old Appledown."

"But look here——"

"I know what you're going to say, sir. But it's no good."

"If you know anything, it's your duty——"

"No, it isn't," said Halliday firmly but respectfully.

170

"Because I don't *know* anything. What I suspect is my own business."

"You may be running a considerable risk."

"I don't think so. But if I must, I must."

"All right," said Hazlerigg. "Don't say I didn't warn you." He went home to breakfast and found Pollock conscientiously bolting his toast.

Hazlerigg had been thinking over the curious attitude adopted by the victim of the last night's attack. He perceived, on second thoughts, that it might prove useful.

"If," he explained, "he really is on to somebody, and somebody thinks that Halliday suspects him, and thinks further that Halliday has explained his suspicions to us then obviously there's no further object in trying to lay Halliday out. If, on the other hand, somebody thinks that Halliday is keeping his suspicions to himself he may have another whack at him, in which case we've only to keep an eye on Halliday and use him as bait. No. Funnily enough the thought of enacting the role of the cheese in the mousetrap doesn't seem to worry him."

Hazlerigg paused,. poured himself out another cup of coffee, and addressing the ceiling rather than his subordinate, added:

"Let's have a frank opinion, Sergeant. How do you think we're doing?"

"We've done a lot of work," said Pollock slowly, "and we've eliminated a lot of possibilities."

"Don't damn us all with faint praise."

"We've opened up a good many trails——"

"I know. Explored every avenue. Like the politicians."

"But after a promising beginning they've all turned into blind alleys."

"Very neatly put," sighed Hazlerigg. "Very neat, in-

deed. Mickie and Prynne and Malthus. So many pictur-
esque cul-de-sacs—or culs-de-sac. And the sum total of
it all is this. Every single suspect for our original time of
the murder has practically eliminated himself. There's
only one answer to that. We must have been wrong about
the time. Simple, isn't it?"

"But we can't have been wrong—we had the whole
thing beautifully watertight. Appledown was dead before
the rain started at ten minutes past eight——"

"Agreed."

"And alive at a minute or so after eight."

"Who says so?"

"The whole choir saw him coming out of his front
door."

"You might as well hear," said Hazlerigg, "what is now
my opinion of that episode. They saw a figure which they
took to be the head verger for two good and sufficient
reasons. Because he had come out of Appledown's front
door and because he was wearing Appledown's type of
coat and rather noticeable hat. That's all. The figure they
saw had its back turned to them and was engaged in pinning a note on to the doorpost. A very natural action for
the owner of a house, you see, and leading to the assumption that the figure so acting *was in fact* the owner
of the house. Also it was an excuse for keeping the back
turned. Clever."

"But surely, it was incredibly risky; one of the
boys——"

"None of the boys saw his face, if that's what you're
going to say. I know, because I asked them yesterday."

Pollock was rapidly assimilating this new notion.

"If it wasn't Appledown, who was it?"

"I'm afraid there's no doubt about that," said Hazlerigg

grimly. "Just ask yourself a few questions. Who had the most obvious motive for killing Appledown—jealousy of a scandal with his wife on the one hand and personal advancement on the other? Who went to see Appledown at twenty-five minutes to eight that evening, and would have conveniently forgotten to mention it if Mrs. Judd (heaven bless her ancient soul) hadn't happened to spot him from her window?"

"If," said Pollock, "it was really Parvin, as you suggest, how did he get to the Victoria and Albert on the stroke of eight?"

"He didn't," said Hazlerigg. "There are two possibilities. Either he's hand in glove with the disreputable Mr. Begg—and remember that Begg has no reason to love the police. Or else—and I rather incline to this view myself—Parvin is relying for his alibi on the fact that on this particular night Mr. Begg's clock was ten minutes *slow*. Not fast, as an honest publican's clock should be, but slow. And relying further on the fact that Mr. Begg, with his known record, would die rather than admit that his clock was slow."

"Then do you mean to say that Parvin killed Appledown, appeared at the front door at eight o'clock to establish an alibi at a time when he knew the choir would be passing, returned to the house, picked up Appledown, carried him to the chapter house, dressed him in hat and coat, dropped him into position, and sprinted up to the Victoria and Albert, arriving there at ten past eight? With due respect, it's not possible."

"Of course it isn't possible," said Hazlerigg. "For the very good reason that it never happened. Parvin went to Appledown's house at twenty-five to eight. On one of a dozen pretexts, which would suggest themselves between one verger and another, he took Appledown out to examine the fastening of the engine-shed door. Both were wearing the very common ecclesiastical blue Burberry (you must have noticed that every other person in the Close possesses one). Appledown was wearing a hat. Parvin was bareheaded. Had anyone seen them crossing the road Parvin would not have killed Appledown. But no one saw them. Parvin had left his walking-stick behind one of the cloister buttresses. With it he kills Appledown. Then he takes his keys, puts on his hat, and watching till the coast is clear slips back across the road into Appledown's house. No great risk really. He sits down and passes the few minutes that are left before the choir are due in scribbling an imitation of Appledown's vile calligraphy. Then he puts on that distinctive hat, and when the choir come past he is busy sticking the note on to the door-post. I like that alibi. To my mind it's the only real touch of genius in the whole thing. Simple, efficient, and foolproof. The moment the choir are out of sight he becomes Parvin again by the very simple expedient of taking off the hat. I should say, as a guess, that he put it back into Appledown's hall—to be rescued much later that night and restored to the corpse."

"By Jove," said Pollock. "Excuse my interrupting, sir. But that explains why the hat was so much less wet than the rest of the clothes. It was something I couldn't understand at the time. If it had really been lying all night under a shower bath from the choked drain-pipe—it would have been pulpy with moisture—whereas, in fact, it was barely damp."

"Good," said Hazlerigg. "I think you're right."

"There's just one snag," said Pollock, who seemed to have abandoned the role of carping critic and become even more enthusiastic about the theory than its begetter. "Even allowing what you say, wasn't that note he pinned up rather a startling piece of forgery?"

"I'm expecting a report of the handwriting from our experts; let's defer judgment on that point until it arrives. A friendly visit to the Victoria and Albert seems to be the next move."

"In our official capacity?"

"I think not. Mr. Begg doesn't sound the sort of man who would respond to official questioning. No, we'll wander in separately and see if anything crops up. Try not to look too like a policeman. You can play darts and engage the local talent in gossip whilst I will stand Mr. Begg a friendly drink and induce him to open to me the secrets of his flinty bosom. And talking about opening, when *do* they open in this confounded hole?"

"Ten o'clock," said Pollock enthusiastically. "So I'm told."

Mr. Begg's flinty bosom was proving an exceptionally resistant and tenacious tract.

The proprietor of the Victoria and Albert was a huge man, who appeared at first sight to be as broad as he was long and was certainly as thick as he was broad. The expression on his face indicated that he had looked on life and found it hollow. Two hands of the size (and colour) of bronze warming-pans rested negligently on the bar in front of him. Unlike young John Brophy he had proved neither an easy nor a fluent conversationalist.

"Fine morning," said Hazlerigg. "Half a pint of bitter, please. Barney's Badger Beer, I see. A fine nutty ale. An excellent choice."

"Eh?"

"I said I admire your choice of beer."

"Fat lot o' choice," said Mr. Begg, exposing the remnant of his front teeth in a wintry smile. "They owns the place."

"Ah, I see. A tied house. Well, that's the only way to get security these days. Perhaps you'll have a drink yourself. It all goes to increase the profits of the company."

Mr. Begg, interpreting a drink as meaning an imperial pint, filled an enormous glass and emptied it as his customer's expense, without mellowing perceptibly. Having exhausted the possibilities of the weather, Hazlerigg enlarged lightly on the coming football season.

"Never watch the game," said Mr. Begg, "silly waste of time." The conversation languished. Hazlerigg paid for another round of drinks and introduced a political note. Mr. Begg expanded a little and condescended to explain, with imaginative detail, what he would do to a number of prominent public men if he had a chance. None of them, Hazlerigg felt, would have derived any pleasure from the treatment. Encouraged by this flow of soul, Hazlerigg bought a third pint for his host and touched on another favourite subject of the working classes, the iniquity of the police.

There could be no doubt at all about the success of this move. Mr. Begg's eye gleamed with a positive animation and he put down his beer half finished (a thing which he hadn't done for several years) in order to explain fully to Hazlerigg his opinion of the Chief Constable of Melchester. Colonel Brabington, it will be remembered, had spoken in an unstinted way about Mr. Begg; sufficient to say that his was a pæan of praise beside Mr. Begg's opinion of Colonel Brabington.

This was all to the good. But even on what was evidently his favourite subject the landlord displayed a curious reluctance to descend from the general to the particular. The police, Hazlerigg gathered, were scum. Further, they conspired to rob a man of his bread. But as to how they performed this robbery no details were forthcoming.

"Make difficulties about closing-time?" suggested Hazlerigg. That, implied Mr. Begg, was putting it mildly.

"Perjuring themselves, I suppose, and swearing your clock was ten minutes slow or five minutes fast, or something of that sort, eh?"

But at the very mention of his clock a change seemed to come over the landlord. Three pints of Barney's Badger Beer were forgotten. The customary look of cold suspicion returned to Mr. Begg's eye.

"What's wrong with my clock?" he said. "It goes all right, doesn't it—what's wrong with it, then?"

Hazlerigg hastened to assure him that his clock was perfectly right, as indeed at that moment it was.

"It's the best clock in Melchester," said Mr. Begg. "And set by time-signal on the wireless every blessed morning, see?"

Hazlerigg saw. He had either to declare his identity and proceed to an official interlocutory, or withdraw. It was no consideration of Mr. Begg's size or ferocity which dictated the latter course. Hazlerigg had subdued larger and more dangerous men, but out of the corner of his eye he could see that Pollock appeared to be in animated conversation with three *habitués* of the four-ale bar. This decided him. Finishing his ale, he bellowed across (it being one of his sovereign rules of life that the louder you say a thing the less attention people pay to it). "See you soon, chum. I'll be at the Cock and Pye. Can't stay there after twelve." Having, like a careful general, established his next base, he withdrew.

Pollock, meanwhile, was playing darts. Not having any desire to win he was soaring to heights of brilliance which shocked even himself. He could do no wrong. Doubles came smoothly to his call. Trebles were legion. He defeated a market-gardener, the local champion, in four and a half minutes in two straight games and accepted half a pint of bitter.

The market-gardener was shaken but not over-whelmed. He summoned his friends Sydney and Harry, and presently Pollock found himself partnered with Harry in a foursome. Any good outsider who played darts in the Victoria and Albert usually found himself paired with Harry before long. The man who could win with Harry on his side was a player indeed. Pollock resigned himself to defeat and won again. He accepted a further half-pint and, in honour bound, took the field again once more.

This time Harry threw so badly—the majority of his darts failed to enter the board at all and were ducked by the scorer—that their opponents succeeded in scraping home. Pollock resigned the board to a second quartette, ordered pints for both his opponents, and retired with them into the chimney corner. He carried with him the full honours of war. All three men plainly regarded Pollock as the *News of the World* darts champion in disguise, and conversation was general and easy. Pollock felt that it was time to broach the real business of the meeting. Both of his opponents had been in the public bar on the Tuesday evening, and when Pollock described Parvin they recognized him at once. Pollock intimated that Parvin was a friend of his. Sydney volunteered the information that Parvin had come in "at about eight o'clock." Pollock pressed him for the exact time, explaining that Parvin had promised to meet him at the cinema at five to eight, but had failed to do so. "He says he waited there till eight o'clock, but if he was here by eight he couldn't have done, could he?" Sydney agreed that he couldn't have been in two places at once. The market-gardener gave it as his opinion that most Welshmen were liars.

"Perhaps the clock was wrong," suggested Pollock delicately. He felt that he could not push the subject much further without appearing unnaturally inquisitive. Sydney grinned. "Better not let old Begg hear you say that. He's touchy about his clock. Sets it by wireless." The market-gardener supported this, and Pollock accepted defeat. He rose regretfully to depart, when Harry, who had hitherto taken more interest in his beer than in the conversation, stopped him. "I can tell you one funny thing," he said. "I was here last Tuesday evening. I didn't stop long because I was going on to the pictures myself. Very anxious to see the news-reel. They told me it came on at twenty to seven. Well, I left here at twenty-five minutes to seven by that clock. Three minutes' walk to the cinema, wouldn't you say? (Three and a half, amended Sydney.) Anyway, when I got there the ruddy thing was finished. It was ten minutes to. Either I'm a perishing loon-attick or that there perishing clock was ten minutes slow, for all his wireless time-signals."

"And that's that," said Pollock to Hazlerigg five minutes later at the Cock and Pye. "It was an unexpected break." Hazlerigg went for a telephone and spoke with the Melchester cinema. He was not away many minutes. When he came back he said in a particularly expressionless voice, "There was no irregularity in the running of the films last Tuesday. Each one started exactly on schedule. Find out the full name and address of that chap at the pub. We shall want him as a witness. I am going down to the station to swear a temporary warrant. You'd better meet me outside the Close in a quarter of an hour. We're going to hold Parvin."

The half-hour after twelve beat out into the stifling air as Hazlerigg and Pollock re-entered the Close. The sunlight felt strong and pitiless. Both men were preoccupied with their thoughts.

"Try his house first," grunted Hazlerigg. They passed up the garden path, and Pollock knocked on the door. There was no response, but they could hear inside the tiny sounds which indicate human occupation. Quick, quiet footsteps, and then the shutting of a door.

"There's someone in there," said Hazlerigg. "Knock again."

Pollock beat a loud and impatient tattoo. When he stopped the close seemed unnaturally silent in the bright sunlight, as though it was listening. But now the noises inside the house had stopped.

Hazlerigg was puzzled and uneasy. He stood for a moment swaying his great bulk backwards and forwards on his heels and contemplating the quiet little garden. Then he made up his mind. He turned and raised his stick. A man who had seemingly been devoting all his energy and attention to clipping the edge of the cathedral verge straightened his back and came up at a lumbering trot.

"Go round the house, Gimblett, and watch the back door and the windows. Shout if anyone tries to get out."

"Right, sir." The man disappeared purposefully. Pollock knocked again, and once more they paused to listen. The silence was unbroken.

"I don't like this a bit," said Hazlerigg. "We've simply

got to get in." Stepping back a pace he swung his foot up, with the sole of the heavy shoe parallel to the face of the door, and kicked. Once, twice, the third kick delivered in the same place, a fraction below the handle, carried away the flimsy lock, and the door caved in. Both men tumbled into the house. Pollock ran to open the back door. Gimblett had seen nobody. Rapidly they searched. Every room was empty.

"Hiding upstairs," said Pollock. They went up with a rush. There were only four rooms, with no cover to speak of. They were all empty. Mercifully Pollock had an exceptionally keen nose. As they stood perplexed, in the upper passage, he caught the well-known smell, sweet and sour at once. "Gas turned on somewhere." For some reason he found himself whispering, "Back here, I think." They raced back to the front bedroom.

"Look for the pipe," said Hazlerigg. "Quick."

It was Gimblett, that amateur plumber, who discovered the gas lead, which ran for a distance along the foot of the wainscoting and seemed to disappear into the wall.

"Cupboard here somewhere," said Hazlerigg, groping with his fingers. It was really a very simple little deception, common to very old and very new dwellings, a cupboard set flush in the panelling of the wall. There was no time for subtlety. Hazlerigg picked up a chair, and using it clubwise broke in the upper panel. Six strong hands seized the ragged edge. A heave, and the door came bodily away. They choked on the thick concentrated wave of gas which hit them.

It was a little clothes cupboard they saw, hung with a few shabby coats and dresses. And huddled up on the floor was Mrs. Parvin. Though unconscious, she still held in her tightly clenched fist the end of the bedroom gas-jet.

"She meant it all right, didn't she?" said Hazlerigg grimly, as they made Mrs. Parvin comfortable on the bed. "Five minutes more and she'd have been away. She'll be all right now, though."

Gimblett was dispatched for the doctor, and as the door closed behind him Mrs. Parvin gasped, coughed violently, and tried to sit up. Then she saw the two policemen, and incongruously burst into tears.

The minutes ticked slowly past, and Mrs. Parvin's sobs grew less convulsive: but no word was spoken on either side until footsteps on the stairs announced the arrival of the constable and the doctor.

Then Hazlerigg leant forward and said in his curiously deep and gentle voice:

"Mrs. Parvin, listen to what I'm saying. That was a very stupid and wicked thing you tried to do just now. Will you believe me when I tell you—he wasn't worth it?"

"Are you going to arrest me?"

"No," said Hazlerigg. "They'll have to take you away to the hospital and look after you for a day or two, but that's all—I promise you. And by the time you're quite well again things will have straightened themselves out." Without shifting his gaze, and in the same tone of voice, he added, "Where's your husband?"

"He's in the cathedral," said Mrs. Parvin listlessly. "You'll not be able to touch him there."

Sanctuary, thought Pollock.

Their mistake, as they realized afterwards, lay in taking the policeman with them. Parvin, apparently unsuspicious of trouble, was actually emerging from the west door as they crossed the lawn in front of it. Hazlerigg and Pollock alone, he might have overlooked. But Hazlerigg and Pollock advancing towards him with a uniformed constable in support provided too obvious a warning to be ignored. He turned and disappeared inside the cathedral.

"More exercise," said Hazlerigg resignedly.

The cavalcade broke into a trot. Pollock's mind was still running on the medieval institution of Sanctuary. For all he knew it still existed, like Livery and Maintenance and the Lord's Day Observance Act and other flotsam cast up by the old tide of law.

They plunged into the cathedral, where everything was cool and dark. Ahead of them a door slammed. "There he goes." They clattered down the aisle and were brought up short in front of an iron-studded door. No flimsy structure this, to be kicked to pieces. Nine inches of oak and bolted on the inside. The policeman plunged futilely against it and succeeded in bruising his shoulder.

"We shall need a locksmith to open that," said Hazlerigg. "I'm afraid we're done."

"If you're in a hurry," said Canon Bloss, appearing apparently from nowhere, "there is an alternative route to the clerestory." He spoke as calmly as though he were showing a party of visitors round the cathedral. "Through the vestry. Follow me." He sailed forward and the pursuit surged behind him. When they reached the canon's vestry, Bloss took a ring of keys from his pocket and swung open a narrow door. "Straight up those steps and through the bell tower. The door is bolted on your side. So you really command both approaches to the clerestory. Be careful not to slip, won't you. It's a terrible place for a giddy head."

At this the constable looked appealingly at Hazlerigg, who said, "You stay and watch both doors in case he cuts back." Then he disapppeared up the narrow winding stairs, with Pollock hard on his heels.

When they reached the bell tower they could appreciate Canon Bloss's sound grasp of strategy. Parvin, by going up the west front stairs, had delivered himself into their hands. He had either to return by the way he had come—and that was now guarded—or make the circle of the clerestory, a course which would inexorably bring him back to the bell tower. They had only to bolt one door—done as soon as thought of—and sally out of the other. They opened the south door and stepped out. The clerestory ledge was wider than it had looked from below —perhaps an arm's span in all. Pollock could have wished it were twice that. He had a fair head for heights. Hazlerigg, he knew, was a mountaineer and sublimely unconscious of them. Eighty feet below, the floor of the south transept gleamed quietly up at them as the sun came pouring through the stained glass.

"We must see him soon," thought Pollock. They had circled the south transept and were passing now, behind and above the huge tops of the biggest organ-pipes, the old "sixty-fours." The next turn would bring them out above the lady chapel. Hazlerigg, who was a few yards ahead, treading silently and confidently in his rubber-soled shoes, suddenly threw up his hand. Pollock stood still and held his breath. Immediately he stood still the ledge seemed to contract, and he wished he could go on again. Hazlerigg was edging softly round the next corner. Pollock crept after him.

What he saw stopped him again in his tracks, and he stood as if turned into stone—the good rugged Melchester stone, which he instinctively clutched for support.

Parvin was poised on the narrow part of the triforium arch where it faced them, across the depth of the lady chapel. He was crouched forward, motionless, and at first sight it seemed that he was staring up into the roof. But his eyes were tight shut. "He's going to fall," thought Pollock. "In a minute he's going to throw himself off." He remembered how, as a very young policeman almost on his first day of duty, an excited man had called him into a factory. A workman (mad they said afterwards at the inquest) had climbed along one of the great girders, and was refusing to come down. Pollock had wondered wildly what he ought to do—vague thoughts of the fire brigade. The workman had saved him further embarrassment by stepping quietly off into space. And the sound as he hit the floor! Ugh! Like a very full suitcase hitting a concrete road and bursting. Parvin swayed forward a few inches. Pollock felt sick.

He was recalled to his wits by Hazlerigg speaking quietly in his ear.

"It's no good rushing him—that would only help him to make up his mind. He'd be over before we'd moved a yard. There's only one quarter of a hope in hell now. We must make him open his eyes and look down. He's hypnotized himself to fall over. If we can make him think about it we might stop him." And raising his voice to conversational pitch, he said:

"Parvin; hey, I say, Parvin." Suddenly, sharply, "Look out, you fool, you'll slip." A tremor passed through the rigid figure, and Parvin opened his eyes. But he continued to stare out in front of him.

"Now look here, Parvin," said Hazlerigg, dropping his voice again, "you can't go clambering about like this in a public building. It's dangerous. It's mad. You'll fall and hurt somebody."

Parvin looked at him out of the corner of his eye, a terrible empty stare.

"It's dangerous enough, you know, without rubber soles on your shoes—you can see that, can't you? But with nailed boots—look at your feet, man, it's madness."

Parvin made no response. His eyes were shutting again. In another moment... !

Hazlerigg played out his last desperate card. All the time that he had been talking he had been edging slowly towards Parvin, and now he had reached the southern-most angle. Without raising his voice, and as though he were saying and doing the most normal thing in the world, Hazlerigg added, "Look how easily you might slip, watch me now." He took a pace to the edge, then another.... Pollock's stomach turned over. When he opened his eyes he saw that Hazlerigg had dropped into a sitting position on the ledge. One hand rested on the pillar and he was swinging his legs.

"So easy to slip, if you aren't careful."

There was no doubt that he held Parvin's attention now. The verger's lips were moving, and he was staring horrified at the detective.

"Such a long way to fall, too. Look at it, man."

Casually Hazlerigg turned on his front and lowered his body over the ledge. The sweat poured down Pollock's face in a steady stream. Then Hazlerigg slipped clear of the ledge until he was hanging by his hands.

Suddenly Parvin started to scream. His eyes were on the stone floor, eighty feet below him. For the first time he seemed to become aware of it. He backed away from it, pressing and flattening his body against the wall behind him—and all the time he was screaming in a horrible high-pitched voice.

Pollock could no more have moved than flown.

So it was Hazlerigg who pulled himself lightly back on to the ledge, stepped up to Parvin, and moved him firmly back along by the way he had come. Though he placed himself on the outside of his prisoner he knew that he had nothing to fear. Parvin's one idea was to keep as close to the wall as possible.

Pollock tottered after them.

XIII • Crossword Puzzle

> What is the crossword solvers' fun
>   This, in a minor key
> The love of things begun and done
>   In welcome symmetry
>
> The piecemeal pitting of the wit
>   Against the wide unknown
> With here a bit and there a bit
>   From sources of one's own.
>   "SEASCAPE." From *The Week-end Calendar*

SO PARVIN WAS TAKEN to the police station and questioned: dazed at first, and saying nothing until Hazlerigg spoke of his wife. When he heard that she was safely convalescing in Melchester Infirmary (they mentioned neither the private ward nor the policewoman everlastingly knitting outside the door) he spoke for the first time since his arrest. He must see her at once.

The words were peremptory, but the tone was pleading, wheedling, almost: very different from his former confident blarney, thought Hazlerigg, finding it difficult to say no. And in the end he gave in, with the stipulation that the interview should be in front of a police officer, who would, if necessary, take notes of what was said. Parvin agreed readily to that: he seemed anxious only to see his wife again.

*   *   *

That evening brought a welcome coolness into the air. The news of Parvin's arrest had sped round the Close, and the consequent relief had produced a very "end-of-term" atmosphere amongst its childlike inhabitants. "Now may canon look canon in the face once more," chanted Prynne to Malthus. The Deutero-Aunt Sylvia was holding a session in Prynne's study. "It is a blessing," agreed Malthus. "At least," he added, a frown crinkling his good-natured face, "I don't quite mean that. A judgment, anyway. Poor Parvin—I can't help feeling——"

"Poor Parvin," snorted Prynne. "Poor Appledown, for that matter."

"Anyway," said Malthus, "it made things much easier."

He was right. At that very moment the Dean was explaining to Halliday, over a cup of tea, that he felt ten years younger. Dr. Mickie, unusually gracious, was listening without visible distress to the Precentor's theories about plainsong. Canon Bloss, alone, was unmoved.

After tea, Prynne called on Canon Trumpington and found him in his library. They were close but undemonstrative friends. Prynne liked Trumpington for the same reasons that everyone else in the Close liked him—because he was unpretentious, possessed a sense of humour, and used to turn if not a deaf ear at least a charitable ear to his neighbour's gossip. If Trumpington had been forced to defend his liking for Prynne before the tribunal of public opinion he might have offered the explanation that a classical education had made him tolerant. Certainly he was the only person who was not afraid of Prynne's tongue. They had got past the stage when they needed to make conversation for each other. Trumpington was coiled into a leather arm-chair, poring over a stout green quarto volume. Prynne stood beside the shelves, picked a book out at random, and ran a long white finger lovingly over the bindings. He knew little about them technically, but could appreciate workmanship.

He slipped the book back and let his eye rove happily about the crowded shelves. They were a democratic company, with no sort of order or precedence. The big "Fortune" Shadwell rubbed shoulders with a standard edition of Webster and a collected Chapman. The old and almost unobtainable "definitive" Congreve lived in perfect amity with the first and only volumes of Ben Johnson which the Oxford Press had so far issued to the world of panting bibliophiles: whilst between the twin spires of the Nonesuch Farquhar peeped that exotic beauty of Fanfrolico Tourneur himself. The wizards of the Nonesuch Press were strongly represented. In addition to Farquhar, Prynne's greedy eye took in Otway, Etheridge, Wycherley, and Vanburgh, all works of conscious craftsmanship.

"You don't deserve them," he said aloud. "And you'll never read a quarter of them." He glowered benevolently at Trumpington, who raised himself with difficulty from the green depths of his volume, and said: "What's that?"

"I said, you'll never read them. Before Whyte gave these books to a Philistine like you he should have exacted a solemn promise—you ought to have pledged yourself to read so many pages a night until you'd finished them."

"I did," said Trumpington simply, and dived back into his book.

"Hey—wake up," said Prynne, stirring him with his toe. "What did you say?"

"I said I'd read them all—in time. Especially the Boswell. We were both rather keen on Boswell, and Whyte had this splendid edition—twelve volumes. I've just started on the *Tour in the Hebrides*." He held the book up for Prynne's inspection. "I'd never read it through before. Whyte knew it by heart, almost." With a casual forefinger—never has the forefinger of Destiny itself been more casual—he flicked over the thick pages.

"That's funny," he said. "Well, that really is funny. And I know that this was Whyte's favourite edition."

"What's funny?" said Prynne.

"Why," said Trumpington, "here's a double page in the middle that hasn't been cut."

"The old hypocrite. The evil that men do lives after them."

"Nonsense. Whyte had read every word——"

"Well, it must be something extra indelicate," said Prynne, "which he thought was better uncut. Do let's cut it and see."

But Trumpington was staring at the book, with a very puzzled and rather frightened look on his face.

"This page isn't uncut," he said quietly, "or not like any page I've ever seen. It's been stuck up—top and bottom as well. And"—he held the book up to the light for Prynne to see—"there's something inside."

The two men looked, first at the book and then at each other, just as Keawe and Lopaka looked at the bottled imp.

"Open it," said Prynne; he sounded irritable.

There was a silence, broken only by the dry crackling of parchment as Trumpington slit the leaves. A small square of paper fell out. When they had unfolded it they saw that it was a crossword puzzle.

"Ah," said Trumpington, with a little laugh—it would be hard to say whether relief or disappointment predominated—"I thought, for a moment——"

"You thought it was a last message from Whyte," said Prynne coolly. "Well, why shouldn't it be?"

Canon Trumpington gaped.

"You were both very keen on this sort of nonsense, weren't you?" went on Prynne, with all the contempt of the non-addict for the addict. "Well, if he wanted to tell you something—something important—it was quite a reasonable proceeding to put it in a book that only you could possibly read, and write it in a language which only you could possibly understand."

"I'm sure," said Trumpington, "that it wouldn't have been anything that—after all, he knew you very well . . . I mean—well, since we found it together let's solve it together."

"I was hoping you'd suggest it," said Prynne with a smile. "I shan't be much use, I'm afraid. How do we start?"

"Typical *Times*' style," said Trumpington briskly. "Obviously derivative. Look here—and here—hoary old favourites. Hidden anagram there—and another. And look at 15 across—I've seen *that* clue before."

"It's Greek to me," said Prynne. "Suppose you start by shouting out the ones you do know. I'll write them down."

"8 across is Opiate—I think it must be. 15 across is Rodeo. 25 across should be something to do with ASS and AM."

"Assam?"

"No, that won't do. Wait a moment—Ned. Short for Neddy, put AM inside. NAMED. What do you think of that?"

"I think it's quite mad," said Prynne, "but don't let me damp your ardour."

"16 down I've seen before—DISENTRY—or Dysentry, the second letter's dead, so it doesn't matter which. Sentry, you see, 'on the look-out.' And 22 down is a concealed anagram of 'O sire.' "

"Quite," said Prynne patiently. "By anagram I take it you mean that the letters have to be rearranged in order to formulate a new word. Let me see, OSIRE . . . I've got it. SERIO—as in serio-comic. Or ROSIE: girl's name."

"Neither," said Trumpington, with the dispassionate certainty of the man who knows. "OSIER."

"I don't see that Osier is in any way superior to either of my suggestions. But I'll take your word for it, and in it goes. 30 across is going to be rather an odd word, isn't it? That antepenultimate 'y' doesn't look very healthy."

"That's very odd—very odd indeed. 'Solve empirically' is given as the clue for 12 down and 14 down, as well as 30 across."

"4 across, too."

"So it is—that's very strange. They can't all be the same, I suppose. No! Two of them have five letters and two have eight."

"We shall have to get the others first and see what we can make of them."

"It's not playing the game," said Canon Trumpington. "Torquemada may indulge in such tricks, but *The Times* has always been a gentleman's crossword."

"Oh, well,"—such distinctions were above Prynne— "I dare say we shall work it out in the end. Here's a quo-

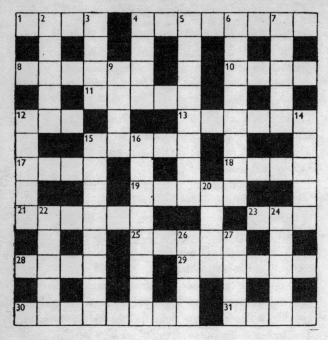

Across

1. Crooked slope.
4. Solve empirically.
8. I a poet? (anag.)
10. Archetype of the manifold varieties of existence.
11. Stare (anag.)
12. Blind beggar's seat.
13. "An envious—broke."
15. Entertainment showing what they did.
17. (with 3 down) The great white water-lily.
18. "She had a tongue with a ——."
19. Two English pronouns in a foreign one.
21. Loll cipherless thrust.
23. Confused end of 8 or 6.
25. A donkey in the dawn? Rather the other way round.
28. The subject of 13 said they bore him barefaced on one.
29. Past scraps?
30. Solve empirically.
31. A typical unit.

Crossword Puzzle

Down

2. 27 to this fruit brings a dear friend in view.
3. See 17.
4. Did they, Blake?
5. White in Spring when added to 2, also a little more than canonical.
6. But where *did* you eat?
7. Merely relative.
9. A monocotyledon of the South Seas.

12. Solve empirically.
14. Solve empirically.
15. Second (two words 6 and 4).
16. Illness—but for the most part one might be on the look-out.
20. Holly.
22. O sire! Excuse me, I got mixed.
24. Ladylike flowers.
26. A drunken confusion.
27. Fluff—and see 2 down.

tation, 13 across. I feel sure that I remember it—wait a moment . . . no, it's gone."

"Say *Hamlet*."

"Of course—Ophelia. Somewhere in Act IV. How did you guess?"

"I didn't guess," said Trumpington modestly. "It's one of the rules—at least one quotation out of *Hamlet* in each puzzle."

"We live and learn. 'An envious sliver,' wasn't it?"

"Six letters—that'll do. Here, wait a moment, though. Are you sure it was Ophelia—look at 28 across. The subject must be masculine, if they said 'him' somewhere."

"We won't argue," said Prynne. "Let's look it up. Pleasure to handle a book like this." He caressed the big red volume. "Here you are."

> *There with fantastic garlands did she come*
> *Of crow-flowers, nettles, daisies and long-purples*
> *That liberal shepherds give a grosser name.*
> *But our cold maids do dead men's fingers call them.*
> *There, on the pendant boughs her coronet weeds*
> *Clambering to hang, an envious sliver broke——*

"Have you ever wondered what the shepherds did call them? Something rather Elizabethan, I suppose. The note says that it's 'wiser not to speculate.' Oh, dear!"

"But this doesn't explain 28 across. The second letter's 'i,' by the way, provided that OSIER is right."

"This is fascinating," said Prynne. "And in this case don't you think rather macabre? 18 across must be Tang —from *The Tempest*; and there's an easy one: 11 across. Anagram of STARE. RATES—got it in one."

"Or TEARS, or TARES, or the Scottish STRAE."

"H'imp. And if you're out to be difficult I suppose one might talk of a pupil who RESAT an exam. But I still think it's RATES."

"I'm inclined to agree with you. Nothing else will fit in with what we've got of 9 down. RATES gives us TA-O; just give me that dictionary: there aren't many possibilities. Here we are—TARO. It doesn't help with anything, but it's nice to know that we're right."

"I'm beginning to see how you crossword fans acquire your reputation for general knowledge. Could 5 down be Blossoms? It looks rather like it—with a sly dig at Canon Bloss."

"Of course—then 2 down goes with it. Apple-blos-

soms. But, then, what do you make of 27?" It was noticeable that he was now treating Prynne almost as an equal
in the craft.

The solution to 27 struck them both simultaneously.

"This is getting rather creepy," said Trumpington.
"DOWN. APPLE-DOWN, I suppose it must be."

"It's of no significance, of course—this must have
been written a long time before——"

"Of course, rather an unfortunate coincidence. How
affectionately he refers to him. Whyte was one of the few
people who seemed to know our head verger well—our
late head verger, I should say. What do you make of 1
across? A ramp is a slope and would fit—but it's hardly
crooked, is it?"

"In the American sense."

"Good gracious, yes. I fear my knowledge of trans-
atlantic terms——"

"Then 3 down seems to be P-AR—what does 'see 17'
mean?"

"Look at clue 17; the two words have to be considered
together—isn't there a lily called a nenuphar? That gives
us an 'n' for this mysterious 12 down. We can't even
guess at it yet."

"Look at 9 across then, how do we work that?"

"Two English pronouns—in a foreign one. Foreign,
of course, always means French in these puzzles. The
first or last letter will be the French pronoun. I see we
already have an 's' for first letter. Then it must be the
reflexive pronoun 'se'—unless it's 'sa'—but that's really
an adjective. We have only three internal letters for two
pronouns. So one must be 'i'—either the second or the
penultimate. The latter, I think, don't you? That leaves
us with 's,' obviously US. And the result"—concluded

Trumpington, with the simple triumph of a man producing a small rabbit out of a large hat—"is SUSIE."

"All right," said Prynne. "I give in. But you mustn't show off more than necessary. Now I think 20 down must be ILEX—the literal botany meaning. But it implies an 'x' at the second of 29 across."

"But that's splendid. 'Past' signifies 'ex'—in the sense of ex-captain. Then 'scraps' is a four-letter word, which——"

"Orts. Exorts. Put it in. We shall soon be finished at this rate."

On which fatal words a doldrum settled on the puzzle, and both solvers stared at it for ten irritating minutes and made no progress.

"Puzzles often go dead like this in the middle," said Trumpington. "But, of course, it's those four blank marginal words which are holding us up. 'Solve empirically.' What on earth does it mean? Do you know, I was sure they went in pairs. 4 across and 30 across the same—and 12 down and 14 down the same. But they can't be. The middle letter of 12 is 'n,' whilst 14 starts R-G, or should do."

Prynne wasn't attending. He gave a litle sigh of satisfaction. "I like this game of yours," he said at last. "I confess it. It gets me. And I think that I am beginning to understand the language. 12 across is PEW—reference Treasure Island. It doesn't help much, since we can't guess 12 down, and the other letters are blank. But I've got an idea for 15 down, which ought to help. What about RUNNER UP? 'Second' in a sporting sense."

"That's good, really—very good indeed. I'll write it down. Now what does that give us? Isn't 30 across going to be an odd word? I don't believe there is such a——

Still, we mustn't speculate. Let's check up by means of 21 across."

"Construe it, first."

"Well, a cipher is nought—in other words, the letter 'o.' But the clue is cunningly set. It might mean one of two things. A word for 'thrust' minus the letter 'o' equals a word for 'Loll.' Or, alternatively, a word for 'Loll' minus the letter 'o' to equal a word for 'thrust.' In either case we can place the 'o'—it's the second letter. Then we have -N-E, and most probably NCE or -NGE; NSE isn't a verbal termination. NNE is uncommon. Some sort of vowel between the 'o' and the 'n.' 'Oa' or 'ou.' It must be

LOUNGE, I think. Yes, of course. Take away the 'o' and you have LUNGE—to thrust in fencing."

"Your bird, Colonel. Now I'm going to cheat. Don't I see a Shakespeare concordance up there? Well, look up 'barefaced.' Only four possibles. 'Play barefaced'—'I could with barefaced power'—only one from *Hamlet*. Listen to this. 'They bore him barefaced on the bier.' That's good enough, isn't it? Sung by Ophelia. Speaking of Polonius. That explains the sex difficulty. Simple enough when you know how."

"Blank letters, all of them," sighed Trumpington ungratefully. "But I own that it's nice to be right. Now that drunken business in 26 down—that's another convention. The finished word has to end in SH. Like a stage drunkard, you know. 'Mess' is 'confusion.' Make it drunk and it becomes 'Mesh.' Rather arbitrary, really. Like the assumption that all Welshmen turn their initial d's into t's, or that all f's become v's in Dorsetshire. That completes that fantastic word at 30 across."

"Haven't we been overlooking rather an easy one at 23 across? It says 'confused end of 8 or 6'—we have 8 across, anyway. That ends ATE. Then 23 across must be TEA—unless it's just plain muddling of the letters—but that's hardly playing the game, is it? I mean, the second one must be a word itself, too, mustn't it? Or don't you play that convention?"

"Certainly it must. But you can also make EAT."

"Confound it, so you can. The Greek letter ETA, for that matter—or would it be spelt with a double E?"

"Taking the alternatives as TEA and EAT, it gives us two possible combinations for 24 down. E-T, or A-T. Do either of those suggest to you a ladylike flower?"

"I can't say they do. When is a flower ladylike?"

"Well, cutting out the ladylike, can you think of any flower beginning with those letters?"

"ASTER—but why the Lady? Oh, of course. Unfair, really, but put it down. That gives us EAT for 23 across. 31 across, by the way, must be NORM—not that it affects the main issue. Then for our key word at 14 down, we have R-G-T."

It was at this point that Prynne made a momentous observation.

"I wonder," he said slowly, "whether perhaps we aren't meant to take that clue at 14 down and the others quite literally—do you see what I mean? After all, the words 'solve empirically' might be taken in two ways. They might be the clue themselves—as, of course, we first assumed that they were—in which case the answer would be something like 'guess' or 'puzzle out.' Or else they might be instructions to us, as solvers. Meaning that we are to get the 'straight clues' first, and then puzzle out what the four key words are by looking at the letters we have got. That's really what 'empirically' means, isn't it —trying all possible combinations?"

"I've seen something of the sort in Torquemada." Trumpington spoke with reverence of the great Inquisitor. "You have sometimes whole sentences or stanzas to guess. But in his arrangement of the frame, of course, there are no hidden letters."

"Then perhaps we can start by guessing 14 down. R-G-T. Unless we are embracing the Latin language— and I don't see any reason to do so—the only word which suggests itself is RIGHT."

"And 12 down? Penal, or——"

"Don't be so cautious—it's PANEL."

"Right, panel."

They were both silent for a moment. It seemed all of a sudden that they had taken a long step nearer to the heart of Canon Whyte's little mystification. Then Trumpington got up and turned the light on. He tried to make his voice sound as matter of fact as possible.

"That's a very clever suggestion. The right panel of what, I wonder? His own library, perhaps—but that's panelled all over."

"Or of his desk?"

"That's more likely. What became of his desk? I believe his son had it—he must have taken it away with him. I do think that Whyte might have been more explicit."

"Aren't we forgetting the other two key words? 4 across and 30 across should tell us all we want to know."

"Of course; we must finish this, Prynne."

"We must, and we will, Trumpington. Advance the standards. What do you make of 4 down?"

"Nothing, at the moment. It seems to leave no point of attack—and which Blake?"

"Sexton Blake?"

"The poet, more probably. What about 6 down, then?"

"One thing we have established: it must end in ATE if the last three letters are an anagram at 23 across. With the 'i' from 'sliver' that gives us four blank letters followed by IATE."

"Well, that's a likely enough ending, in all conscience. An adjective, like collegiate or branchiate—or a verb, perhaps—officiate."

"All good sound suggestions—except that they've got too many letters——"

"And nothing to do with the clue."

"True. What about 7 down?"

"Well, I have a feeling, based on many similar subterfuges, that the word 'merely' has been put in with intent to deceive—the nucleus of the clue is 'relative.' "

"Five letters, and ending in 'e.' UNCLE."

"Or NIECE."

"Confound you, yes. It might be 'niece.' What a hard world it is. And 10 across is quite incomprehensible."

" 'Archetype of the manifold varieties of existence.' But it does seem to mean something, doesn't it? I mean, it's not just sheer gibberish, like 'Why is a mouse when it spins?' Now, how would you define an archetype?"

"I shouldn't. I should look it up. Here we are. It means a prototype."

"Well, that's very helpful. And a prototype means— don't tell me. I've guessed it. It means an archetype."

After this pronouncement a gloomy silence prevailed. Once again it was Prynne, the amateur, who came to the rescue.

"Idea," he said firmly.

"You've had an idea?"

"No. Yes. I mean 'idea' is the answer to 10 across. It's an Aristotelian definition. I knew I had met it somewhere."

"Are you sure? That's very remarkable. I don't wish to look a gift horse in the mouth, but if you'll pass the dictionary. Yes, indeed. 'An image of an external object formed by the mind—notion—thought—product of intellectual action. An archetype of the manifold——' Prynne, that's absolutely brilliant."

"Write it in," said Prynne. "We're in the straight now. 7 down has got to be 'niece,' of course."

"And 6 down seems to suggest a word now:—I-IATE,

-ICIATE, -ILIATE, -ITIATE. 'Initiate.' That 's right, it must be. Taken in four separate words. 'In it I ate.' "

"I don't wish to damp your ardour, but 4 across doesn't look any more like a word than 30 across. What letter are you going to suggest between the 'i' and the 'n?' A vowel —or another 'n.' Or a 'g'—that gives it a sort of French look, finishing -IGNE."

"There are too many possibilities. We shall have to get 4 down. I feel that it's the poet Blake that is referred to. I haven't a copy of his works——"

"I have," said Prynne. "I'll fetch it. And we'll dig it out if it means reading through the whole boiling issue."

A moment later the door had slammed behind him.

When he came back with a fat volume of Blake's poems one look at Trumpington's face told him that he'd had his journey for nothing. "Have you got it?" he cried.

"Women's Institute. I thought of it as soon as you'd left."

"Of course. Why, it was only last week that we had it—and did those feet——? Put it in, anyway."

"There!" They stared at the finished product.

"That top word, now. It should be easy enough, with the first letter 'f' and the third letter 'b.' Where's that dictionary? I'll start with the FAB's. No good. FEB—'Febrific' would do—if niece is wrong. And it means feverish, or 'producing fever,' which is quite appropriate. FIB—no use. FOB—FUB—nothing at all."

"Try FYB," said Prynne desperately. "It must be something. . . . Well, it's a rotten dictionary, then."

"This is the only dictionary Whyte ever used." Trumpington gazed lovingly at the tattered, dog-eared edition of Chambers' *Twentieth Century*—the crossword solver's vade-mecum.

"Try that gazetteer."

The gazetteer produced a number of towns, rivers, inlets, and hills starting with F-B, but nothing of eight letters to fit the data except "Fabriano" which they discovered to be a cathedral town (population 23,200) in the neighbourhood of Ancona in Italy.

"And Whyte was never in Italy in his life," wailed Trumpington—and broke off short at the sight of Prynne's face.

"Don't talk," said Prynne simply, "and I may remember it. I don't promise anything, mind you. Somewhere, somehow. Oh, Lord, what a muddled head I've got. Fabriano. But it's not a place at all—it's a person. That's it. Exhibition of Italian art. Where's that dictionary of biography?"

Feverishly he turned the pages. "Fabriano, Gentile da—(1348?–1428?) Italian painter. Born at Fabriano and known after his native town. Painted at, etc., etc. Adorned the Lateran Church with many beautiful frescoes—a series of five beautiful miniature triptyches.' There you are," he finished simply.

In complete silence Canon Trumpington wrote FA-BRIANO into the top right-hand corner of the puzzle and TRIPTYCH into the bottom left-hand corner. Then he got up.

"That must be the one he gave the Dean," he said; "we'd better go and look at it now. Come on."

XIV • Being Dead, Yet Speaketh

> "Let it be enjoined that those who kill themselves by
> sword, poison, precipice or halter, or by any other means
> bring violent death upon themselves, shall not have a
> memorial made of them . . . nor shall their bodies be car-
> ried with Psalm to burial. . . ."

"CHECK," said Halliday regretfully: "and it really is mate
this time."

"Nonsense, Halliday. I can still move back. Oh, your
knight, I see. So it is." The Dean collected the remaining
pieces from the board. "We'll start again, and I'll take
black. You've plenty of time for another game, haven't
you?"

"Afraid not. No late choir practice to-night—and that
means evening class. Scripture, Second Kings. Such an
embarrassing book. I always prepare two chapters ahead.
I promise you your revenge to-morrow evening."

As Halliday was letting himself out of the front door
he saw Pollock and Hazlerigg coming up the path, and
forthwith regretted his own conscientiousness. If only he
had stayed five minutes longer, he reflected, he might
have heard the very latest tidbits of news about Parvin—
and no one in the Close appreciated early and exclusive
news more than Halliday. However, he supposed it *would*
look a bit odd if he turned back again, so he flung the two

policemen a reproachful "Good evening," and trudged off into the darkness.

"Sit down, Inspector. . . . A cigarette—and you, Bobby?"

Business over, status of nephew resumed, thought Pollock, and lit his pipe.

"I asked you to come round here to-night," went on the Dean, "so that we could talk things over quietly, and see whether something couldn't be done to make things a little easier for—well—you know what I mean. There's no need for Mrs. Parvin to suffer unnecessarily——"

"Parvin——" Hazlerigg was beginning when the maid arrived to build up the fire, and there ensued one of those silences which arise all the world over, when the movements of domestics suspend private conversation.

"I can scarcely believe it even now," continued the Dean when the maid, having done her best to put out a perfectly good fire by emptying a scuttle of coal on it, had at last removed herself. "Parvin was a man who had, perhaps, a certain weakness for the bottle in his hours of duty: scarcely what one looks for in a verger: but apart from that——"

"I was going to tell you," said Hazlerigg patiently, "that Parvin——"

Again he was interrupted. They had not heard the bell, but now the sound of trampling feet in the hall announced the unceremonious arrival of Trumpington and Prynne. One glance at their faces brought all three men to their feet.

Trumpington was spokesman.

"Something very important has happened," he said—and in a quiet voice he explained to them the chain of circumstance which had resulted in the discovery of

Canon Whyte's last message. When he had finished the silence was broken unexpectedly by Hazlerigg.

"Who was Canon Whyte?"

"Why," said the Dean guiltily, "didn't I tell you about Canon Whyte? I was sure you'd heard about Canon Whyte. Such a distressing business. He fell from the roof of the cathedral—practically on the spot where Appledown——"

His voice died away. Pollock thought Hazlerigg was going to explode. But when at last the inspector found his voice its very softness was more explosive than violence.

"Three days," he said. "Three days; everyone under suspicion of murder, and some of you in actual danger of your lives, and you never thought it worth your while to tell me the one thing that really mattered. Never mind, it can't be helped now. With your permission, Mr. Dean, we'll open that triptych."

The Dean, feeling obscurely guilty, fetched a paper-knife and prized up the thin matchboarding which formed the back of the right-hand volet of the triptych. Between the wood and the figured panel, and exactly fitting into the cavity, lay a flat envelope of oiled silk, of the type much used by lawyers for the preservation of deeds. The Dean removed this, and seeing that it was sealed handed it after a moment's hesitation to Trumpington.

"I think it was meant for you," he said. Trumpington looked from the Dean to Prynne, who was openly grinning; to Pollock, desperately interested, but simulating a polite unconcern; to Hazlerigg, impassive as ever.

Then, "Excuse me," he said, as simply as if he had been at his own breakfast-table, and slitting open the envelope he drew out the one sheet of notepaper which it contained—a large sheet, folded twice, and covered back and front with Canon Whyte's neat handwriting.

He read carefully for a few moments, gasped, scrutinized a line or two ahead, then said in a choking voice:

"You'd better all see this. I suppose it's—I mean to say——" he turned to the Dean. "Look here, sir, would you read it out to us? It's addressed to you as well."

The Dean looked inquiringly at Hazlerigg, who said, "Please do." So he took the paper from Trumpington's outstretched hand, and started to read without more ado in his quiet unemphatic voice.

"'Dear Trumpington, and you, Mr. Dean, and others who may be present at these my last obsequies and rites. When I decided to end my life, I was determined on two things. The first, that there should be no shadow of an idea in anyone's mind that my death was premeditated. This was important for many reasons. Principally, because my dear daughter was about to be married, and my son, may God bless him and help him, was on the point of entering on his career in the diplomatic service. The news that I had destroyed myself might have been disastrous to both of them in a number of easily imaginable ways. I am sure that they will forgive me this innocent deception, should it be necessary to tell them of it.

"'Now to my second resolution. It was that the cause of my taking this step, though hidden at first, should eventually be known in the proper quarters (and there alone).

"'Faced as I was with this dual problem, you will wonder why I did not employ the device of leaving a message—to be opened at some definite period after my death. The answer is that the mere fact of having done so would have aroused those very suspicions which I was most anxious to avoid. A lawyer, left with such instructions, must, I understand, open a confidential letter if he suspects a breach of the law—for *felonia de se*, remember, in this enlightened country of ours, is a crime. No. What I wanted was some device by which the message I had to leave might be dispatched, but *delayed* from reaching its destination—hidden away until the time was ripe—and then falling into the right hands. You will perhaps agree that I showed some little ingenuity in my dismal task.

"'To you, Trumpington, my very dear friend, I left my books. You remember the promise I exacted, that you would try to read them all! Spoken half in jest, but I knew you wouldn't forget. And the Boswell above all. How often has your unenvious soul envied me my books. I felt that I was safe in leaving my clue interred in the volumes of the *Tour to the Hebrides*. How soon did you reach it, I wonder? I made many attempts before I could get that crossword puzzle just right. Not too hard—but hard enough to defeat anyone else in the Close but yourself. To you, Mr. Dean, I left my Fabriano triptych—thus subtly, you see, have I appointed you and Trumpington the executors and trustees of my secret.

"And what is this secret? Perhaps you have guessed it already.'"

The Dean here paused for a moment, having come to the end of the page, and the crackle as he turned the stiff parchment over sounded electric in the heavy silence.

"'For many years Appledown has been blackmailing me. The secret on which he based his demands concerns my early life in India, and I do not propose to set out any of the facts here. When, for the prosecution of Appledown or any other purpose whatever, it becomes necessary to discover them, you will apply to Colonel

Deighton at Room M.19 in the Special Branch at the India Office. I will say only this. I was entirely in Appledown's hands, and I could not put an end to his power except by ending my life in Melchester—on the one hand by exposure, imprisonment, and disgrace—or on the other hand, by death.

"'I chose the latter alternative, fortified by the knowledge that I might use my death to good purpose—or rather that you, my good friends, might use my death for me. Have no scruple in doing so. For I tell you now, solemnly and sanely, that Daniel Appledown is the cruellest and most heartless scoundrel that I have ever met—and in the roving commission of my life I have met not a few. As I watch him, this benevolent white-haired old man, walking sedately about the cathedral Close, he seems to me to be literally inhuman—amoral, if you want a grand word for it. He affects me so strongly as something altogether vile and unnatural that it is only with an effort that I can bring myself to talk to him, or be near him. If he were to touch me, even by accident, I should be sick. He is a venomous snake. And there is only one treatment for snakes—the heel of your boot. For make no mistake about this. *I am not the only victim.* I know as a fact that he is practising his vile trade on the second verger, Parvin. I am not quite sure what his hold over him is, but it concerns his wife. I give you this information in confidence and in the trust that you will not have to use it. I suspect that two—and perhaps three— more people in the Close are being victimized. You are so particularly defenceless in this Close community, aren't you? One breath of scandal!—and how Appledown knows it, and plays on it, to the satisfaction of his own cold-hearted lust and greed.

"'One last word. You, my trusted executors and exe-cutioners, now that I have presented you with your case, use it to the full, but—stir up as little of the mud as possible. I see no reason why anyone but myself should suffer. Except Appledown, of course. . . .'"

When the Dean had finished reading he laid the paper down on the table in front of him. The thick, triangular writing stood out firm and bold, with never a tremor to the end. Prynne voiced all their thoughts when he said, "That's a type of courage which I can appreciate but could never aspire to."

"He played his part well," said Trumpington. "He must have been planning this for many weeks before the end."

"Months—not weeks," said the Dean. "Months or even years. His will was dated, remember, nearly six months before his death."

The four men were silent again as they contemplated with a feeling akin to awe the relentless machinery which old Canon Whyte had built and set into motion—ma-chinery which had not, even yet, ceased to turn. Trum-pington was thinking of Whyte as he had known him in the last months of his life—struggling with *The Times* crossword or smiling at some happy pomposity of the great Boswell—a happy and harmless old clergyman, you would have said; but to those who really knew him there was something more than that: a deceptive quality; a lambent inner flame. And Trumpington remembered being surprised when Whyte had once expressed a very warm admiration for "the greatest Frenchwoman of all time." He had supposed that Whyte meant Jeanne d'Arc. "No," said Whyte, "Charlotte Corday." And he had added in a tone which Trumpington had never forgotten,

"She had the additional grandeur of complete failure."

Again Prynne was the first to break the silence.

"In a way," he said, addressing himself to Hazlerigg, "I suppose this simplifies matters, for it supplies what has all along been lacking—a convincing motive. And yet— well, I know it's no part of your job to entertain any human feelings, but in your place I should not be too happy about hanging Parvin. I should be more inclined to congratulate him on doing a necessary and salutary job. When you think of the money that Appledown must have squeezed out—— By the way, *was* he very rich?"

"Yes," said Pollock, "we discovered that he had a lot of money; but it was mostly salted away."

"Must the real reasons for Parvin's action be dragged into the light," said Trumpington. "You remember what Whyte said—that it somehow concerned Mrs. Parvin. She, anyway, could have had no hand in the murder— couldn't she be left out of it?"

"Look here," said the Dean, "this won't do. We're trading on a position of confidence to embarrass the inspector. He will, of course, have to do exactly what he thinks fit."

And last of all Hazlerigg spoke. He had been silent for a long time. He sounded very tired.

"You ought to know," he said, "that Parvin——"

And incredibly for the third and last time the interruption came. The quick crunching of feet on the gravel, the bang of the front door, footsteps in the passage heavy and hurried, the agitated voice of the Dean's parlourmaid uplifted in protest, "But he's with the detective gentleman from London—he wasn't to be disturbed." A further rush of footsteps: a menacing cross-fire of whispers; and then a loud, imperious voice. "I tell you, I must see the Dean."

Then the door burst open, revealing the wild figure of
Doctor Smallhorn, and behind him, looking even more
frightened, Vicar Choral Halliday.

"Well, Dr. Smallhorn," said the Dean, "what's the
matter?"

"Mr. Dean," said Dr. Smallhorn thickly. "It's murder.
It's happened again."

To obtain a correct idea of the events of that memorable Friday evening, we must follow Vicar Choral Halliday, whom we left on the Dean's doorstep. Seven o'clock
had struck and he was sitting in the senior classroom at
the choristers school, waiting with ill-concealed impa-
tience for the dilatory members of his divinity class.

It really was a mistake, he reflected, having class so
soon after the evening meal. The boys were sleepy, and
one hadn't the heart to chivvy them—however, there
were limits. "Come on, boy—come on." A crimson in-
fant, his mouth still bulging with currant cake, shot into
the room. "Hewlett, of course, you beastly little pig.
Empty your mouth *before* coming into class, can't you?
Now are we all here? Two still missing. Bird and Brophy.
What are they doing? Still eating, I suppose."

Hewlett, having disposed of a cubic foot of cake,
opined that they were "turning." He referred to the time-
honoured custom by which two boys, on non-practice
night, were allowed to visit the cathedral to prepare the
music for the next day's service—a task which a grown-
up would have thought particularly onerous, but which,
for some reason, appealed to the mind of youth as a de-
sirable privilege.

"All right." Halliday viewed with resignation his
bloated and apathetic scripture class. Young Green would

215

be asleep in a moment. Really, evening class was a mistake. "All right—we'll start. Second Kings, chapter twelve—dash it, though, we can't. I lent my Bible with all the notes in it to Brophy."

"It's in his locker," screamed Hewlett, scenting a promising distraction. "Shall I get it for you?"

"Sit down, boy, sit down. I can perfectly well get it myself. Why is it that all you boys keep your lockers in such a horrible mess? Brophy, for instance, appears to be making a collection of used blotting-paper."

His head disappeared deeper into the locker, and the form settled once more into apathy.

The sound of the door opening caused Halliday to extricate himself. "Ah—it's you, Bird. You're late—nearly ten minutes late—not the early bird this time——"

The jest was received with a complacent laugh by the rest of the form, but got no response at all from Bird. And his face looked strangely white in the strong unshaded light. Halliday hurried forward.

"What is it?" he said quietly.

"It's Brophy," said Bird. "He's fainted or something—I fell over him as I was coming through the precinct gate——"

"All right—nothing to be upset about. It's probably the heat." The evening had suddenly got oppressively close, he noticed. "You run up to Matron. Tell her to get a bed ready. And she'd better look after you, too, my lad, if you feel upset. Horner, go and fetch the headmaster. And the rest of you—*keep quiet*."

The senior divinity class, feeling that the whole affair had been staged expressly for their benefit, sat gripped with pleasurable excitement. Hurrying steps across the court—Dr. Smallhorn's voice, quiet but perfectly audible, "Have you got a torch, Halliday?" The click of the precinct gate. And then—listen as they would—complete silence. The minutes ticked by. And then a rather horrible sound—the shuffling footsteps of people who carry a heavy weight. Still no sound of talking. The footsteps passed down the passage, and the silence became distinctly unpleasant.

"We found him lying on the grass, just inside the gate," said Dr. Smallhorn. "I'm very much afraid——" he left the sentence unfinished.

"You've got a doctor, of course," said the Dean. "The doctor's with him now," said Halliday. "He didn't hold out much hope. The back of the skull is cracked, you see: just like——"

"No," said Dr. Smallhorn, so suddenly and fiercely that they all stared at him. "No—it can't be—it's just an accident, that's all. He fell and hit his head on the gatepost. I see it now. It's quite obvious. You mustn't think, just because Appledown—— It's absurd—absurd even to imagine it. Why, he's only a child, you know, Inspector. Scarcely thirteen. Who in the world could want to hurt him?"

"It is horrible," said Trumpington. "And it makes one feel so helpless. I'd go over if there was anything I could do; but one would only be in the way."

"I suppose you realize," said Prynne slowly, "that this lets out Parvin—he's the only single person in the whole Close who couldn't possibly——"

"Don't." Dr. Smallhorn turned on him quite savagely. "Don't keep saying that. What reason have you. What right have you——"

The telephone shrilled. The Dean picked up the receiver.

"Yes. It's the Dean speaking. Who are you . . . oh, yes, Doctor. The inspector is here—he'll speak to you."

Hazlerigg took the receiver and listened for a few minutes. He said nothing. He had not spoken since the interruption. "Very well," he said at last, and rang off. Then he turned and looked at the five men—dispassionately, as if he were seeing them for the first time, and weighing them up before he spoke.

"Brophy's dead," he said at last. "I have just spoken to the police surgeon. He tells me that there is no question of accident. That boy was murdered."

"But if Parvin——" began Prynne.

"Two murderers!" exclaimed Trumpington.

Dr. Smallhorn said nothing. Since Hazlerigg had spoken he seemed completely dazed.

Once more the inspector considered his audience gravely before speaking.

"Parvin escaped this evening." (Pollock gave a start of surprise.) "He asked to be allowed to go to the hospital to see his wife. Foolishly, perhaps, I consented. There were two policemen in the car and two more went into the hospital with him. The three of them were walking up the passage which leads to the room where his wife is being kept, when Parvin, as I understand it, simply jumped through an open door and slammed it behind him—and bolted it. In the few seconds before the door could be broken down he ran through a connecting door, climbed an interior staircase, and came out into the passage above. A nurse said later that she saw him crossing it, but mistook him for a patient. That was the last that was seen of him. Of course," he finished cheerfully, "it won't be long before we have our hands on him again."

"Then he's at large!" exclaimed the Dean. "Good heavens, he may be lurking in the Close at this moment! You must give us a guard, Inspector——"

"If he's in the Close," said Hazlerigg grimly, "he won't get out of it."

"He must be mad, I suppose," said Prynne.

Curiously enough this suggestion, which alarmed the others more than they would have cared to admit, seemed to afford Dr. Smallhorn a very slender ray of comfort. "That's it," he said. "The man's mad, of course. I knew there could be no other reason for such a horrible senseless, brutal thing."

There was a great deal to do.

The least pleasant task the Dean naturally shouldered himself—as he had been quietly shouldering all the tiresome and unpleasant burdens in the Close for the last fourteen years. He called on Colonel Brophy—a widower, who lived in a big, rather empty house on the outskirts of Melchester. What the colonel said to him and what words he found for the colonel in that black hour will never be known; but it was well after midnight when Sergeant Brumfit heard the knock he had been listening for on the Close gate and hurried out with a torch.

"I'm afraid I've kept you up," said the Dean in a very quiet flat voice. "It has got rather close again, hasn't it? More thunder coming, I think."

"Afraid so, sir."

"Good night, Brumfit."

"Good night, sir," said Brumfit in a fatherly tone of voice. He thought the Dean looked very tired.

The Dean was tired, but he didn't go to bed. And for hour after hour a light shone out from the oriel floor window in the south corner which was the Dean's private sitting-room—and, in time of need, his private chapel.

After the necessary formalities had been completed Hazlerigg and Pollock walked back to the Bear together. Pollock was badly on his dignity. It was some time before Hazlerigg appeared to notice that anything was amiss; then he suddenly suspended an eloquent discourse on the futility of judging by appearances, and peered at his subordinate.

"What's up, Sergeant? Swallowed a fish bone?"

"There's nothing up with me, thank you," said Pollock politely.

"Then, if there's nothing wrong," said Hazlerigg, equally politely, "would you have the goodness to explain exactly why you are looking and walking like a constipated crab with tonsilitis."

"I'm sorry," said Pollock stiffly, "I had no idea——"

"Good Lord—of course." The inspector slapped his leg softly. "You're fed up because I never told you about Parvin's escape. Gross lack of confidence in my subordinate, eh?"

Since that was precisely what had been annoying Pollock he naturally hastened to deny it.

"Of course not," he said. "There's no reason why you should tell me any more than you want to——"

"Don't be an owl," snarled Hazlerigg. "There was just one excellent reason why I couldn't tell you of Parvin's escape. It never happened. As far as I know Parvin is safe and sound in Melchester police station, being tucked up and put to bed by Uncle Palfrey."

"Then, why——"

"No, don't ask stupid questions. Work it out for yourself. Do it out loud if you think that'll help. It will be illuminating to see if your brain works as quickly as mine had to."

Pollock gathered the scattered remnants of his wits. "I suppose," he began slowly, "that you never had any doubt that the same person did both murders?"

"No doubt at all—same man, same method, same weapon. The doctor saw both bodies—he thought so, too."

"Well, then: the second murder simply couldn't have been done by Parvin. Almost anybody else, but not Parvin. Therefore the murderer—the double-murderer—was somebody else in the Close. Somebody we hadn't even dreamed of."

"Correct so far."

"That somebody must have been very happy when we suspected Parvin. Very happy indeed. Then why did he go and spoil it all by murdering a harmless and helpless little boy—putting his own neck into danger again, and letting out Parvin? He must either have had a very strong reason—or else—he's mad."

"He's not mad," said Hazlerigg.

"Conceding that he's not mad he must have realized the new risk he was running from now on. He would have to be doubly—trebly—careful. But all of a sudden——"

"Yes?"

"All of a sudden he hears that he has had an amazing stroke of luck. Parvin has escaped. Far from exculpating Parvin the second murder has redoubled suspicion on the wretched verger. Once again the real murderer can go on his way unsuspected. He relaxes."

"Before God," said Hazlerigg solemnly, "I hope he does relax, for if he doesn't make a mistake soon I don't think we shall catch him, and then Parvin will hang for the murder of Appledown—a murder he never committed."

The second half, anyway, of Hazlerigg's prediction was immediately proved false. They found awaiting them a chastened Inspector Palfrey. Parvin had been left in the charge of Inspector Palfrey at the police station, and it afforded the inspector very little pleasure to have to tell Hazlerigg that his prisoner had committed suicide in the charge-room by cutting his throat with the station-sergeant's scissors.

So that it was very late indeed—long after midnight —when Pollock and Hazlerigg finally got back to their hotel. Every star was hidden, but the storm delayed and the night was oppressive with the undischarged artillery.

Pollock went straight to bed and tried to read himself to sleep with the seventh and dullest book of Wordsworth's *Excursion*. He read till the words danced in front of his eyes:

> *Memories—images . . .*
> *That shall not die and cannot be destroyed.*

He thought of Parvin.

Hazlerigg had no intention of going to bed. He knew —none better—that so far he had failed: failed all along the line, and the realization combined unpleasantly with the heaviness of the night and forbade any thought of sleep. He had, as Pollock had once pointed out, proved to his own satisfaction that a number of prime suspects were innocent. He had shown who hadn't done the murder, but that was poor consolation. He had unearthed and exposed the rather pointless little manoeuvres of

Vicar Choral Malthus. The most important discovery—
the only important discovery—had been made by Trumpington and Prynne. Appledown the blackmailer! It was
rather a staggering thought. And it supplied a strong motive: one of the oldest and strongest in the world. But the
devil of it was it was a motive that would fit anyone.
Canon Whyte's words came back to him—"Two—and
perhaps three—more people in the Close are being victimized." But who were they? Mickie, the organist, for
one. Hazlerigg felt that this was a good guess. It explained
Mickie's otherwise inexplicable agitation and his very
dangerous secrecy. The thought of Canon Whyte brought
Hazlerigg's mind back again to Parvin. Poor little Parvin
—what a beautiful, watertight case they had worked out
against him. And now it looked as if the case and the
prisoner had gone west at one blow. It was black undis-
guised defeat.

And yet—and this was what maddened Hazlerigg—
the whole answer was there, before his eyes, under his
fingers. He knew it: he felt it. And for want of under-
standing he could not grasp it.

Three lives gone—first Appledown, and then that boy
—and now Parvin. Who was going to be next? "There
must be no more of it," said Hazlerigg, and found he had
spoken aloud.

With a deep sigh which was equal parts weariness and
disillusionment, he pulled out every paper connected
with the case, stacked them on the table, drew up his
chair, and started all over again.

He didn't skimp his work, and the long hand had gone
round twice before he had done. He had many qualities
which went to the making of a good police officer, but
one above all others: a quality which was destined to raise

him afterwards to the heights of his profession. Concentration. Tireless, relentless, implacable concentration. And yet something more than that. Selective concentration. "The essence of all police work is sound elimination." And here there was so much that was superfluous. Carefully he recalled the essentials, and above all the three points at which, as he had told Pollock, he had first glimpsed the possibility of a controlling mind. Mickie's ghost. And two voices. First the old, high tones of Mrs. Judd. "I've still got good hearing... I heard things... wicked things. Later that night. Much later. Footsteps creeping, doors creaking." That was one voice. Then Prynne's precise tones. "I saw a light go on in his front room and his shadow jerking about on the blind." There was a key there.

And the anonymous messages—what was their connection with the murder? He had outlined three possibilities to Pollock—there was, of course, a fourth. He had just seen it. Hazlerigg experienced a little tremor of excitement.

He had once watched a water diviner—a "dowser" he called himself—at work with his forked hazel rod. He had seen the man step quite listlessly on to a patch of gravel and then—the change. A tiny, almost imperceptible trembling of the stick. Then a quivering. Then a triumphant dip. Five minutes later they were digging the well.

Hazlerigg was far from striking water yet, but he had felt the first magical tingling of an idea. Painstakingly he swept backwards and forwards from it. It was all there. Every word, every fact. He was sure of it. He had only to believe what he had seen and heard. The evidence of his eyes and ears—eyes and ears. The stick trembled, and then stopped. Hazlerigg repeated the words slowly to himself—"The evidence of eyes and ears."

And at that moment the idea was born. It came to life curiously with a quotation from Pater about "dumb inquiry over the relapse after death." Hazlerigg whispered the well-known words to himself. "At last, far off, thin and vague . . . a passing light, a mere intangible external effect." The conviction was growing stronger now. "A dream that lingers a moment, retreating in the dawn," but this dream was going to stay, "a thing with faint hearing": that was it—one could feel the stick dipping strongly now—"faint memory, faint power of touch: a breath, a flame in the doorway, a feather in the wind."

The storm had passed for that night at least, and the stars were beginning to pale when Hazlerigg got stiffly to his feet, and rolled, almost with one motion, into his bed.

And the great Melchester mystery was a mystery no longer.

XV • The Threads Are Picked Up

THE FOLLOWING DAY was Saturday and it opened with an hour or two of mixed endeavour.

"Go to Colonel Brophy's house," said Hazlerigg, "and see if you can get hold of some specimens of John Brophy's handwriting. I needn't tell you to be tactful. . . ."

Pollock found himself, ten minutes later, in front of a big house on the outskirts of Melchester. It spoke of the retired military man from its regimented flowerbeds and tightly shaven lawns to the inevitable relics of shikari which adorned the front hall. A schoolboy's blue and white cap still hung from a peg in the hall beside the big Benares gong.

Pollock was preparing his gentlest opening when the old colonel cut him short. "Ask what you like, sir! Turn the house upside down if it will assist you in any way whatsoever. Let's get hold of this fellow and hang him. Letters? Yes, I've got most of what he ever wrote to me. Come in here."

He led the way into the study and opened a desk.

"Here's his last letter," he added.

Pollock looked at it closely and got the greatest shock he had sustained in the case.

There was absolutely no doubt about it at all.

John Brophy was the writer of that last anonymous letter which the Dean had received.

The colonel was looking over his shoulder.

"He always signed himself J.B.," he explained. "He was in some respects rather an old-fashioned boy."

Forty years in the army had at least taught the colonel to discipline himself.

Hazlerigg met Pollock by arrangement at the Mayflower Café, and inspected the letter before folding it carefully away.

"I've had a tussle," he said. "Bank officials. The usual sticky crowd. They seem to think that if an ordinary customer's account is sacred a clergyman's must be doubly so. I had to talk for a quarter of an hour on the phone to their head office. Trunk call, too. It all goes on that rates. . . ."

After that they marched back to the Close, crossed the green, through the wicket-gate outside the late Appledown's house, and a few minutes later they were talking to Biddy, Halliday's housekeeper. Halliday and his sister were out, but Biddy proved unexpectedly enlightening.

"Try to remember, please," said Hazlerigg, "on that night when you were standing in the hall with Mr. Halliday. Did you or Mr. Halliday actually go outside into the garden or into the porch?"

Biddy, whose deafness appeared to vary in proportion as she was being "flustered" or not, at last opined that they had not gone out. Mr. Halliday had come out into the hall, and they had stood in the hall for a moment talking together, and then the Foxes had arrived.

Hazlerigg stood for a moment, half in and half out of the front door. He turned his head to the right and looked into the stone-paved front court of the school: then to the left and into the front garden of the Appledown *ménage*. The pillar of the front porch, to which the famous note had been pinned, was clearly visible from where he stood. He seemed hardly to be listening to Biddy's voluble explanations, and Pollock got the impression that he was simply waiting for something or somebody; an impression that was heightened when he caught the inspector glancing surreptitiously at his watch.

"Nip across to the school and see if Dr. Smallhorn is in," he said to Pollock. "I'd like a word with him before lunch."

As Pollock departed on this errand the mellow cathedral bell embarked on a leisurely announcement of midday, and out of the corner of his eye he saw Hazlerigg turn to address a further remark to Biddy.

It was only then, as he afterwards realized, that he got the first inkling of the truth for himself.

Dr. Smallhorn, extracted from a Latin class, welcomed Pollock in his study. Hazlerigg joined them a minute or two later.

"I have got to take you into my confidence to a very real degree, Dr. Smallhorn," said Hazlerigg, "and I want your promise that you will say nothing whatever to anyone of what I am now going to tell you. Not to anyone at all. Even to the boys. Mrs. Meadows will have to be taken into your confidence, but to a more limited extent."

"You may rely on me implicitly," said Dr. Smallhorn,

his Adam's apple giving a gratified bob.

"First point, then. Supposing you found a boy in possession of something which you considered undesirable or dangerous: an—er—weapon or implement, or perhaps even reading matter of an undesirable nature—what would your reactions be? Apart, I mean, perhaps, from punishing the boy for possession of the forbidden property, would you consider yourself justified in 'confiscating' (I believe that is the correct word)—in confiscating the article in question?"

"I must confess," began Dr. Smallhorn, joining the tips of his fingers together in a way which had intimidated three generations of choristers, "that I fail to see the immediate pertinency of your question—but my answer is a most decided negative. I am not a believer in confiscation. Indeed, I fail to see that my status as a schoolmaster gives me any rights over the property of my pupils at all. I may be wrong. If the article in question was an undesirable one I should call on the boy to destroy it: if, on the other hand, it was, as you suggest, a dangerous toy or implement of some sort, then I would have it returned to the boy's parents, who could take what action they wished in the matter."

"I see," said Hazlerigg. He ticked off an item in his notebook. "Now this is what I want you to do."

As he talked, Dr. Smallhorn's amazement grew.

"We've time to snatch some lunch before we see your uncle at two o'clock," said Hazlerigg. They had left the school and were strolling back along the western edge of the green. The oppressive heat made all exertion unpleasant. They had nearly reached the wicket-gate and were about to turn through it when something made the Chief

Inspector pause. He glanced back sharply at Appledown's cottage. In the prevailing stillness Pollock heard—and as he heard, saw—the front door closing sharply. Thoughtfully they retraced their steps, and a moment later were knocking at the (now fast-closed) door.

There ensued a good deal of shuffling supported by a certain amount of grumbling and some ostentatious "noises off": then the door was flung open and Artful blinked out at them. An overcoat, which appeared to have been hastily discarded, was lying over the back of a chair, and the end of a suitcase caught Pollock's eye, sticking out through the curtains of the alcove and imperfectly concealed by them.

"Flitting, eh?"

Artful blinked, but said nothing.

"Now you listen to me." The Chief Inspector's bulk filled the tiny hall and his finger was an instrument of indictment which impaled the shabby finger in front of him.

"Just you listen to me. I know all about you, and I can't say I like much of it. You were living with your brother and you were living on your brother. You were in with him in all his precious schemes. That's to say you had a share in the proceeds and you knew who it came from—don't interrupt. You were an accessory after the fact to his dirty blackmailing business, and if it was worth it I'd charge you with it and send you up. I'm giving you the very slender benefit of the doubt, however, and assuming that though you knew *who* was paying the money you didn't know *why*. I think your brother Daniel was too close for that."

Pollock perceived that this shaft had gone home.

"But if you try to run away, I'll let you in on a little

secret. It wouldn't do you any good if you did decide to run. There are forty policemen sitting round the Close now. They're almost holding hands. So stay put and stay happy."

Hazlerigg backed out, and Pollock followed. Artful appeared to have nothing to say, but his little red eyes winked fearfully.

Back at the hotel a telegram was waiting for them. Pollock read it over Hazlerigg's shoulder. It ran:

"Very interesting suggestion. Probably powdered rhodamine on a grease base. Letter follows by hand soonest."

It was signed by a name so celebrated in the world of forensic science that even Pollock recognized it.

"Parvin," said Hazlerigg, "has been our stumbling-block all along." They were sitting in the Dean's study, and the inspector had just brought his two listeners up to date about the fate of the unhappy second verger.

"Even though he is dead and we ought to think kindly of him, yet I find it difficult to forgive his unwarrantable intrusion into what might have been a simple case. What happened is this. Parvin was being blackmailed by Apple-down. One of our head verger's filthy little ten-shilling-a-week efforts, which I find so much more loathsome than grander larceny. Parvin dropped in that night, as we know, to see Appledown at about seven-forty. Why? Probably Tuesday was pay-day. At all events he goes up to the house: knocks and gets no answer. He's a bit puzzled, but finally tries the door and finds it open. So he goes in.

231

Looks into one or two of the rooms, including the kitchen, and soon discovers that there is nobody at home."

"But——" began the Dean.

"Here, wait a bit now——" began Pollock.

"He discovers," repeated Hazlerigg inexorably, "that there is nobody in. The dinner, I fancy, was uneaten on the plates, the clock ticking on the mantelpiece. *But there was nobody at home.* He waits for a minute or two and then begins to get uneasy. The silence gets on his nerves. Remember, Appledown was a creature of habit as everyone has told us. Absolutely regular. Out every afternoon to cathedral at four o'clock, 'regular as clockwork,' Artful told us. Back at a quarter to seven. Very unlikely to go out after that, and if he did, *always* left a note on the door. No—Parvin is badly worried. Particularly worried, because as far as he knows, if anything has happened to Appledown *he* will be the number one suspect. Blackmailer's victim (I don't suppose he knew he wasn't the only one) and also next for promotion and so on. After a minute or two it gets too much for him, and he exits cautiously and pushes off home. He has a few words with his wife (Mrs. Judd, who saw him go out but was at dinner and missed his return, heard a man's voice and jumped to the worst conclusions about Mrs. Parvin). Mrs. Parvin says, 'Don't worry, go and have a drink and forget about it.' Parvin pushes off to the V. and A. and has his drink. Happens to notice that Begg's clock is ten minutes slow and only registers eight o'clock as he gets there: this fact being filed for future reference."

Pollock was following with breathless attention and doing some wild discarding from his previous hand.

"Now that's not conjecture," went on Hazlerigg. "I got it from Mrs. Parvin in hospital this morning and missed lunch to do it. Once I heard she'd decided to talk I knew we'd get something, and I wasn't disappointed. You see what it all means?"

They were beginning to do so.

"Parvin lied about seeing Appledown at a quarter to eight. He lied to save his own skin. Because he knew that *we* thought Appledown was alive at eight, and *he* had an alibi for eight o'clock. He was hoping against hope in the first place that no one had seen him go into the house at all. When Mrs. Judd firmly blew that particular gaff he had to improvise. If he told the truth and said that the house was quite empty then we should have—we must have—suspected the eight o'clock business straight away. We might quite likely even have thought that it was Parvin who had rigged it. He might have done, you know. It was physically possible, I mean."

"But was it not incredibly risky to lie about such a cardinal point," protested the Dean. "Wouldn't it have been much safer in the end to tell the truth?"

"Of course it would," said Hazlerigg wearily. "If people understood that, sir, how simple our job would be."

"I am afraid," observed Mr. Scrimgeour, the fourth member of the party, who had as yet taken no part in the conversation, "that I must support the inspector there, Mr. Dean. From my early experiences in London I can assure you that witnesses in murder cases—even well-meaning and impartial witnesses—very often seem to be hypnotized into mendacity by the seriousness of the occasion. I need only remind you"—he turned to Hazlerigg—"of the classic example of the carman who so nearly hanged Robert Wood."*

Pollock could contain himself no longer.

"Then what you are telling us is that Appledown was already dead when Parvin called at his house at a quarter to eight. His body was already lying behind the buttress —but why? How? Damnation take it (excuse me, Uncle), but are we going to start all over again?"

"Indeed not," said Hazlerigg, "for most of the main construction stands. We have only to put the time of the murder back a little farther. Appledown was—shall I say induced?—to go round to the engine shed immediately after the end of evening service. The murderer, as I see it, was waiting there for him. He hit him on the head, hid the stick, dragged the body a little farther out of sight— slightly grazing the face as he did so—picked up the hat, which had rolled off, and walked calmly up the path to Appledown's front door, letting himself in with Apple-down's key. He then—however, I mustn't waste the time of two very busy gentlemen in conjecture."

Neither of the two busy gentlemen referred to looked at all adverse to a little more of this inspired conjecture, but Hazlerigg gave them no time to voice a protest.

"I and Dr. Smallhorn have worked out, with Mrs. Meadows, the school matron, a little plot which I hope may help us. Now what I want you to do is this. Will you and Mr. Scrimgeour go over to the school together, tim-ing yourself to arrive there at a minute before four o'clock?—we must remember to synchronize our watches before I go. The maid will let you in, and you will say

---

*Mr. Scrimgeour was referring to the Camden Town murder case of 1907 which was just before Hazlerigg went to London.

that you have come to see Dr. Mickie. He will be in his study at that moment, and there will be someone with him. He will come out to meet you, and you will all meet in the hall."

The Dean nodded, and Mr. Scrimgeour made a methodical note.

"You will explain that you have come to clear up a few points about young Brophy's effects—Mr. Scrimgeour will be able to add the necessary legal touches there. Dr. Smallhorn will be standing in the door of the study so that anyone who is already inside will be unable to push his way out without rudeness and so will naturally be able to hear all that you say. Take your time, and make it sound natural, please."

The Dean thought of disastrous attempts at charades at deanery parties, and groaned in spirit.

"You will particularly ask Dr. Smallhorn whether all of John's effects have been gathered together and where they have been put. Dr. Smallhorn will probably appeal to Mrs. Meadows—she struck me as being a most competent woman, by the way. She will say something to the effect that they have all been collected and put in the linen-room: his trunk and handbag packed, and his few personal belongings parcelled up with the luggage."

His hearers nodded.

"One of you—I think Mr. Scrimgeour—will then ask whether John had much in the way of personal belongings, and the matron will say 'No, just one or two books and some old letters and papers,' and Dr. Smallhorn will say 'Would you like to take charge of it at once?' You gag a bit, and then conclude that 'to-morrow morning will do.' Then change the subject and go on talking about anything you like. I think the third party will push off at this juncture—all correct?"

"Don't you think," said the Dean anxiously, "that we ought to rehearse it a bit?"

"I had thought about that," said Hazlerigg, "and I should say it would be better not to. It'll never sound quite so natural once it loses its first fresh bloom. We must go now and fix our end of it. Au revoir."

"At Philippi," said the Dean gravely.

Half an hour had gone by.

Hazlerigg and Pollock, having climbed two garden walls and slipped through the kitchen quarters of the choir school (happily empty at that time), were now ensconced in the stifling discomfort of the school linen-room. This was a large and functional apartment on the first floor, its shelves filled with best and second-best suits and heaps of well-darned vests and pants and poplin shirts.

Near the door a green canvas trunk strapped up bore the initials J. B., with a handbag and a brown paper parcel on top of it.

A ready-made hiding-place had been found behind a row of bath towels hanging from a crossbar.

It was very hot.

"Whilst we're waiting," said Hazlerigg quietly, "I think I might improve the shining hour by telling you what we are waiting for. The only thing which prevented me from doing so before was an overdeveloped ego and a natural desire to surprise." He looked at his watch. "Five to four. Plenty of time yet. On second thoughts, Sergeant, supposing you tell me first how far you've got."

"All right," agreed Pollock. The steamy atmosphere

was combining with the heat of the day to make him feel terribly sleepy, and talking might serve perhaps to keep him awake.

"The first questions came, I think, from the body. I remember thinking, 'Clothes that were too wet and a hat that was too dry.' We soon got on to the fact that the clothes were so wet because a jackdaw's nest had stopped the gutter and at some period there had been a regular overflow—probably an hour or two after the rain had started. But this only made the dryness of the hat odder still. The only conclusion was that it had been put there considerably after the rest of the outfit—perhaps as much as six hours later, when the rain had steadied to a drizzle and the gutter was no longer spouting. How I see it now —in view of what you've just told us—is this. The murderer needed to use the hat as part of his own disguise in walking the short distance to Appledown's front door. He left it somewhere in Appledown's house, and came back for it late that night. That was Mrs. Judd's footsteps 'later that night, much later' and the wicket that squeaked."

"Bull's-eye there," said Hazlerigg.

"One thing beats me," went on Pollock. "If he was as clever as all that, why didn't he simply hold the hat under the scullery tap until it was as wet as hell, and then we shouldn't have noticed anything."

"He didn't know how wet the body was going to get," grunted Hazlerigg. "Keep your voice down—time's going on. On the contrary, he had a good deal of data to show how very dry the buttress and the shed between them would keep anything lying between them on a wet night."

Pollock looked his query.

"I think he'd rehearsed once or twice, before the great day. He took a bowler hat and a Burberry out on a number of wet and stormy nights and left them behind the shed to see how wet they'd get."

"Good God, of course! Mickie's ghost."

"That's it—he saw a coat and hat stretched out on the asphalt—possibly padded up a bit, and his imagination did the rest. Do you know, the fellow has my professional admiration there. Lots of people might do a murder if sufficiently provoked, but the number is much more limited who would get up on a beastly night beforehand to study the comparative wetness of hats and coats in a given position. Pity in a way that the jackdaw upset his plans——"

"The fowls of the air shall make their habitation—and the wicked shall be confounded."

"Whssst."

They strained their ears.

An imprisoned bluebottle was bumbling resentfully round the inside of the dusty window, and in the slanting sunlight the dust-motes danced and swam. A board creaked.

Quite suddenly the door opened and Vicar Choral Halliday walked in. He went over quickly but very quietly to Brophy's pile of belongings and started to undo the string round the parcel: then to probe among the contents. Two or three books came out, followed by a packet of papers, through which Halliday glanced eagerly.

Suddenly a little gasp burst from his lips, uncontrollably and as if in spite of himself. He picked out one of the envelopes and tore it open.

"I wrote that," said Hazlerigg in his blandest voice. "Get to the door, Sergeant. It's no good struggling. Come along."

XVI • The Real Work

But he had not the supreme gift of the artist, the knowledge of where to stop.
CONAN DOYLE. *THE RETURN OF SHERLOCK HOLMES*

"I FEEL," said the Dean, without levity, "that nothing
will have power to surprise me further. Has Halliday confessed to both the murders?"

"Not him," said Hazlerigg. "By the rules of fiction, I
know, he should have made a full confession, neatly
clearing up all the doubtful points, and then committed
suicide. I'm afraid he's done neither. We're in for some
real work before we can build a case that'll stand up in
court. And that's why I've asked you gentlemen to give
me your time this morning."

There were present in the chapter house, besides the
inspector and Pollock, nine people. The Dean, with Mr.
Scrimgeour at his right hand: the four residentiary
canons: Minor Canons Malthus and Prynne, and the
Precentor. It was nine o'clock on the Sunday morning,
the storm had finally broken during the night, and the
world looked and felt fresh again.

"As originally planned, you know, it was a very simple
murder. Halliday was a young, strong fellow, quite an
able chap—and the possessor of what I should describe as
a good 'chess' brain. Appledown himself recognized that

239

he was a most dangerous subject for blackmail—quite in a class apart from poor little Parvin or old Canon Whyte —from whom the most he had to fear was that they might break down and make a clean breast of everything. And Appledown did, in fact, take very special precautions with regard to Halliday: he told him plainly that all the details of his crime or indiscretion, or whatever it was, were on paper, cached somewhere: and that if he as much as suspected that Halliday was planning to attack him, a letter would go to the Dean. In the first instance it would only be a warning letter, telling you, sir, that *should* anything unexpected happen to your head verger you were to go to such and such a place and recover a letter which would give you fuller details, but binding you to take no steps immediately. This would have been his first answer to a threatening move from Halliday, and a very unpleasant one too, as you can imagine."

"Is this deduction or induction?" asked Bloss keenly.

"Neither," said Hazlerigg. "I've seen the letter. Mrs. Meadows gave it to me yesterday. But to proceed. The scheme, in its conception, was simple. Halliday noticed that he was about the same size as Appledown, and his first step was to buy a blue burberry—not an uncommon garment in the Close—similar to that worn by the head verger. He also cultivated the habit of himself going about bareheaded on every possible occasion. His idea was to wait for a suitably rainy, blustery night, when there wouldn't be too many people hanging round the cathedral, and then get one of the choristers, in the vestry, just before Evensong, to tell Appledown that 'the engine-shed door had been left open.'

"Immediately service was over, Halliday reckoned to slip quietly off in the darkness of the cathedral, out of the cloister door and then through the window, which, you remember, is a pivot type fastened by a latch on the inside. This would bring him out almost behind the engine shed, where I expect he would pick up the stick he had previously left there. A few minutes' wait—arrival of Appledown—and pausing only to take his hat and his keys (which are all on one ring and clearly labelled), he walks back to Appledown's house, imitating, for the benefit of Mrs. Judd and other possible witnesses, the head verger's rather peculiar tottering gait. Immediately he is safely inside he turns on the light in the living-room—again to deceive any possible watchers—goes through the house, out of the back door, across the intervening two lawns, and in through his own study window. The whole thing, from the striking of the blow to the moment he reaches his study, can be done inside five minutes without hurry. I've tried it.

"I'm told that it is Halliday's custom to attend to his private devotions for five or ten minutes after Evensong every night. It was a strict rule in that household that he must never be disturbed during those few minutes."

Canon Trumpington raised his voice for the first time.

"Inspector," he said, "how *could* a man—a man of his calling—say his prayers to God within five minutes of taking a life? I can accept all the rest if you tell us it is so, but this seems to me to be psychologically impossible. Let us say, 'he pretended to say his prayers.'"

His good-tempered face wore a positively comical look of indignation.

"I think," said Canon Fox unexpectedly, "that you haven't really understood his outlook on the matter, Trumpington. I have no doubt that he felt he was under a species of duty to rid the world of an evil man. It was a

241

crusade that he was embarked on."

"It was," agreed Hazlerigg, "and of course it made him ten times as dangerous. Well, now, the strength of the scheme was its simplicity. It could hardly go wrong. If Appledown didn't come round to see about the door, then the whole business could be put off—no one was committed. If he had left it just like that, then I think that he must have got away with it. But he couldn't leave well alone. He started to elaborate on two or three of the points. I've already told you how careful he was about the wetness of the mackintosh and the hat, and how that very piece of carefulness gave us a line on him. Well, he decided to tighten up in two other respects, both equally fatal.

"First of all he worked out the additional eight o'clock alibi, with the choir and the note pinned to the doorpost. This was in itself a very brilliant idea, to make the whole choir a witness to his innocence: and we'll go into the mechanics of it in a moment. But observe one evil result at once. Instead of being able to do the business on any night when Artful was away—and that happened every other Tuesday—he had also to fit in a choir practice and the invitation to the Foxes to play cards, with the addition of dirty weather if he could get it.

"This meant that he had to be pretty certain that once he had started the ball rolling the thing would go through. That when Appledown had once been told about the engine-shed door he *would* come round after the service to look at it; and that was precisely what he was *not* able to be certain about. Appledown was a confoundedly lazy old man and would be more than likely to forget about the whole thing or leave it until the next morning—particularly on a rainy night.

"That was why he started the anonymous letters. Most of them, you will remember, harped on the theme that Appledown was getting inefficient—old—past his job. One of them, I don't know with what truth, accused him of having left the cloister doors unlocked one night. The immediate effect of all this was naturally to make Appledown seek to disprove the allegations by being twice as punctilious in the performance of his duties. Morgan noticed it at once. He told me he had 'never seen the old man work so hard' as during that week.

"Rather a cumbersome device, you might think. But effective, and in point of fact quite safe. Even now I don't think it's going to be possible to prove that he had anything to do with this part. He prepared it all before he went away for his holiday. Hid the flag, put the anthems in the cupboard, and made his arrangements with his more or less innocent accomplice at Starminster to send on the letters. Then he went off and let the fun begin."

The Dean had obviously been boiling up for a protest for some time.

"But what about my wall?" he said, as Hazlerigg paused. "That must have been done on Sunday night, and Halliday was still down in Devonshire. You checked up on it yourself. Don't tell me he came sneaking back that night——"

"No. Certainly not. The whole point of the anonymous attacks was that they should be conducted with perfect safety to Halliday. They were designed to lead suspicion away from him, not towards him. And they weren't important enough to be worth taking any serious risks over."

"Then if he didn't come back until Monday, and the

writing was done on Sunday night—you're being a little obscure, Inspector."

"Who says that the writing was done on Sunday night?"

The Dean looked slightly dazed.

"Myself—and Hubbard, my gardener—and all the domestics in my house. Surely you don't fancy we're in some conspiracy to——"

"Of course not," said Hazlerigg. "I put the matter very clumsily. What I should have said was, 'How do you know the writing wasn't there *before* Sunday?' I know that you didn't actually see it. I don't think you were meant to. No—wait a second, please. Tell me this. Was Halliday in your garden at any time within a few days before going on his vacation?"

The Dean, who was still looking as if he thought that the strain had been too much for Hazlerigg, made a strong effort at detachment and remembered that Halliday had visited his garden on the afternoon before he left. He couldn't remember why. People used each other's gardens very freely in the Close.

"Quite so," said Hazlerigg. "Well, I expect that was when he wrote his message on your wall. He wrote it with a crayon of grease, mixed with some substance like rhodamine, which reacts to water—the same principle as most of our invisible inks and paints. He reckoned that the first shower after he had left would 'develop' his message, but actually, as you remember, the weather kept exceptionally clear and dry for the whole of that week— right up until the evening before he returned; then the thunderstorm did the job with a vengeance.

"You probably remember remarking that though the wall was wet the writing was set and dry: which would be

244

the case with this particular substance: the water runs off the grease, printing the letters scarlet. You remember I said that all this elaboration was fatal; well, this is one point where it may prove so. Rhoadamine is by no means a common substance, and it's not unlikely that we can trace the purchase.

"His second elaboration was the one which actually gave the game away. He decided that he needed an additional alibi for eight o'clock, and he also wanted to mislead us by suggesting that Appledown had gone out at about that time—on his way, as we should be expected to presume, to the fatal rendezvous. And this was how he worked it out.

"His sister always liked to change for these little social evenings and would hurry upstairs after she had tidied the room and set the card-table. Halliday retires to his study, possibly saying to his sister, 'I've got a little work I'd like to finish before the Foxes come, so don't disturb me.' The time is about ten to eight. It's the work of a minute to get back into Appledown's house and dispose of the cold supper in a convincing looking way by tipping it down the lavatory! Then he takes his stand inside the front door. Out of the porch window he can see both approaches. If you"—he turned to Canon Fox—"and your good wife had been early he would have had to leg it back pretty fast, but again, no harm done."

"I should not dream of arriving early at any after-dinner invitation given by a member of the Close," said Canon Fox. "Your hostess would never forgive you if you found her making the coffee, or worse still assisting with the washing up. One knows that these tasks have to be done, but like the Queen of Spain's legs, they are not referred to in public. It is a safe rule to arrive from five to ten minutes later than the time given in the invitation."

"I see," said Hazlerigg. "Well, he was batting, possibly, on a better wicket than we imagined. Anyway, he waits until he sees the choir approaching, and then opens the door, turns his back on them, and is actually pinning the notice up as they go past. Immediately they are safely past he nips back into the house, back the way he had come, and into his study.

"Here is where he had to rely on luck a bit, but everything goes smoothly. He goes out into the hall, opens his own front door, and rings his own front door-bell. This bell actually rings in the kitchen and is one of the few noises which Biddy, from long experience, can be calculated to hear. She comes pattering up into the hall and meets Halliday. He evinces surprise, says No, he hadn't heard the bell ring. He'll just open the front door to make sure. Of course no one is there; and as they stand talking in the hall he adds, 'There's eight o'clock striking: the Foxes will be here any minute now.'

"Biddy, who is not only deaf, but like a lot of old deaf people extremely touchy about admitting it, agrees that she can hear eight o'clock striking and goes back to her kitchen.

"Now here we come to an indisputable fact. I stood in that hall with Biddy this morning, on a very still clear day, with the door wide open whilst the cathedral clock was striking midday. Half-way through, on a pretext of having left my watch behind, I asked Biddy if she could tell me what the time was. And without batting an eyelid she said, 'I'll go and have a look at the study clock!'

"So much for the value of that particular alibi. It was five past eight, *not* eight o'clock at all, when Halliday talked to Biddy in the hall, and Biddy didn't hear the clock strike for the very good reason that it wasn't striking and even if it had been she wouldn't have been able to hear it."

"I should certainly have said," agreed Canon Fox, "though it's difficult to swear to, that it was five past eight at the least when I left my house. I must ask my wife. She will be more likely to know about a thing like that."

Prynne said, "What put you on to the truth first, Inspector?"

"You did," said Hazlerigg.

Prynne looked absurdly gratified. "I'm pleased to have helped," he said. "I have a strong suspicion it was something I said when describing my encounter with Appledown—or the person I took to be Appledown—as I was on my way to the cinema. I knew at the time that something was amiss there. Don't misunderstand me. I'm not claiming to have recognized that it wasn't Appledown I had seen—no such thought entered my head. But I *was* conscious that I had definitely seen something out of place."

"Go on," said Hazlerigg, "this is most interesting."

"Well, it's no good. I've thought from then till now, on and off. I think it was something I saw but failed to understand. It made me so confoundedly nervous—now don't laugh—that I got an unpleasant feeling half-way through the first film (it was a murder film too) that perhaps someone might be murdering Appledown. Possibly all those anonymous letters had something to do with it. But, anyway, I determined that whoever else was implicated I wasn't going to be. I made quite a fuss—I don't suppose they've forgotten it yet."

"They remembered all right," said Pollock.

Hazlerigg tried hard to imagine what all this would sound like to a jury, and then fell back on his notes.

"I'll read out exactly what you said to me about that evening. Here it is. 'I looked up and saw Appledown crossing the road. He must just have left the cathedral. By the time I got up he had gone indoors, but I saw the light go on in his front window and immediately afterwards his shadow jerking about on the blind.' That's as you remember it?"

"Quite right," agreed Prynne.

"Then who had drawn the blind down?" said Hazlerigg, "and when?"

There was a longish pause in the chapter house whilst a number of theologically sharpened minds concentrated on this point.

"I mean," went on Hazlerigg slowly, "that Appledown had left the house in broad daylight, at four o'clock in the afternoon and hadn't been back. His brother left even earlier. And up to the time of Appledown's supposed return the house had been empty. By this time it was almost dark—inside the house it must have been pitch black. You've seen that room, full of gimcrack tables and furniture. Can you suggest any single logical reason why a man should go into it, feel his way across it, pull the blind down, and then—and not till then—go back again to the door and switch on the light?* Except for the real and very obvious reason that we know of now—that he daren't risk being recognized. An old figure in hat and coat tottering up the path is one thing—easy to make a mistake about him. But a man standing facing you in a lighted window—that's quite a different position."

The Dean turned to Prynne.

"That *is* what you saw, I take it?"

---

*Pre-war, of course.

"Oh, yes," said Prynne. "No doubt about it. The blind was down when the light came on. The first thing I saw was the light go up, and then the shadow against the blind. It wouldn't be easy to make a mistake about a thing like that. If Appledown had turned the light on and then walked over to the window and drawn the blind it would have presented a very definite and different sequence."

Hazlerigg thought again about the jury and reflected that crime in the Close had certain compensating features. He did not see Prynne easily shaken under cross-examination.

"Well, we've nearly done now. I've told you how I think Halliday first plotted the thing; and then how he elaborated it. But I still doubt most sincerely whether we should ever have got near our man if it hadn't been for the really desperate piece of bad luck which he experienced over those letters."

He turned to Pollock.

"You remember I told you once that our only real chance would be if something went wrong for the murderer and he lost his nerve?"

Pollock nodded.

"That is exactly what had already happened. Something *had* gone wrong with a vengeance. Something so unfortunate that Halliday must have seen the hand of Providence in it. He had that sort of mind."

The Dean said, "I guess it was something to do with John Brophy, but I can't even begin to see where he came into it. Please go on, Inspector."

"Appledown," continued Hazlerigg, "as I said a moment ago, had taken certain safety precautions against Halliday. He had written an account giving the details of Halliday's sins and lodged it in some safe and accessible place. He had further threatened that if Halliday showed fight he would straightaway inform you of the existence of this reading matter, asking you not to investigate it unless and until something should happen to him of a violent and untoward kind. You might, of course, have felt bound to override your verger's wishes—in any event the situation would have been very awkward for Halliday.

"Now I fancy that Appledown knew pretty well who was behind the anonymous letter campaign—though he didn't, of course, see why it was being done. I think he took it all at its face value and imagined that Halliday was trying to get him the sack. The fact that the whole thing coincided with Halliday's vacation rather increased his suspicions, and as incident followed incident he got furiously angry. More than probably he had it out with Halliday the moment the latter got back; told him the thing must stop at once. I can imagine him patting his pocket and saying that if the attacks didn't stop he had a letter for the Dean which would soon settle matters.

"That threat, as we can imagine, didn't worry Halliday—his plans were well matured. But I should think that after killing Appledown he took the precaution of running through his pockets and his desk too, later that night; and I dare say it worried him to find no letter there—though not too seriously, at first.

"He was far from guessing the truth: that Appledown had already sent the letter. He had sent it that evening. Just before Evensong something must have happened to arouse his suspicions—I cannot at the moment divine what it was."

"Do you suppose," said Bloss, "that he might have overheard Halliday telling the chorister to give him that message about the engine-shed door?"

"It's an idea—but I think on the whole it's unlikely. If Appledown *had* overheard it, he would never have risked going near the place. He was pretty nervous of Halliday, you know——"

"*Et pour cause,*" agreed Prynne.

"Whatever his motives may have been we have a number of witnesses—choristers—that Appledown gave Brophy the note and asked him to 'drop it in' at the deanery. Brophy put it in his pocket and again we've plenty of witnesses that he stepped out of the line (they remembered it because it was a breach of rules) on his way to choir practice that night at seven o'clock, and dropped 'a note' in at your door, Mr. Dean."

The Dean saw light.

"I had an idea the handwriting was familiar—developed sort of writing for a thirteen-year-old. But then he was a rather grown-up sort of boy—signed J. B., too."

"And liberally covered with his finger- and thumb-prints on both paper and envelope."

"But I still don't understand," said Prynne. "The letter you received, Mr. Dean, had nothing to do with Halliday or his goings-on. . . ."

The Dean felt glad that he at last could enlighten a colleague.

"The letters, I take it, had got mixed up in Brophy's pocket. He unwittingly retained the note Appledown had entrusted to him and dropped one of his own composition in at my front door."

"Surely," said Canon Fox, "if I recollect the letter you did get on that occasion, it was rather an *unusual* missive for a boy to be carrying round in his pocket."

"Not at all," said the Dean. "I expect he had a packet of them. Dr. Smallhorn, you remember, told us that the boys had started a great game of passing anonymous notes and that sort of thing, influenced no doubt by what was going on round them in the Close. Excuse me, Inspector, please go on."

"I'm glad you saw the point so easily," said Hazlerigg, "because you'll appreciate now how quickly Halliday jumped to the right conclusion, once he heard about the note you had received that night. From then on he knew that there was more than a strong possibility that John Brophy was walking about—maybe quite unconsciously —*with a most damning exposé of the whole business in his pocket*.

"When he saw the original J. B. note—I think you showed it to him after your tea-party, sir—he was then absolutely sure of what had happened, and his reactions became correspondingly more vigorous.

"He made no less than four attempts to get it back— not including, of course, the fifth, which he made yesterday afternoon after the suggestive little conversation which we forced him to overhear in Dr. Smallhorn's hall. Only by that time, as I said, the note was in our hands.

"His first shot at getting it was pure burglary. He broke open the outer door of the school buildings and searched Brophy's private desk. Having drawn blank there, he tried again and called in on Mrs. Meadows while that worthy woman was at work in the linen-room. Helping her fetch and carry gave him plenty of opportunities to search Brophy's Sunday suit and spare suit. I saw him doing it, though it didn't register particularly at the time. However, still no luck.

"It was immediately after that, at the tea-party, that most of the really deadly things in this case happened. First of all I heard from Dr. Smallhorn about the boys' habits of passing notes to each other. Halliday, as a master, knew about it already, of course, but he can't have been best pleased when I came to share the information.

"Then afterwards you, Mr. Dean, showed Halliday a copy of the J. B. note. No one can blame you, by any stretch of imagination—but that act was actually the cause of John Brophy's death."

Catching a glimpse of the Dean's face, Hazlerigg wished he had put this rather more tactfully, and hurried on.

"The next night Brophy and another boy were late back from cathedral, and they came over separately. Halliday was waiting for them. I don't suppose that he meant to kill the boy, but it is of course a matter of great delicacy, even for a professional, to stun without killing. And I think it hardly affects the moral blame, whether he intended to kill him or not."

"Or the legal," observed Mr. Scrimgeour with some satisfaction.

"When Brophy was down he searched his pockets quickly—and drew blank yet again. But he wasn't quite done yet. He had an evening class to take at the school; so he hurried in and, on the pretext that he had lent Brophy his Bible, he quite openly searched his school-desk—did it in front of the whole class. And still he found nothing. Actually, by the way, the letter was in a book on a shelf, at the head of John's bed. I think that's all."

"Then Halliday made up the whole story about the attack on himself outside my house," said Trumpington. "He certainly did it very convincingly."

"Possibly—but there is another explanation there. I think someone was on the look-out for Halliday—had seen him go to the deanery, had crept to the door and heard him talking to the Dean after the party. Had bided his time outside, determined to serve him out a little of his own medicine."

"Artful," exclaimed Pollock. "Is that who you mean?"

"I think it's probable," said Hazlerigg. "Artful is a truculent old man, and family affection aside he can't have enjoyed seeing his income cut off. There's no need to press the point, however. We don't intend to make it part of our case, and if Halliday raises it in defence he is open to the imputation of having invented the whole story."

"I think I can enlighten you on one point," said Bloss. "By a curious coincidence I stumbled, a few months ago, on the facts which probably formed the basis of Appledown's blackmail of Halliday. I will let you have them"—his limpid gaze swivelled round the assembly—"afterwards."

"Quite so," agreed the Dean hastily. "No sense in unnecessary revelations at this point. We've got Miss Halliday's feelings to consider, amongst other things."

As the morning service-bell began to sound overhead, Hazlerigg climbed to his feet.

"I've told you all this," he said, "and I know that it's as much in your interests as it is in mine to keep quiet about it. In return I want every scrap of information you can give me. I've never faced a more difficult case."

"Perhaps if Halliday had stopped after his first murder," said the Dean, "you wouldn't have found us so keen; but as it is—well, I'll speak for everyone, and say that you can rely on our discretion—and our help."

"Thank you," said Hazlerigg. "And it's with the profoundest respect that I must differ over that last proposition. When I find myself thinking that way, as I sometimes do, I remember those meticulous rehearsals which Halliday made with the hat and the raincoat. When a man reaches that stage of God-like detachment, he really is too dangerous to live."

For nearly an hour after the others had gone Hazlerigg and Pollock worked quietly over the papers, sorting, listing, and docketing the case to be presented. The rhodamine powder—the early anonymous letters—the walking-stick which they had taken that morning from where it stood quite openly in Halliday's hatstand. The ferrule to be measured against the plaster-cast of those sixteen little holes in the ground behind the engine shed. Might not microphotography match it up further with the tiny splinters found in John Brophy's hair? And the inside of the bowler hat. There was a possibility, but no more, that a hair or two of Halliday's might still be found there—unlike him, though, not to have remembered to wipe it.

And so it went on.

Pollock got up to stretch his legs and wandered out into the cloisters. Quietly he opened the door of the south transept and stepped inside. From where he stood he could see the faces of the clergy and choir framed by the iron trellis screen behind the pulpit. They were singing the anthem—part of Twelfth Ecclesiastes to Steggall's lovely settting—and had reached the treble solo with which it ends:

Remember now thy Creator, in the days of thy youth,
In the days of thy youth.

The canary notes went up and up, higher and higher into the dim roof of the cathedral.

Pollock tiptoed out.

He felt an overmastering desire for a steak—done red —and a pint of milk stout.

Since it was the summer of 1937 he got both without difficulty.

27 million Americans can't read a bedtime story to a child.

It's because 27 million adults in this country simply can't read.

Functional illiteracy has reached one out of five Americans. It robs them of even the simplest of human pleasures, like reading a fairy tale to a child.

You can change all this by joining the fight against illiteracy.

Call the Coalition for Literacy at toll-free **1-800-228-8813** and volunteer.

**Volunteer
Against Illiteracy.
The only degree you need
is a degree of caring.**

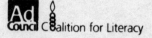